TOO CLOSE
for COMFORT
A Sgt. Windflower Mystery

"Be prepared to be charmed by Windflower,
a food-loving sergeant who could possibly be
Canada's most polite Mountie."
— *Halifax Chronicle-Herald*

I0635688

Award-Winning Author
MIKE MARTIN

Ottawa Press and Publishing
Copyright © Mike Martin 2024

ISBN BOOK: 9781990896224
ISBN EBOOK: 9781990896231

Cover design: Joanna D'Angelo

Interior layout: Patti Moran / Patti Moran Graphic Design Printed and bound in Canada

Interior Book Format and Design (Amazon) Joanna D'Angelo

Library and Archives Canada Cataloguing in Publication

Title: Too close for comfort / by Mike Martin.

Names: Martin, Mike, 1954 author

Description: Series statement: A Sgt. Windflower Mystery; 15 Identifiers: Canadiana (print) 20240442296 | Canadiana (ebook) 20240445252 |

ISBN 9781990896224 (softcover) | ISBN 9781990896231 (ebook)

Subjects: LCGFT: Detective and mystery fiction. | LCGFT: Novels. Classification: LCC PS8626.A77255 T66 2024 | DDC C813/.6—dc23

TOO CLOSE FOR COMFORT

THE SGT. WINDFLOWER MYSTERY SERIES
BOOK 15

MIKE MARTIN

ACKNOWLEDGMENTS

I would like to thank a number of people for their help in getting this book out of my head and onto these pages. That includes beta readers and advisers: Mike MacDonald, Barb Stewart, Robert Way, Denise Zendel, Karen Nortman and Lynne Tyler. Allister Thompson for his excellent copy editing and Alex Zych for final proofreading.

To Joan:
Thank you for your unwavering support.
I am so happy we are on this journey together.

CHAPTER 1

It was a quiet morning in Grand Bank, Newfoundland. A wonderful early fall morning. Sergeant Winston Windflower had just come from breakfast at the beautiful B&B that he and his wife Sheila owned and operated. He didn't have to cook, which was an added bonus, and he didn't even have to clean up, which was even better. Windflower was an RCMP officer again after a short sojourn away as the community safety officer for the area.

He was now on a one-year assignment as the acting inspector not for just Grand Bank, a tiny community on the edge of the Atlantic Ocean, but for all the region, including the much larger town of Marystown. That was where he was headed next, right after he stopped into his office to see his administrative assistant, Betsy Molloy. He was hoping for a quiet day, but something inside him told him that was not going to be today.

His first hint was the smell of smoke when he stepped out of the B&B. Then he heard the sirens. He jumped in his car and followed the noise, just like half of Grand Bank, by the size of the crowd that was standing in the laneway of a house that backed onto the cemetery. The Grand Bank Volunteer Fire Department truck was already on the scene, and a handful of the crew were hauling a hose towards the fire that was leaping out of the second-floor window.

Windflower managed to squeeze through the crowd and then used his vehicle to block any further access. He watched as the firefighters fought a losing battle against the fire, which was now threatening to spread. They diverted their efforts to keep the flames from attacking the nearby houses while the nervous neighbours watched on, likely in shock, thought Windflower.

An hour later, the flames had been diminished, and the exhausted firefighters and neighbours looked relieved. It was only then that Windflower approached the fire chief to get information. Chief Roy Pike had only been on the job for about six months after the retirement of the longtime fire chief, but he clearly knew how to fight and contain a fire.

"Good job, Chief," said Windflower.

"Thanks," said Chief Pike. "I guess all our Wednesday night training is paying off."

"Was there anyone living here?"

"No, another vacant property fire," said Pike. "That's the third one this year. We're lucky it was a fair distance away from other houses. That's my biggest worry. If we get one in the middle of town, we may not be as fortunate."

"Too early for cause?" asked Windflower.

Pike nodded. "But if it's the same pattern, we don't expect to find any accelerant. Whoever is doing this knows how to start a fire without leaving much evidence. We suspect they are using a bag of chips to get the fire going. Once something like a sofa or curtains get going, the rest goes up pretty fast."

"A bag of chips?" said Windflower. "That's a new one to me."

"I hear that's how people start fires in prison," said Chief Pike. "They can place the bag where they like and have a couple of minutes to get out before the real fire starts. We first started hearing about this with vehicle fires. But it works just as well with houses."

"But somebody would still have to start the fire," said Windflower. "This is not spontaneous combustion or anything."

"No, someone definitely set this fire," said Pike. "And the others."

And someone definitely saw something, thought Windflower as he looked around at the large crowd on onlookers. Maybe even one of these people right here.

He walked away and called Betsy on his cell phone. "Are you at the fire?" asked Betsy. "It's horrible."

Windflower didn't have time to give her a full report. Right now, he needed help. "Can you call over to Marystown and ask Corporal Tizzard to send over somebody right away? We need to interview people."

"Yes, sir," said Betsy.

"And, yes, Betsy, it is horrible," he added as he hung up.

"Will your guys secure the site?" asked Windflower as he went back to the fire chief.

"We will," said Chief Pike. "There are often flareups after we put out the initial fire. But we got here early, so the structure may still be okay. We'll go in tomorrow morning and start poking around to see if it's safe to inspect. Right now, it's just mop up and monitor."

"Great," said Windflower. "I've got somebody coming over to start talking to people. See if we can't find somebody who saw anything."

"Good luck with that," said the fire chief. "So far, they've been pretty careful. Picking houses at the end of the road and just before dawn when nobody is up yet."

"Thanks," said Windflower. "I'll put some police tape up in the laneway and check in with you later. Call me if you see anything interesting."

"Will do," said Pike as he turned his attention back to the work his crew was engaged in.

Windflower walked back to his car and got the roll of yellow tape from the trunk. He wound the tape across the laneway in front of his car, tying one end to a fence post and the other around a large oak tree. He could feel what felt like a hundred eyes watching his every move. He turned around and spoke to the crowd.

"This tape means that this area is a crime scene. No one is permitted on this property until the chief completes his investigation."

People nodded, but he could almost feel a rumble from the crowd. After an awkward moment of silence, one of the women spoke up.

"You got to do something about dis situation," she said. "We're skeared to go to bed at night."

"I hear you," said Windflower. "We want to stop whoever is doing this. But we need your help. If anybody saw anything out of the ordinary. Any strange cars or people that aren't usually around here."

"It's dem fellers from Saint Pierre," said one of the men in the crowd.

The crowd murmured their agreement with this sentiment. "We don't know that," said Windflower.

The man who had spoken earlier stepped forward. "Dere over here buying up everything they can," he said. "Dey wants to drive us out and take over."

"Let us and the fire chief do our jobs," said Windflower, a little more firmly than before. "Don't jump to conclusions until we get evidence. We don't want to cause any more trouble than we already have, do we?"

The crowd seemed to sag a little at this pronouncement,

and the man moved back a little. "One of our people will be here soon, and they will talk to all of you. If you have any evidence or have seen anything unusual, we want to know. Thank you."

With that, Windflower got into his car, and as he began to back out of the laneway, the crowd parted to give him room. But he could feel their rapt attention on him until he finally got to the road and drove away. Almost at his office, his cell phone rang. He pulled into the parking lot and looked at the number displayed on the screen. It was Eddie Tizzard.

CHAPTER 2

Corporal Eddie Tizzard was one of Windflower's closest friends and someone who'd been involved with the RCMP in the Grand Bank area for as long as he had. Once he'd been Windflower's 2IC but now was working at the region's headquarters in Marystown. Windflower had been the acting inspector for a while but was quite comfortable stepping back when his old friend, Eddie, had agreed to take on the inspector assignment. Neither of them were quite sure how this would work, with Windflower overseeing everything from Grand Bank and commuting to headquarters two days a week, but they were both happy to continue working together.

Another complication, albeit a very happy one, was that Tizzard's partner, Carrie Evanchuk, also an RCMP officer, had just had their second child and was still off on maternity leave. It was complicated because Carrie had been assigned to Windflower as his assistant, and now Tizzard had to scramble to fill in that hole with whoever might be available.

"Morning, boss," said Tizzard.

"Good morning, Eddie," said Windflower. "You got somebody on their way over?"

"That would be me," said Tizzard. "That's the third arson in Grand Bank. I thought you might need some help. I'm just out of Marystown. Be there in half an hour."

"Great," said Windflower. "I'll brief you when you get here. How are Carrie and the baby doing?"

"Mother and Princess Sophie are doing quite well," said Tizzard. "My sister, Margaret, is over this week to help out with things, especially Hughie."

"How is Hughie doing with his little sister?"

He's doing good for an eighteenmonthold," said Tizzard. "As long as Margaret is there, he gets plenty of attention. We'll have to watch how he reacts when it's just him and Carrie and Sophie."

"Fun and games," said Windflower. "My girls are all about dance and figure skating. We're not that interesting to them anymore." Windflower's phone buzzed with another call. It was Sheila. "I gotta go," he said. "See you when you get here.

"Good morning, beautiful," he said into the phone.

"Compliments will get you everywhere," said Sheila. "I

heard about the fire. People are getting scared now. You have to do something."

"That appears to be an almost unanimous opinion this morning," said Windflower. "We have just started the investigation, you know."

"It's the third one," said Sheila. "It feels bigger than just a few isolated situations."

"I agree," said Windflower. "And people are looking for someone to blame. Me and the Mounties, of course. But some are suggesting that it might be folks from Saint Pierre."

"That's just talk," said Sheila. "As long as I can remember some folks would blame 'those Frenchmen,' that's what they called them, for everything from shoplifting to if they got a flat tire."

"I guess it's easier to blame an outsider than think it might be someone in your own community doing this. We'll figure it out. Give us a little time."

"That's all you have," said Sheila. "A little time. Speaking of which, would you have time to be here to meet the bus when it comes this afternoon? I'm meeting some potential suppliers in Garnish and may not get back in time."

"I think I can manage that," said Windflower. "I guess you have to keep that warehouse stocked in Marystown."

"You laugh sometimes at our 'little operation,'" said Sheila. "But we employ four people fulltime and provide a steady income for about fifty women on the peninsula."

"I don't laugh," said Windflower. "I heard a good one the

other day. Shakespeare said, 'Laughing at your own mistakes can lengthen your life.' But Shakespeare's wife reportedly added 'Laughing at your wife's mistakes can shorten it.'"

"Good one," said Sheila. "Okay, I'll leave the girls to you. Oh, did you see Molly this morning before you left?"

"I can't recall seeing her," said Windflower. "That cat doesn't really pay attention to me. I don't think she likes me."

"She's a cat," said Sheila. "She barely tolerates any of us. In any case, she's not here. Did you leave the screen door open out back?"

There was a dreaded moment of silence as Windflower pondered his options. Tell the truth and face the consequences or fudge and take his chances. "Sorry, I gotta go," was his choice. "I'll take a look around when I get home. Love you."

Breathing a sigh of relief that he recognized might be shortlived, he walked into the office to see Betsy.

"What a way to start the week," said Betsy. "Would you like a cup of coffee?"

"That would be grand, thanks, Betsy," said Windflower. "Can you also get me the files on the two previous fires?"

While Betsy got his coffee and files, Windflower took a look at the stack of paper that was overflowing his in-basket. He had forgotten how much paperwork was involved with policing, especially the RCMP. Not his favourite part of the job, that was for sure.

He was still looking at it when Betsy came back with two

file folders, a cup of coffee and a tin that she offered to Windflower. "Partridge berry muffins," she said. "My Bob picks 'em and I cooks 'em."

Windflower took one and passed the tin back. "No, take them home with you," said Betsy. "I'm sure Sheila and the girls might like one." She waited until he took a bite and pronounced it "delicious."

"Isn't this awful?" said Betsy. "Right here in Grand Bank. Someone burnin' down people's houses. Folks are some upset."

Windflower finished his muffin and took a sip of coffee. "Betsy, will you see if the Lions Club is available for a town meeting this week?"

"I can tell you that it's busy tonight, 'cause Bob's dart league is in there. But tomorrow or Wednesday night might work. What time are you looking at?"

"Seven o'clock?"

"Half-past six might be better," said Betsy. "Most people has their supper around five or five-thirty."

"Good," said Windflower. "See if you can arrange it for tomorrow evening at six-thirty. Thanks."

CHAPTER 3

Betsy went to make her phone call, and Windflower started to look back at his pile of paper. He picked up a couple near the top that Betsy had marked as urgent and signed or initialled them as directed. He was about to move to the next level when he saw and heard Eddie Tizzard speed into the parking lot.

The next thing he heard was Betsy and Tizzard laughing, and then Tizzard bounded into his office with a cup of coffee. "Betsy tells me you've got the goods," said Tizzard.

Windflower smiled and handed over the muffin tin. "Ah," said Tizzard. "Nothing better than homemade muffins."

"You say that about everything you eat, and you eat everything," said Windflower.

"Not everything. I'm not big on vegetables."

"Name one you don't eat," said Windflower, snatching the

tin back from Tizzard, who was going for his second muffin. "Those are for Sheila and the girls."

"I don't eat cauliflower," said Tizzard after thinking about it for a while. "My dad says that 'a cauliflower is nothing but a cabbage with a college education.'"

"I think that's Mark Twain," said Windflower.

"And my dad," said Tizzard.

"Okay, I give up," said Windflower. "Let's go through the first two fires."

"The first one was down by the beach, wasn't it?"

"Last house on the block. Nobody living there for years. Fire started sometime in the night. By the time anybody noticed and called the fire department, it was gone. Almost burnt to the ground," said Windflower.

"No accelerant found and no witnesses," said Tizzard.

"Three weeks ago?"

"Correct on all fronts. Although I wasn't here at the time. We were in St. John's for back-to-school shopping."

"The second one was out at L'Anse au Loup," said Tizzard. "You weren't here then, either, were you?"

"Nope," said Windflower. "Stella had a figure skating tournament in Mount Pearl. But the file said nobody saw or heard anything. How is that possible in a small community like this?"

"I don't know. Makes you think that they might be local, though, doesn't it?"

"I'm more inclined to think that, too," said Windflower. "More than the 'Frenchmen from Saint Pierre' theory."

"Easier to blame the outsider."

"Well, neither theory nor blame will get us anywhere," said Windflower. "We need some solid information. Are you going to do the interviews?"

"That would be your assistant," said Tizzard.

"My assistant, your partner, is off on maternity leave."

"Your new assistant," said Tizzard. "Temporary, like everything in the RCMP these days, but they should be here soon. Ron Quigley freed up a position so that we could back-fill behind her."

"That's good news," said Windflower. "I was wondering how we were going to manage this. And I only made the request last week."

"I guess Superintendent Quigley didn't want to lose another acting inspector," said Tizzard. An inside joke, since he had abruptly quit not so long ago.

"When is she coming?"

Tizzard looked out the window and pointed. "She's coming right now." Both men watched as the RCMP constable parked the car and walked across the parking lot to the building. She was tall, almost six feet, thin, and had a firm and confident stride. Betsy came in to introduce her.

"Sergeant Windflower, this is Constable Samira Gupta. Did I say it right?"

"Perfect, Missus Molloy," said the female officer. "Nice to

meet you, Sergeant. I have heard many good things about you. Good morning, Corporal Tizzard."

"Nice to meet you, too," said Windflower. "Sit down. We are just going through the files on a string of fires in Grand Bank. Arson, we believe."

"I've heard about them as well," said Gupta. "It must be terrifying for the people in a small town like this."

Both Windflower and Tizzard nodded.

"Here are the files. Why don't you take a quick look?" said Windflower as he passed over the files to Gupta. "Once you are done, maybe Corporal Tizzard can take you over to the scene of the latest fire. The fire department is still there, and Chief Pike can give you the latest update. Then, I want you to interview everybody who lives on that street and anyone who is hanging around. We desperately need some information."

"Certainly," said Gupta, who took the files and started scanning them.

"Great," said Windflower. "I'm going to talk to Betsy. She's trying to set up a community meeting to talk about all this." Windflower left and Tizzard followed him out. "She seems bright," said Windflower.

"She's one of the best," said Tizzard. "She was working on community liaison and had made a ton of friends and allies in Marystown. She's perfect for this job."

"Thanks," said Windflower. "Listen, once you've got her set up, why don't you meet me at the Mug-Up for lunch?"

"Now you're talking my language," said Tizzard. "See you then."

Windflower spent a few minutes going over the preparation for the meeting tomorrow night. Not that he had to do much. Betsy had the hall booked, coffee and tea and snacks ordered, and had a draft of the notice that would go out.

"I'll send it to the media, but I don't think we'll have any trouble getting people out to this," said Betsy. "What are you going to say?"

"That's a good question," said Windflower as he waved goodbye to Gupta and Tizzard, who were heading over to the fire scene.

He was still thinking about that half an hour later when his grumbling stomach reminded him it was lunch time.

"I'm going for lunch," he mouthed to Betsy, who was on the phone as he was leaving. A few minutes later he parked outside the best and only café in Grand Bank, the Mug-Up. Mug-Up was an old Newfoundland term for a snack and a cup of tea, and if you wanted delicious homemade lunches and the best cheesecake on the island, then this was the place for you.

CHAPTER 4

The Mug-Up used to be owned and operated by Sheila, but she sold it to her friends Moira and Herb Stoodley after a car accident that slowed her down considerably. She and Moira remained close, and Windflower and Herb had also developed a strong friendship based on some shared interests, including trout fishing and a love of the law. Herb was a retired crown attorney, and he often offered Windflower free advice about how the system actually worked. That was helpful, but more interesting was their common love of classical music.

Herb was a true aficionado of the genre, and he was tutoring Windflower in its many variations and intricacies. Windflower, for his part, was an attentive student, and he found that almost nothing could soothe his savage brain like a drive through the barren countryside with some Mozart or Beethoven or Schubert playing in the background.

But Herb wasn't at his usual place near the cash register at the café today, and Windflower waved to the young waitress as he took one of the last remaining tables in the crowded lunchtime room. He could feel everyone's eyes on him again as he settled into his chair. When he looked up, they all turned away. That wasn't a good sign, he thought. But his attention was soon drawn back to the task at hand, and he ordered a coffee and a grilled cheese sandwich. He thought about having cod au gratin but resisted in the faint hope that he might be able to squeeze in a piece of cheesecake for dessert.

His sandwich had just arrived when Eddie Tizzard came in, spotted him, and walked to his table.

"It may be hot in here, but I definitely feel the cold shoulder," whispered Tizzard.

"You got that, too?" asked Windflower, putting his sandwich down and sipping his coffee. "The fires?"

"I'd say so," said Tizzard. The waitress came by to take his order. "I'll have pea soup and one of those sandwiches."

"Will that be enough for you?" asked Windflower.

"I'm saving myself for a cupcake," said Tizzard. "They have those specialty salted caramel ones today. I have to bring some home for Carrie."

"How did it go with our new assistant?" asked Windflower.

"She was doing fine," said Tizzard. "She has a way of making friends with all the women, and the men are a little intimidated by her. She gets the job done. If anybody knows anything, she'll suss it out."

Tizzard's food came soon after, and there was quiet at their table until Tizzard finished up. When the waitress came to clear the table, Tizzard ordered four cupcakes, one each for him and Windflower and two to go. Windflower did not resist the offer.

After lunch, Tizzard left to go back to Marystown. Windflower was about to go back to the office when Herb Stoodley's van pulled up in front of the Mug-Up.

"Winston, how's she going b'y?" asked Herb in the familiar Newfoundland greeting.

Windflower gave the appropriate response. "She's going good, b'y."

"Just back from Marystown with supplies," said Herb. "Are you coming or going?"

"Heading back to work," said Windflower.

"Another fire this morning," said Herb. "What's going on?"

"Still trying to figure that out."

Herb shook his head in sympathy. "Good luck with that. People are some upset, b'y."

"I know."

"Anyway, that's work," said Herb. "We haven't seen you or Sheila and the girls in ages. Moira and I would like to have you over for supper. I've got some lovely sea trout in the freezer with your names on them."

"That would be nice," said Windflower. "Let me talk to Sheila. We're so busy now with the girls back in school."

"No problem," said Herb. "Oh, and I almost forgot. I have something for you. I think you'll enjoy this one." He went back into his van, came out with a CD and passed it to Windflower.

Windflower looked at the cover. "Rafał Blechacz, Chopin," he said. "Blechacz is an expert on Chopin," said Herb. "He's been playing and recording Chopin's works since 2007. In my opinion, he's the best."

"Thank you, Herb, I'm sure I'll like it," said Windflower. "Now, I have to get back to work. But I'll talk to Sheila and let you know about supper. Thanks again."

Windflower tucked the CD into the glove compartment and drove off, waving to Herb along the way. He thought about driving back to the office but turned back towards the fire scene instead.

The fire fighters were still cleaning up the area, and the crowd of onlookers had thinned dramatically. He was about to turn around when he saw an RCMP cruiser come up the road behind him. It was Constable Gupta, and it looked like she had somebody in the car with her. Not a prisoner, because they were riding up front with her. When they got closer, he recognized another familiar face. It was Eddie's father.

"Good day, Sergeant," said Richard Tizzard.

"Mister Tizzard, nice to see you," said Windflower.

He must have looked puzzled because his female constable stepped in. "Mister Tizzard thought he saw something this morning," she said. "I'm glad we found you."

"Well, I'm not sure I saw very much," said the older man. "I'm up before dawn every morning. Something that an old fisherman like me can't shake. Anyway, my dog, old Felix, started growling. He don't really bark much anymore. Too old, I guess. But when I heard Felix, I thought I'd take a look outside. I didn't turn any lights on, just wanted to check it out, you know."

"What did you see?" asked Windflower.

"Like I told your young constable here, I didn't see much," said Richard. "But there was a guy on a bike. Only he wasn't on the bike. He was just wheeling it alongside him. I didn't think anymore about it until I heard the commotion across the road this morning."

"Did you get a look at the person?" asked Windflower. "Was he old or young, do you think?"

"I couldn't see much in the dark," said Richard. "He moved pretty quick, so that suggests he wasn't oldish, but as far as his age, I couldn't really say."

"But you did see one thing that might be important," said Constable Gupta.

"Oh, yes," said the man. "He passed under the streetlight for a second. I couldn't make out what clothes he was wearing, 'cause it was too dark. But he had a hat on. One of them Frenchmen's hats."

"A beret?" asked Windflower.

"That's it," said Richard. "A beret."

"Anything else?" asked Windflower.

"No, b'y, that's it," said the elder Tizzard. "Sorry I can't be of more help. This is an awful situation going on right now. I hopes you catches whoever is doing this."

"Thanks," said Windflower. "You've been a great help."

"I can give you a drive back, now, Mister Tizzard," said Gupta.

"That's okay," said Windflower. "I can give him a ride. I'll let you finish your work."

Gupta nodded, got into her car and drove away. Richard jumped into Windflower's vehicle, and he drove them both to Tizzard's little house down by the beach.

CHAPTER 5

"You missed your son this morning," said Windflower as they parked in the driveway.

"He's over here all the time now," said Richard. "Him and his two beautiful little people. I love that Hughie. He reminds me of Eddie when he was small. Always poking into everything. Not a bad kid, just nosy."

"Still the same," said Windflower, laughing. "How are you making out over here by yourself?"

"I'm never alone," said the older man. "Brenda or Margaret are always dropping in with soup or homemade bread."

"How are you feeling?" asked Windflower. "With your heart and everything."

"Since I had my operation and got these new meds, I am perfect," said Richard. "Other than getting older, I'm great.

I've always thought that 'life would be infinitely happier if we could only be born at the age of eighty and gradually approach eighteen.'"

"That's a great quote," said Windflower. "One of yours?"

"Courtesy of Samuel Clemens, a.k.a. Mark Twain, one of my favourites," he replied. "Thanks for the ride, and good luck with your investigations."

"See you again soon," said Windflower. He thought again about going to the office and then remembered he had to be home to meet the girls coming home from school. He had a few more minutes, so he decided to drive down to the beach to catch a little more of this fabulous September air.

It was certainly a beach, but there was very little sand. There was sand down there somewhere, but it was covered by a million beach rocks of every size, shape and colour. Windflower wasn't looking for sand to lie around on anyway. He just wanted to stare out at the endless ocean and feel the sea breeze on his face. Today was a perfect day to do just that.

He thought a little about Richard Tizzard as he sat on a large boulder facing the Atlantic Ocean. How upset Eddie and his sisters had been when he had his heart attack. He was clearly recovering well from that episode. He also remembered being with Richard after Eddie, his only remaining son, had been shot by a deranged criminal a few years back. He felt the love and kindness of the elder Tizzard, and he had made a point of staying connected with Richard ever since.

Enough lingering, he said to himself as he managed to get up and back to his car. He arrived at his driveway just before the yellow school bus pulled to a stop and his two little girls, Amelia Louise and Stella, climbed out.

They were surprised but happy to see him. Even more so when he showed them the partridgeberry muffins. They got him to warm the muffins up in the microwave and then slathered them with butter.

Lady, their Collie, stood hopefully in front of the microwave, and while she didn't get a muffin, Windflower did get her a Milk Bone after he laid out the muffins and glasses of milk for the girls.

"That's the way Mom makes them," said Stella. She was in grade three now and very much the leader of the two girls.

Amelia Louise, however, made sure that she took all of the space available to her. "I like blueberry muffins better," she said. "Especially the ones that Mom makes."

"What happened at school today?" asked Windflower.

"We're practicing our reading," said Amelia Louise. "The teacher said I'm very good."

"We're doing math," said Stella, sounding very much like the older sister.

"And we're doing numbers, too," said Amelia Louise, not wanting to be outdone.

The girls finished their snacks, and Windflower directed them as they loaded their glasses and plates into the dishwasher.

"I've got to do my exercises for my figure skating," said Stella.

"And I've got to practice my dancing," said Amelia Louise.

"That's great, but didn't you notice that somebody is missing?" asked Windflower.

"Mom?" asked Stella.

"She'll be home soon," said Windflower. "Where's Molly?"

Both girls jumped up and started looking around the house. Windflower could hear them running all over calling out the cat's name. They came back a few minutes later, panting.

"She's not here," said Amelia Louise.

"Where is she?" asked Stella.

Windflower could tell the girls were getting upset. He bent over and called them both close to him. He hugged them even closer.

"Sometimes cats wander off," said Windflower. "One of us probably left the back door open and she got out."

"It wasn't me," said Stella.

"Me, either," said Amelia Louise.

"It's nobody's fault," said Windflower. "Do you want to go out and look for her?"

That made both girls and Lady happy. They weren't as happy when they returned half an hour later with no sign of Molly. At least Sheila was home now to help console them.

"Maybe somebody has seen Molly and might have even taken her in," said Sheila. "Let's make up a poster, and we can put it up on the telephone poles and at the stores."

"That's a great idea," said Windflower. "But I have to go back to work for another hour or so. I'm sure it'll be great." The girls thought it was a great idea too and were soon absorbed with their mom in creating the poster for their missing cat. He gave Sheila a peck on the cheek and went back to work.

As Windflower approached his office, Constable Gupta was pulling out.

She stopped and got out to talk with him.

"I've got a few more people to see, so I'll be back over in the morning.

But nothing new, not yet anyway," she said.

"Okay," said Windflower. "We should meet in the morning, and I'll give you an update on what else is going on."

"That would be good," said Gupta. "I was also planning on attending the meeting tomorrow night, if that's okay."

"Sure," said Windflower. "See you tomorrow, and thanks for your work today."

Betsy was still on the phone when he came back in, but she paused her call to let him know that someone was waiting for him in his office.

He was very surprised to see a smiling, healthylooking Bernard Thibault sitting in the visitor's chair.

"Bernard, you look great," said Windflower.

"I've been clean for six months," said Thibault. "Even gave up the weed. Couldn't stand all the hacking."

"Congratulations," said Windflower. "What are you doing over here?"

"I'm living in a sober house in Marystown, but my cousin needed some painting done, so I'm in Grand Bank for the week," said Thibault. "I also wanted to say thank you."

"I didn't do anything," said Windflower.

"You pointed me in the right direction," said Thibault. "I was in bad shape. Using, OD'ing, I thought my life was over. But when we met and did that job together, and you said I could have a better life. I guess that was what I needed to hear."

"That was crazy," said Windflower. "You got captured by those bad guys. I was worried we wouldn't get you back."

"I know that if it wasn't for you, the other Mounties would have given up on me," said Thibault. "You didn't. It meant a lot. Still does."

"I'm just glad we all survived that insanity."

Thibault laughed. "Anyways, I gotta get going."

"It's good to see you," said Windflower. "Oh, did you say you were painting? Inside or out?"

"I can do both," said Thibault. "But I'm better inside, I think. I used to be a painter before all that dope screwed me up."

"I might have some work for you over at the B&B if you're interested."

"Sure," said Thibault.

"Let me talk to Sheila, and I'll let you know," said Windflower. "I think I have your cell phone number."

"I got a new number," said Thibault, scribbling it on a scrap of paper. "Too many bad guys on the old one."

"Gotcha," said Windflower. "I'll call you."

After Bernard left, Windflower took a couple of moments to reflect on the newlooking Bernard Thibault and their adventures together earlier in the year. Windflower, who was out of the RCMP at that time, had agreed, somewhat reluctantly, to be part of a sting operation in Nova Scotia. Bernard was an active drug user who was recruited to make the actual transaction and pick up the contraband. Things went awry, and Thibault was taken hostage. At Windflower's insistence, they let the bad guys go, temporarily, so that Thibault could be released.

Everything somehow worked out at the end, and Thibault and Windflower were reunited. That's when they had their heart-to-heart that Thibault had referenced. It obviously had the right effect, thought Windflower. He was smiling to himself as Betsy came in to say that she was leaving for the day.

"You should be pleased with yourself," said Betsy.

"What do you mean?"

"Bernard told me what you did. What you said," said Betsy. "I knew his family from years ago. They gave up on him a long time ago. And look at him now. You gave him hope. I can see it in his eyes."

"It was already in there," said Windflower. "'The miserable have no other medicine. But only hope.'"

"True enough," said Betsy. "My Bob says that every child needs a little bit of hope and someone who believes in them. You believed in Bernard."

"He finally started to believe in himself," said Windflower.

"See you tomorrow, Sergeant," said Betsy.

"Bye, Betsy," said Windflower as he started to clear off his desk and closed his computer. He was getting in his car when his cell phone rang. It was Sheila.

CHAPTER 6

"Can you see if Warren's has any of that corn on the cob left?" she asked. "I was hoping you could barbeque hot dogs and we could have corn and a salad."

"No problem," said Windflower. He turned right instead of left and was soon at the allpurpose grocery store in the middle of Grand Bank. Warren's was a special place run by the same family for generations, and they literally had everything from soup to nuts. And if they didn't have it, all you had to was ask and they would bring it in for you. Windflower loved that they had their own little butcher shop in the back and would have loved to see what meats they had on sale today, but that wasn't his mission. He found the bin with the corn, which had been picked over quite a bit, but still managed to find half a dozen cobs that would suffice for this evening. He was paying when he saw the poster. There was Molly, live as life, staring back under a Missing Cat notice. He couldn't say she was smiling. He didn't think she ever did. She could barely give a sigh of contentment after he gave her a special treat of leftover salmon. But tonight, somehow, he felt she looked sad. But maybe that was him projecting.

The sadness of his two little girls was real enough. And the fact that they didn't immediately hear anything from their poster made them despondent. He dropped off the corn to Sheila and tried to cheer them up.

"Sometimes it takes a bit of time," he said to Amelia Louise and Stella, who were sitting quietly on the living room floor. They never sat quietly anywhere.

The girls looked like they were going to cry. Stella started, and soon Amelia Louise joined in. "Come here," said Windflower, holding out his arms. He held them both very tightly. "One thing I've learned as a police officer is never to give up hope."

"But she's gone," blubbered Stella.

"She's not here right now, but until we know anything else, we have to keep hoping that we'll find her," said Windflower. "Molly has to be somewhere, right?"

"But where?" asked Amelia Louise.

"That's what we'll find out, if we keep looking," said Windflower. "And remember, the Mounties always get their cat."

"Is that true or are you just making that up?" asked Stella.

"Ask your mother," said Windflower.

The girls ran to Sheila, who had the corn on to boil and was making the salad for supper.

"Is it true?" Amelia Louise asked.

"Do the Mounties always get their cat or is Daddy fibbing?" asked Stella.

"If your dad said it, he believes it to be true," said Sheila. "I believe that Molly is somewhere. We just have to find her."

"Can we look for her again after supper?" asked Amelia Louise.

"For a few minutes, but tomorrow is a school day," said Sheila. "Maybe you can take some posters to school with you and ask your friends if they've seen Molly, too."

The girls now had a mission and a plan and went back to being their normal boisterous selves.

Windflower, with Lady close behind, was happy to get out to the back deck to start the hot dogs for supper. During their meal, the sad thoughts about the missing cat were replaced by stories from school and upcoming events for the girls. Stella was one of the best young figure skaters in the province. Her coach had said that she had a chance to be junior champ if she worked hard and continued her progress. Amelia Louise was more artistic but still competitive when it came to her sister, so she announced that she was going to be the champion of her dance class.

After supper, Sheila cleaned up while Windflower, the girls, and Lady continued the search for Molly. Tonight, they wandered down by the brook, where they were greeted by many ducks and sea birds, but no cats. A little down, they headed back home, where Windflower cheered them up with hot chocolate before Shelia got them ready for bed. Windflower took Amelia Louise while Shelia got Stella for bedtime stories.

Amelia Louise picked two books for tonight's reading. The first was *Girls Can Do Anything*, a marvellous book that gave a great message to little girls that they could do and be anything they wanted. Windflower loved that right after they read this book together, Amelia Louise would always say as loud as she could, "I'm a girl and I'm proud of it."

Windflower laughed every time.

The second book was called *Carson Crosses Canada*, one of Amelia Louise's new ones from the library, and it told the story of Annie and her dog Carson who were travelling across Canada from British Columbia to Newfoundland. Windflower and Amelia Louise both laughed out loud at their antics and their bologna sandwiches. When she finished, Amelia Louise asked him if they could take a trip like that sometime.

"Maybe," said Windflower. "But we would have to have a better car than Annie and Carson."

Amelia Louise laughed at that, too, and then grew very quiet. "Daddy," she said. "Can we say a prayer tonight for Molly to come home? At Sunday school, they say to pray if you really, really want God to help you with something."

Windflower was not particularly religious, but it seemed like absolutely the right thing to do. After their prayer, he kissed her goodnight and went downstairs, where Sheila had made some fresh tea.

"They're pretty upset," she said.

"I know," said Windflower. "Amelia Louise got me to pray for Molly with her."

"That's not like her," said Sheila. "I guess she must be learning something in Sunday school."

"Probably got it from Stella," said Windflower, pouring himself a cup of tea. "I guess we keep looking. She'll show up one way or another."

"That's not a very pleasant thought."

"Here's something more pleasant then," said Windflower. "I saw Herb Stoodley today, and he invited us over for supper."

"That's a great idea," said Sheila. "If we can tear ourselves away from dance classes and figure skating. I'll call Moira. Any more good news?"

"Yes," said Windflower. "Bernard Thibault came to see me today. He's in recovery and doing well. Over here to help his cousin with some painting."

"We need some painting done at the B&B," said Sheila.

"My thought exactly," said Windflower. "Do you want to try him out?"

"Is he really okay? We don't want to be bringing any trouble into our business."

"Fair enough," said Windflower. "Painting the exterior of the B&B is relatively straightforward. We can monitor his progress, and Levi will keep an eye on him. But he looks good, and I'd like to give him a chance."

"Everyone deserves a second chance."

"How about you?" asked Windflower. "How was your day?"

"Great meetings and new suppliers on board," said Sheila. "Our little co-op keeps growing and growing. I think I need to set up a trip to Halifax to line up more distribution. Our warehouse in Marystown is almost at capacity."

"That would be nice," said Windflower. "I was thinking that it would be good to take a road trip with the girls. They haven't been anywhere except for St. John's and Gander. Although Amelia Louise was with us when we went to Pink Lake for Auntie Marie's service."

Windflower paused when he thought about his late aunt. She had been like a mother to him after his own had passed young back in his home community of Pink Lake, a Cree community in Northern Alberta.

"Are you okay?" asked Sheila.

"I'm good," said Windflower. "Just thinking about Auntie Marie and Uncle Frank."

"You miss them a lot, don't you?"

"I do," said Windflower. "But every so often I feel them with me. It's funny. Like a ray of sunlight on your arm makes you feel warm inside."

"That's nice," said Sheila. "A trip would be nice, too. But we'd have to take the girls out of school."

"That wouldn't be too hard," said Windflower. "I'd also have to clean up the mess around here."

"Oh yeah, how's that going?" asked Sheila. "Everybody is talking about the meeting tomorrow night. I hope you're ready and have some answers. They have a lot of questions."

Windflower sighed. "We're doing our best."

"I know," said Sheila. "People just want some reassurance that they are going to be safe."

Windflower nodded. "I'm going to pop out with Lady one more time."

"Okay," said Sheila. "I'll leave a light on for you."

CHAPTER 7

Lady was more than ready to go for a walk. But even she seemed a little down tonight, thought Windflower. Maybe she was missing Molly too. But once outside, Lady perked up considerably as she and her master strolled around their quiet neighbourhood. Windflower loved a lot of things about Grand Bank, but one of the best was the near silence that enveloped the community after nine o'clock at night.

Part of that was that this was an older, retirement community. And getting older and not younger. But also because people seemed to love sitting inside their snug and comfortable houses and settling in for the evening. A few random dogs barked at their intrusion into what they believed was their personal space, but other than that, man and dog had Grand Bank completely to themselves for their half-hour stroll about town.

When they got back, Windflower filled Lady's bowls and gave her a treat. He stared wistfully for a moment at Molly's dishes and then on a whim filled them up too. Why not? he thought. Might as well be hopeful. He thought of the Shakespeare quote about hope: "True hope is swift, and flies with swallow's wings." This cause appeared as righteous as any to him, and with luck, maybe tomorrow would bring good news. Or two very disappointed little girls. He turned off the last light and went upstairs to bed.

He snuggled in beside Sheila, who was reading her book, and soon fell asleep. Then he woke. Well, almost woke. He woke inside a dream. He knew it was a dream because he could look down and see himself and Sheila in the bed below. He was floating in the air. That had to be a dream. Windflower's whole family, led by his maternal grandfather, were dream weavers. They had taught him to understand and interpret dreams, for themselves and others. Although so far he had only been able to partially understand his own, with a lot of help from his late Auntie Marie and his recently deceased Uncle Frank, who were both master dream weavers. As he felt himself rise in his dream and float away from his bedroom and his house and Grand Bank, he wondered if he would have any contact with them.

His people, the Northern Cree, weren't all dream inter-preters. That seemed to be a particular trait of his mother's family. But they all somewhat believed that they could connect with their ancestors through the dream world. As Windflower drifted farther away from his home, the dark sky faded, and it almost became as bright as day. He came to rest on what looked like a cloud. But it was firm enough to stand on, so he started to look around and see what would happen next.

The first thing he heard was two voices, almost arguing, but in that friendly, familiar banter that could often be heard from a married couple. He recognized the man's voice first. It was his Uncle Frank, a distinctive, almost baritone sound. But it was really the laugh that gave him away. Despite his deep voice, he had an almost childlike laugh. Windflower would know that sound anywhere.

The woman's voice was also easily recognizable as his Auntie Marie. It was kind but firm, and in conversation with her husband a little sceptical, bordering on sarcasm. As if to say, how could you be so dumb? But said much more nicely and smoothly than that.

"Auntie. Uncle. Is that you?" asked Windflower.

"Sorry, Winston," said his aunt. "Your uncle is being a dumb lummox."

"I was only making a suggestion," said Uncle Frank.

"Why can't I see you?" asked Windflower. "Usually, when you come to me in dreams, you have some kind of body or even an animal shape."

"My body is in the shop," said Uncle Frank.

"That's what gets you in trouble," said Auntie Marie. "Somebody asks you a question and you make a silly joke."

Windflower heard something that sounded like "harumph" from his uncle.

"Sorry, again, Winston," said Auntie Marie. "We actually have no need for bodies up here. We only use one when we go down there. Mostly to make people feel comfortable."

"It is so nice to hear your voices," said Windflower. "Are you okay up here?"

"It's Heaven. What could be wrong?" said Uncle Frank. "It's perfect."

"We can see you're having some difficulties, though," said Auntie Marie.

"And you haven't been smudging or spending much time in nature," said Uncle Frank. "Men need to be out with Mother Earth. That's how we connect with the world and with our spirit."

"I know," said Windflower. "I guess I've been busy."

"We know how busy family life can be," said Auntie Marie. "Two little girls and a beautiful wife to be with and look after. But you must look after yourself. Especially in here."

Windflower thought he felt a gentle but firm push on his chest.

"We will watch over you and help you," said Uncle Frank. "But you have to connect with us to do that. We only get so many visits out."

"Is that true?" asked Windflower.

"No, your uncle is joshing again," said Auntie Marie. "But he is right that our ability to assist you is limited unless you ask first."

With that, the voices faded, and Windflower could feel himself slipping off the cloud and slowly falling until he could see the ground far below him. As he descended, he could see Grand Bank come again into view, and before he knew it, he was back in bed with Sheila. He lay on his back, completely still, and thought about what had just happened. Was it just a dream? Maybe. But he knew what his family had told him was true. He had to reconnect to his spirit to be a good person, a good father and partner, and even a good police officer. He closed his eyes, and despite the recent excitement, he fell into a deep sleep and didn't stir 'til the morning.

CHAPTER 8

After his dream-world visit with his aunt and uncle, Windflower was determined to do better in looking after his spiritual side. He knew he'd been slipping in that regard, and one of the best ways to remedy that was to start his day with smudging and prayer. Smudging was a way to cleanse his body, mind and spirit, and so before anyone else got up, he snuck downstairs and let Lady out back to do her business. Then he gathered up his smudge kit and brought it outside with him.

Inside the kit were small packets of his four sacred medicines: cedar, sage, sweetgrass and tobacco. There was also an abalone shell, a small box of wooden matches and an eagle feather fan that had been gifted to him by his grandfather many years ago. After lighting the herbs using a wooden match, he used the fan to waft the smoke from the medicines over all parts of his body.

He spread the smoke over his eyes and head to help him see and think clearly, over his heart to keep his thoughts pure, and even under his feet to help him walk a straight and honest path. Then, when finished, he laid the ashes on bare ground so all negative thoughts and feelings were absorbed by Mother Earth. Lastly, he prayed.

He started with gratitude for the gifts he had already received. Uncle Frank had taught him to always start with thanks because what you were grateful for, you got to keep. He also told him not to pray directly for himself but to ask for blessings for those he cared about and those who might really need it. Today, he had a long gratitude list, and then he added his prayers for others, including one for his daughters that they find their missing cat. Maybe that was for him, too, but he decided to sneak it in anyway.

Prayers finished, he and Lady went back inside to get breakfast started.

Usually, breakfast was simple: cereal and toast. But this morning, after he put the coffee on to brew, he decided to make waffles. By the time Sheila and the girls came down, he had the first batch of waffles and a bowl of fresh fruit on the table.

"Wow, this is a special morning," said Sheila as she grabbed a cup of coffee.

"I thought we all needed a bit of cheering up this morning," he whispered in her ear as she came closer.

"Good idea," she said as she surveyed their two unusually glum daughters sitting at the kitchen table.

The waffles helped temporarily improve morale in the Windflower-Hillier household, but maybe that was the sugar in the maple syrup, thought Windflower as he waved goodbye to the yellow school bus that was taking his daughters to school in Fortune. He kissed Sheila goodbye and headed over to his office.

When he arrived, Betsy was sitting with Chief Roy Pike. "Great, you're here," said the fire chief.

"Good morning to you both," replied Windflower.

"I need to speak with you. In private," said Pike.

"Sure, come on in," said Windflower, glancing back at Betsy for some clue about what was going on, but she simply shrugged.

Pike walked in behind Windflower and closed the door. "We found a body," he said.

"Inside the house?" asked Windflower.

"It finally cooled down enough for me and Greg Rose to go in this morning. We found him in the kitchen."

"Was he badly burned? Did you recognize him?" asked Windflower.

"He was burned, but not extensively," said Pike. "The fire wasn't likely started in the kitchen. And no, we didn't recognize him. He's not from around here."

"Is he the person who started the fire?" asked Windflower, thinking the man might have gotten trapped or overcome by smoke.

"Very unlikely," said Pike. "The kitchen area had the least amount of fire damage, which almost certainly means the fire originated in another room. Probably the living room, by the looks of it. Easy to get the curtains going, and once that happens it spreads quickly."

"So, he came in after the fire got started?" asked Windflower.

"That's a good probability," said the fire chief. "But here's the really interesting thing. He didn't die from the fire, although I'm sure he had smoke inhalation."

"Why do you say that?"

"Because he had a large bloodstain on the front of his shirt," said Pike. "We didn't do any more than to see if he was dead. Didn't want to disturb anything. And I came over right away. My young guy is pretty upset. I told him to wait in his truck until I came back and not to let anyone else into the house."

"That's good," said Windflower. "We don't want any information getting out on this until we can get in there and have a look around. Can you stay here? I have a couple of phone calls to make."

"Yes," said Pike. "Although we need to get someone over there soon to help Greg out."

"Will do."

Betsy was waiting for him when he came out of the office.

"Betsy, we need forensics over here as quickly as possible," he said. "There's been a body discovered over at the fire scene. We'll need the paramedics to come over, but can you ask them not to use their lights and sirens? And can you also check with Constable Gupta to see when she'll be here?"

"Yes, sir," said Betsy. "That's awful. Do we know who it is?"

"Not yet," said Windflower. "And can you keep this whole thing as quiet as you can for now?"

"Absolutely," said Betsy. "My lips are sealed."

Windflower knew he could count on Betsy's discretion. She liked almost nothing better than knowing what was going on in Grand Bank. She would make arrangements with everybody and get the formal processes going. Windflower would go over with Chief Pike to help his young firefighter and to get his own first look at the scene.

He followed Pike and pulled in behind the chief's vehicle and a pickup truck parked just outside the police tape. Greg Rose was puffing on a vape when he saw his boss and the RCMP vehicle arrive. He stepped out of his pickup and walked towards the chief.

"You okay?" Windflower heard Chief Pike ask him.

"I will be," answered Rose. "Once I can get out of here."

"Just a couple of more minutes while we show Sergeant Windflower around, okay?" asked Pike.

Rose nodded, first to him, and then to Windflower, who had approached them.

"Let's go," said Pike. He led the other two men in through the back of the house, the area closest to the kitchen.

CHAPTER 9

The smell of smoke and burnt things was overpowering.

Chief Pike noticed Windflower's discomfort. "It's all the chemicals. Treated wood and laminate and things that are sprayed on to protect surfaces. It's better today, but still pretty bad. But I guess we're used to it."

"Not a pleasant part of your job," said Windflower as they stepped gingerly around areas that definitely looked unstable. He had a quick look above him as well, just in case. But this part of the house hadn't been completely wrecked by the fire.

Pike saw him looking up. "This side is still relatively okay. But the second floor has collapsed on the other side. The house is a write-off."

Finally, they came to the kitchen, and Greg Rose stood

back while Chief Pike led Windflower to the body lying on the floor. Some of the area around the body had been scorched, but the fire chief was right; there was minimal damage in the kitchen. The same could not be said for the man lying facedown on the floor. His body was starting to lose its stiffening, by the looks of it, thought Windflower. He knew enough to know that rigor mortis usually started about two hours after death and then stayed for up to twenty-four hours afterwards. That meant a time of death sometime early yesterday.

But all that could wait for forensics. What couldn't wait was for Windflower to do his own initial assessment of what was starting to resemble a crime scene and maybe a potential arson. That was clear from the startling red stain on the dead man's clothing that Chief Pike had warned him about. A large pool of congealed blood underneath the body. The man's face, frozen in time from whatever had happened in the early hours of yesterday morning, made it hard to determine his age, but a wedding ring on his finger gave some indication that he wasn't a loner. Windflower put on a pair of gloves and did a quick search of the pockets but didn't feel like there was a wallet or anything there. He would leave the full search to the paramedics and forensics, whoever came first.

He stood up and took a long look around the kitchen. Not much out of the ordinary. No sign of a struggle, if there was one. He looked under the table and saw it: a dark-blue beret sitting by itself. He reached in, pulled it out and laid it beside the dead man. Then he took the tablecloth off the kitchen table and laid it over the deceased.

"We're good for now," said Windflower.

He followed Chief Pike and Greg Rose out. After a quick chat with the chief, Rose was sent home with a warning not to speak about this situation to anyone but to call Pike if he had any difficulty.

"It's hard for young people to see things like this," said Pike.

"It never gets easy," said Windflower. "I was on highway patrol out west. Have you seen a lot of this?"

"I was in the military," said Chief Pike. "Afghanistan. I still have dreams about it sometimes, but I got help for my PTSD."

"Good for you," said Windflower as they saw the ambulance come up behind their vehicles. Windflower lowered the police tape so they could get through and motioned to the paramedics to drive right up to the house. He noticed that they were starting to gather an audience of onlookers. Not surprising. Police, fire and ambulance all at one location would always draw a crowd, especially in Grand Bank.

When the paramedics came closer, Windflower and Pike brought them into the back of the house and the kitchen where the man lay on the floor. They left them to do their final check and went back outside.

While they were waiting, Windflower was also pleased to

see another RCMP cruiser show up. He was particularly pleased that there were two people in the car. Looked like Tizzard had come along with Gupta this morning. He was happy to see them both. "Excuse me, Chief," he said as he walked over to the other two RCMP officers,

"Good morning to you both," he said. "I was expecting you, Constable, but thank you for coming, Corporal."

"'Morning, Sergeant," said Gupta.

"I got the info about the death and thought you might need a hand," said Tizzard. "There was no one else around, so I hitched a ride with Constable Gupta. So, what's going on?"

"Come over here," said Windflower. "Away from prying eyes and ears." They walked over near Chief Pike, where the new officers greeted the fire chief.

"Chief Pike and one of his men found a body this morning. The paramedics are in there right now," said Windflower. "I'm going to take them in for a quick look."

"Be careful," said Pike. "We have no idea how structurally safe that place is. I suspect not very much."

"Thanks, Chief," said Windflower. "Gupta, can you get your camera? We'll need some scene shots before we can let the paramedics move the body."

Constable Gupta ran back to her car and grabbed a camera out of her trunk. She joined the other two RCMP officers as they walked into the house. The paramedics were wrapping up their work in the kitchen.

"He's dead," said one of them. "But we'll have to get a doctor at the clinic to confirm."

"Whenever you're ready, we can take him out," said the other. "Any idea on identity?"

"Not yet," said Windflower. "Can you wait outside for a minute? We're going to take a few pictures."

The paramedics went outside to wait for further instructions while Gupta started photographing the crime scene. She probably took a hundred pictures while Windflower and Tizzard stood by and watched. When she was finished, she nodded to Windflower.

"Good job," said Windflower. "Now it looks like we have a murder scene in addition to the arson."

"Anything stand out to you?" asked Tizzard. "Other than the fact that our late friend here had a traumatic chest event."

"I didn't look underneath," said Windflower. "But I would suggest that he was shot. Likely at close range. Not much spattering like you'd see in a stabbing. And not much sign of a fight."

"That sometimes means they knew their attacker," said Gupta.

"Or were taken completely by surprise," said Tizzard.

"And the beret, sir," said Gupta. "Didn't our witness talk about seeing a man with a beret?"

"That was my dad," said Tizzard. "He phoned me last night to tell me about his ride in a police car."

"Richard did mention that," said Windflower. "I know that it might suggest somebody from Saint Pierre. "But let's be careful about going down that road until we know more."

"Agreed, sir," said Gupta. "More than a few people I interviewed claimed that this was being done by 'those Frenchmen.'"

"We should check with the gendarmes in Saint Pierre all the same, though," said Windflower. "I'll get Betsy to send a picture over and see if they can identify our deceased. Gupta, can you run the pictures back to the office and check on forensics to see when they're coming? Me and Eddie will stay and look after this place. Send the paramedics in when you go out."

"This is an unwelcome development," said Tizzard.

"It is indeed," said Windflower. "Although it could be worse. It could be a local. Then the place would be in a complete uproar."

Tizzard grimaced at that thought as the paramedics came in with their gurney. They carefully loaded the corpse and covered it with a sheet. One of them reached down and placed the beret on top.

"Can you place that underneath the sheet?" asked Windflower. "Evidence," he explained. The paramedics did as told and carefully wheeled the gurney back out.

"That was smart," said Tizzard.

"The less fodder for the rumour mill, the better," said Windflower.

"'On Rumor's tongue continual slanders ride,'" said Tizzard.

"Good one," said Windflower. "You must have been practicing. 'Foul whisp'rings are indeed abroad.'"

"You have time for coffee?" asked Tizzard. "I'm starved."

"Let me check with Chief Pike, and then we'll go over to the Mug-Up," said Windflower.

CHAPTER 10

A couple of other volunteer firefighters had shown up to help with the cleanup and were talking with the fire chief when the RCMP officers emerged from the house. All eyes were on the ambulance that was slowly making its way down the road, heading over to the clinic. The crowd of spectators had also grown in their absence, and as the paramedics drifted away, their attention turned to Windflower and Tizzard.

Windflower called the chief over. "What can I tell them?" asked Pike.

"You can tell them that we have discovered a body in the house," said Windflower. "And you'll have to suspend your operations and investigation until the forensics team gets here."

"That's fine," said Pike. "I'll get one of my guys to stick

around until they get here, and then we'll wait until they give us the green light to go back in."

"Thanks," said Windflower. "One of us will be back here soon."

Windflower and Tizzard left the scene in Windflower's vehicle and drove to the Mug-Up.

The café was full this time in the morning with the usual coffee crowd, but Windflower and Tizzard found a seat in the corner and ordered their coffee and a raisin tea biscuit. They were happily spreading butter on their piping-hot snack when they heard a familiar voice greeting them.

"Good morning to two of our finest," said Doctor Vijay Sanjay, an old friend and the retired coroner for the area.

Both men stood to greet him, and Tizzard borrowed a nearby chair so that he could join them.

"Well, this is a pleasant sight," said Sanjay. "Repa is getting her hair done, and I thought I would stop in for a cup of tea. It is so nice to see both of you."

"I'll order your tea," said Tizzard. "Do you want a tea biscuit as well?"

"No, thank you," said the doctor. "Just strong black tea, please." Tizzard went to get the tea.

"How have you been?" asked Windflower. "We haven't seen much of you lately."

"Repa and I went to Ontario to see our new grandchild. A beautiful young girl," said Sanjay. "She would have stayed longer, but I wanted to come home. I love this time of year."

"Me too," said Windflower.

"I am happy you are back with the RCMP," said Sanjay. "It makes us all feel safer."

"Well, not everybody," said Windflower as Tizzard returned with the doctor's tea.

"Oh, I know people are upset about the fires, but I have confidence that you will resolve the situation. And young Tizzard, how is that family of yours? We haven't seen your little boy for quite some time. You must bring him for a visit. Repa was wondering about when we would see your new daughter too."

"We'll be over to Grand Bank soon and pop in to see you," said Tizzard. "Things have been a little hectic lately."

"Enjoy your little ones while you can," said the doctor. "Too soon they will fly away."

"Have you completely retired now?" asked Tizzard.

"Yes, even from giving medical advice to my loving spouse, who seems to prefer the young doctor at the clinic," said Sanjay. "But if I can ever be of service to either of you, please let me know."

"Thanks, Doc," said Tizzard.

"Now I must take my leave and pick up Repa. Enjoy your day, gentlemen. Unless you have other plans." Sanjay chuckled to himself as he walked away.

"He is such a nice man," said Tizzard.

"Indeed," said Windflower, finishing his coffee. "He was

one of the first people in Grand Bank to befriend me. He said that we Indians had to stick together."

As the two officers were leaving, Doctor Sanjay came rushing back into the café. "I almost forgot," he said breathlessly. "I have a new Scotch that you simply must come try. It's a Benriach and one of the best reviewed single malts of the year."

"I would love to do that," said Windflower. "I'll call you to set up a visit."

"Perfect," said Sanjay. As he started to walk away again, Constable Gupta came by in her cruiser.

"*Shubh prabhaat,*" said Gupta to Doctor Sanjay, bowing slightly.

"*Suprabhaat, mere bachche,*" said the doctor, returning the bow.

"You know each other?" asked Windflower.

"How could we not?" said Sanjay. "We are only a few Hindi speakers on the whole peninsula. She's from Mumbai, but I promise not to hold it against her," he added with a laugh.

Constable Gupta laughed as well. "The doctor is quite famous among the East Asian community. He has been very kind to me."

"She is a sweet girl," said Sanjay. "Although I probably shouldn't say things about a woman of her authority. In any case I must take my departure. Goodbye, my friends. *Hamaare punah milane tak.*"

"Until we meet again," translated Gupta as all three officers waved goodbye.

"Forensics will be here by noon," said Gupta. "And Betsy is already checking with the people in Saint Pierre."

"Great," said Windflower. "Can you go back to the scene and make sure it stays secure until forensics arrive? Maybe Tizzard can drop you off and take the car. I need him to go over to the clinic and find out whatever he can about our dead friend. I'm going back to the office. I guess we'll have to put out a statement about his death before everybody in town gets wind of it."

All three Mounties headed off on their tasks with Windflower arriving soon after at his office. Betsy was there to greet him.

"Shocking about the death," she said. "Are we going to put out a statement?"

"Yes," said Windflower. "Can you draft it up? Something simple. RCMP announces that a man's body was discovered this morning at a fire scene in Grand Bank. An investigation is underway. More details to follow."

Betsy looked at him as if to say is that all there is? "That's going to generate more questions than answers."

"Sorry, that's all we really know as yet," said Windflower. "We'll need to confirm his identity and get some idea on cause of death. Did you hear anything back from Saint Pierre?"

"Not yet," said Betsy. "They're not as fast as we are, usually. I don't think their technology is as good."

Windflower nodded. The islands of Saint Pierre and Miquelon were only ninety minutes away by ferry from nearby Fortune. But the French territories were far from their homeland and had much fewer resources than their Canadian counterparts. The only good news was that they were tapped into the French system, so that meant they could search the entire European continent. He had dealt with the local police many times over the years, and he could confirm that while they were very polite, they were also sometimes slow to respond.

"Once we get more information on cause of death, even a preliminary decision, we can schedule a media conference," said Windflower. "Tizzard is at the clinic right now. Maybe he'll have something to report soon."

It was Betsy's turn to nod as she took her notepad and went to put the media notice together. Windflower was starting to go through his in-basket when his cell phone rang.

CHAPTER 11

"Hi Sheila, what's up?" he asked. "If you're calling about the dead man, we don't know anything yet."

"What dead man?" asked Sheila. "I was calling to tell you that we think there's been a Molly sighting. Tell me what's going on. Is it somebody we know?"

"A man's body was found in the house that was on fire yesterday," said Windflower. "We don't have any more information yet. Where did they say they saw the cat?"

"A woman who lives over across the brook not far from Doctor Sanjay's house thought they saw her getting a drink of water this morning," said Sheila. "They saw the notice at Warren's and just called."

"I'll take a run over around there," said Windflower. "What's the woman's name?"

"Sharon Herridge," said Sheila. "On Greenwood Avenue."

"Okay, I'll let you know if I find anything."

Passing Betsy, he said, "I have to go out for a minute." He drove over to see the woman who had reported seeing Molly. She didn't have much more to add, and no, she hadn't seen the cat again or where she went.

"No, b'y," she said. "I only seen her the once this morning. I called out to her, but I guess I must have frightened her, and she ran away."

"Are you sure it was Molly, our cat?" asked Windflower.

"Well, it looked like she," said the woman. "And you seldom sees any cats out and about round here."

"Thanks very much," said Windflower. "If you see her again, please let us know." He spent a few minutes circulating around the neighbourhood, but no sign of Molly. He called Sheila.

"I guess it's good to know that she's still alive," said Sheila. "If it really was Molly."

"If you have time, maybe you and the girls could come over and have a look after school," said Windflower. "She might come out if she's hiding and hears your voices. I'll try to come, too, but the situation is a bit chaotic at work."

"Understood," said Sheila. "Any more news?"

"Not yet. I'll keep you posted."

He was going to drive back to the office when he shifted

gears and went back to the fire scene, now a murder scene as well. It was good timing, since the large white forensics van was just pulling into the laneway. Gupta was now almost physically holding people back who were starting to creep in closer to the house to get a better look. They scattered when they saw Windflower.

"It's not about you," said Windflower. "They just know me."

"Sorry, sir, I do think it is," said Gupta. "But I'm glad you're here."

"I'm going to leave it all with you," said Windflower. "I wanted to stop by and say hello to the forensics team."

There were two technicians and a team leader who got out of the forensics van. Corporal Ted Brown waved to Windflower.

"Brownie," said Windflower. "You still doing this?"

"A few more years 'til retirement," said Brown. "But why stop when you're having fun, right?"

"Corporal Ted Brown, this is Constable Samira Gupta," said Windflower.

"Nice to meet you," said Gupta as she and Brown shook hands.

"She'll be the lead," said Windflower. "I have to deal with the body and the media. Chief Pike over there and one of his men discovered the body this morning. The remains are at the clinic, and Gupta has pictures. I'll leave it with you."

"Thanks," said Brown. "Does that café still have cheesecake?"

"Best in Newfoundland," said Windflower. "You both know how to reach me."

Windflower got back in his car and was almost back to his office when his cell phone rang. It was Tizzard.

"Can you come over to the clinic? I can give you a verbal update or you can get it directly from the doctor."

"I'm on my way," said Windflower.

The waiting room at the Grand Bank Medical Centre, known locally as the clinic, was busy this morning, full of older people, of which there was a preponderance of in Grand Bank, waiting to get their flu shots. They could get them at the drug store, but they preferred to go to the clinic, where they could get their booster and maybe some juicy gossip as well. All eyes in the room turned towards him as he entered and burned a hole through his back as he went down the hallway to the ICU.

There was little need of an ICU at the clinic, since most serious accidents and patients were almost immediately transported to the much larger hospital in Burin. So, it served as emergency triage in case anyone was bleeding or in cardiac distress, and for special occasions like this morning when an unexplained death turned up on their doorstep.

Windflower saw Tizzard talking to a female doctor and walked over.

Another familiar face today, Doctor Danette White.

"Good morning, Doctor," said Windflower. "How are you this morning?"

"I am well, thank you, Sergeant," said Doctor White. "The clinic is slow, as you can see, except for our flu shot clinic, which is capably run by our nurse practitioners."

"Have you had a look at the deceased?" he asked.

"I have," said the doctor. "Male. Caucasian. Mid-forties. He was shot, most likely at close range. Three bullet holes that are easily visible. I won't know for sure until we open him up, but I'd say that they punctured one of his lungs and probably his heart as well."

"Do you still perform that procedure here?" asked Windflower.

"We do everything here that we can't send to Burin or St. John's," said the doctor. "But it won't be for a few days. Do we have any idea who his next of kin is?"

"Nothing on that yet."

"This might help," said the doctor, walking over to where the dead man's body was being held behind a curtain. She rolled the body over enough so that Windflower could see two tattoos, one on each shoulder. One said *Un Pourcent*. The other was the distinctive symbol of the Outlaws Motorcycle Club, a small skull on motorcycle handles and below it a stylized *S.S.*

Windflower and Tizzard shared a glance. They had both

had dealings with criminal biker gangs over the years, none of them pleasant.

"That might indeed," said Windflower. "Anything else of interest?"

"Not from the outside," said Doctor White. "I'll call you when I know more."

"Thank you, Doctor," said Windflower. "We'll leave our friend in your capable hands."

"Very interesting," said Tizzard as they walked back down through the waiting area.

"Let's talk outside," said Windflower. "Too many eyes and ears around here."

"Well, whoever he is, he has or had biker connections," said Windflower once they got to the parking lot.

"Outlaws, that's not good news," said Tizzard. "They haven't had much of a presence around here. And in case you're wondering, they're not over on Saint Pierre, either. Too small for biker culture."

"Might be French, as in France," said Windflower. "I know what one percent means. Proud to be an outlaw biker. But you're the expert on biker gangs. What's the *S.S.* stand for?"

"I think it's the symbol for someone who's committed a murder on behalf of the club," said Tizzard. That comment sent a chill through both Mounties, even as the sun warmed up this September day.

"Goes from bad to worse," said Windflower. "Can you

start looking into our late man's connections with the Outlaws? Both here in Canada and across the pond. Looks like he may have been a serious member. If that's the case, somebody has a file on him. Then, go back and check in on Gupta. Forensics is there. I am going back to the office."

CHAPTER 12

Tizzard drove off, and Windflower went back to see Betsy. She was waiting with a media release, simple and to the point.

"They are already calling," she said.

"I know," said Windflower. "We can add male, aged approximately forty-five. Treating death as suspicious."

"That will help with the initial questions," said Betsy. "But it will only spark more, I'm afraid."

"It'll have to do for now," said Windflower. "Let's set up a media conference for the morning. That will keep them overnight."

"Good plan," said Betsy. "You'll have to deal with this tonight as well. The media will be at the meeting."

"I can manage the media," said Windflower, although he

had to admit that he hadn't really thought about that aspect. "I'll have Gupta there to help me."

"Now, that's a good plan," said Betsy as she went to go make her revisions and send out the media release.

Windflower only had a few moments to himself before Betsy came back in. "Do you have time to see someone? I can send them away. It's Bernard Thibault."

"No, send him in, I need to talk to him," said Windflower.

"Sorry to bother you," said Thibault. "But I'm finished up with my cousin and heading back to Marystown."

"No worries," said Windflower. "I think I have some work for you at the B&B. The front exterior needs a touch-up. Is it too late in the year for that?"

"No, b'y, I think that's fine," said Thibault. "As long as the weather holds like this, it should be good. I could start next week. I'll need scaffolding and somebody to help me move it around."

"No problem," said Windflower. "I can have the scaffolding over on Monday morning, and we'll keep it for the week. Levi at the B&B can help you set it up. I think he has a friend who can help out as well. I'll talk to him. We have some paint left over in the basement, and I'll order more as you need it."

"Perfect," said Thibault. "Like I said, if the weather holds half-decent, I can start scraping on Monday. If I have someone to help with that, I can get the main painting done fairly quickly afterwards. Then, the trim. Easier to do it section by section. That way it will look nice from the road even if the weather turns bad and we get slowed down."

"Good plan," said Windflower. "Do you want to do a fixed price or paid by the hour?"

"By the hour, if you don't mind," said Thibault. "I don't have much credit. I charges twenty-five bucks an hour. Is that okay?"

"More than okay," said Windflower. "I'll get everything set up, and we'll see you on Monday."

"Thank you very much," said Thibault. "I won't let you down."

Betsy came in with the final media release for his approval as Thibault was leaving. He initialled it and handed it back. He called Levi Parsons, the manager at the B&B, and arranged for him to look after the scaffolding and paint. Levi was happy to help out and would talk to his friend who could help them with the scraping and setup.

"There's only two guests tonight and a few more reservations for the rest of the week," said Levi. "Tourist season is winding down. I think we only have one booking for next week, so it's a good time to get the painting started."

"Thanks," said Windflower. "Appreciate your help with this."

"So, any news on the dead man this morning?"

"You heard already?" asked Windflower.

"It's Grand Bank," said Levi. "Somebody was live streaming the paramedics coming and going. Now they're watching to see what the forensics people are up to. It's the only show in town."

"Nothing to report," said Windflower.

"Doesn't hurt to ask," said Levi. "See you tonight?"

"Are you going to the meeting?" asked Windflower. "Why? You're a young person. You must have more fun things to do than that."

Levi laughed. "I wouldn't miss this for anything."

"Thanks for your support," said Windflower, just a little sarcastically. Levi laughed again and hung up. He had hoped to get out of the office and back over to see how the forensics team was coming along, but that was not to be. Betsy popped her head into his office.

"Superintendent Quigley is on the line for you."

Ron Quigley and Windflower had known each other a long time, even before Windflower had gotten to Newfoundland. He'd met Quigley in Nova Scotia, where they worked on a few cases together at the Halifax airport. Ron was originally from St. John's, the capital city, and had spent time there and in Marystown, where he'd served for a time as inspector, Windflower's current role. It had been Quigley who persuaded him to take the job, despite some serious misgivings on the part of both Sheila and Windflower. Now, Quigley was in charge of the whole Atlantic Region for the RCMP. What did he want?

"Good morning, Ron," said Windflower.

"Good morning, Winston. Why does everyone sound nervous when I call them?"

"'Tis the eye of childhood that fears a painted devil,'" said Windflower.

"That's a good one," said Quigley. "Although did you just call me the devil? You have little to worry about with me. 'Be just and fear not.'"

"I'll spare you the next one, then," said Windflower. "How can I help you today, Superintendent?"

"That's better," said Quigley. "I saw the media release."

"We don't know much more."

"And that's been how many, three fires in the last little while?" asked Quigley. "What's going on in Grand Bank?"

"That's a good question. On the good news front, I have a new assistant that I'm guessing I also have you to thank for."

"Nice diversion, and you're welcome," said Quigley. "But tell me your plan for getting out of this mess."

"Well, having Tizzard over here for a few more days will let us dig a bit deeper into both the fires and the murder, and yes, I said murder. Shot, three times the doctor at the clinic suspects. We don't know who he is yet, but it looks like he has connections with the Outlaws. Might be here or over in France. Tizzard is checking on that right now."

"Is there a Saint Pierre connection? Have you checked in with the gendarmes?" asked Quigley. "I know a deputy captain, a guy named Edouard Nougue. I can check in with Eddie if you want."

"That would be good," said Windflower. "Betsy sent photos over, but I'm not sure she even got a response."

CHAPTER 13

"And what are you doing to quell the restless burghers of Grand Bank?" asked Quigley. "I'm sure they can't be pleased with the fires and now a murder, too."

"Correct," said Windflower. "I've got a town hall meeting tonight and a media conference tomorrow."

"Okay, if you need anything else from me, just let me know," said Quigley. "Oh, and how would you like to come up to Halifax for a visit? I'm organizing a session with the Halifax Regional Police on community policing, and I'd like you to be on a panel. It's in two weeks."

"Assuming we are not in the same shape as right now, which I hope to heavens we're not, I'd like that," said Windflower. "Could I take a week's vacation around it? Me and Sheila were thinking about taking the kids on a road trip, and she needs to go to Halifax for business."

"Sure, that would work," said Quigley. "You can still take the ferry from Argentia to North Sydney until the end of September. That would be a great trip. I'll send you the dates when I have confirmation. Trust me, I'll look after you."

"'Modest doubt is called the beacon of the wise,'" said Windflower.

Quigley laughed. "Ah, my old friend, being the boss is not easy. 'Sometimes to do great thing we have to do a little wrong.'"

Windflower thought as fast as he could but couldn't come up with another Shakespeare quote until he realized Quigley was gone. His grumbling stomach reminded him he hadn't had lunch. Nor had Gupta or Tizzard, either, probably. He called Tizzard.

"We're starving, b'y," said Tizzard.

"I'm sure you'll survive," said Windflower. "Why don't I pick up some sandwiches and bring them over?"

"Sounds good," said Tizzard. "Maybe get some for our forensics buddies, too."

Windflower called the Mug-Up and ordered a tray of sandwiches and half a dozen cold drinks. When he arrived, both Herb and Moira were out, but the manager, Doris, was starting to put full cheesecakes into the fridge alongside the cash.

"What kind did you make this week?" he asked.

Doris started rhyming them off. "Brownie Swirl, Coffee Crisp, Strawberry Cheesecake, Luscious Lemon, Chocolate Peanut Butter, Swiss Chocolate, Banker's Delight."

Windflower stopped her. "Did you say chocolate peanut butter?"

"Yes," said Doris. "Do you want a piece?"

"Can I have the whole thing?"

"The whole thing?" asked Doris. "I guess so."

"It's not all for me," said Windflower. "I'm going to share. Can you cut it into pieces and put in a few paper plates and forks with my sandwiches?"

"Sure," said Doris.

A few minutes later, Windflower, burdened down by a boxload of sandwiches, soft drinks and his precious cheese-cake, was on his way over to see his fellow officers at the crime scene.

His lunch basket was greatly appreciated by all the assembled RCMP officers who sat around the back of the forensics van and enjoyed their sandwiches. When Windflower opened the cardboard box with the cheesecake, there were audible gasps from more than one of them, including Brown.

"I hope nobody is allergic to peanut butter," said Windflower.

"I'm not," said Brown. "But even if I was, I might still have a slice."

In fact, Brown had two slices, along with Tizzard, of

course, while the rest, including Windflower, were happy to bask in the cheesecake glow.

"You find anything interesting yet?" asked Windflower as Brown licked the crumbs off his paper plate.

"Some shell casings, .38 calibre, pretty common gun used by the look of it. We tried to get some prints. But it's hard when there's smoke and water damage. Even though there wasn't as much damage in the kitchen as the rest of the house, no luck, I'm afraid."

"Okay," said Windflower. "You got much more to do?"

"Nah," said Brown. "There's been too much traffic up and down the driveway to get any tire prints, so we'll get some more pictures and start wrapping up. Then we'll upload all the pictures and scan them to see if anything pops out. I'll let you know."

"Perfect," said Windflower. "Gupta, can you stay until they're finished up and then come over to the office? Tizzard will come with me. Thanks for your help," he said to Brown and his crew.

"Thanks for the cheesecake," said Brown.

Back at the office, the media calls were starting to come in. Betsy handed Windflower a stack of yellow slips. He scanned them. Local radio and newspaper and a few from St. John's.

"Here you go," said Windflower as he handed the yellow slips to Tizzard.

"What am I supposed to do with these?" asked Tizzard.

"Call them back."

"What do I tell them?"

"Everything you know," said Windflower. "Listen, you know the drill. We don't have anything to say, and they're going to ambush me tonight after the meeting anyway. Just give them the routine response. I've seen you do it a dozen times. You're good at it."

"Doesn't mean I like it," said Tizzard.

"I'm the boss, remember," said Windflower.

"I'm beginning to regret my decision to step down," said Tizzard.

"You'll be great," said Windflower. "I've got to work on some notes for this evening. I'll see you in an hour." He told Betsy he was going out and left handling the media in their capable hands for now. He'd do his share tonight and then again tomorrow.

CHAPTER 14

He needed some time and space to clear his head and think. One of his favourite places to do that was at the T at L'Anse au Loup. It was a few minutes outside Grand Bank, with a rough, unpaved roadway that led from the highway down to a narrow strip of land in the shape of a T that jutted out into the ocean.

It was often deserted, save for another dog walker or solitary soul, so it made for a great place to walk and think. Both of which Windflower needed today. He didn't need to solve the crimes that were plaguing his community, but he absolutely needed to give the residents some sense that they were safe in their own homes. Right now, many of them did not feel that way.

As the sun warmed the air around him and the wind blew in from the Atlantic Ocean, he felt a sense of peace and calm come into him. It felt like he wasn't alone, and he realized that he could sense other beings or spirits around him. He thought it might be his Auntie Marie in the sunshine and his Uncle Frank in the wind. Each of them was bringing him a gift to help him on his journey. He remembered his aunt telling him always to speak the truth, even when it was difficult or uncomfortable. He thought about his many walks with Uncle Frank, who always insisted on staying in the moment and not drifting off to remember the past or worry about the future.

"Good advice," he said out loud, taking a quick peek around him to make sure he was really alone. "Thank you," he added as he walked back to his car. He knew how he would handle the meeting this evening.

When he got back to his office, Gupta was sitting with Betsy.

"Forensics have left, nothing new to report," said Gupta.

"Thanks," said Windflower. "You're staying for the meeting tonight, right? I think Tizzard has to get back. New baby and everything. I'd appreciate your support and your observations afterward."

"I was planning to do just that," said Gupta. "Betsy has offered me a bed for the night any time I need it. And I'd prefer not to travel back and forth to Marystown at night."

"I understand," said Windflower. "We've had three serious moose accidents already this year."

"Four, if you include Johnny Anderson, who drove off the

road avoiding one," said Betsy. "It's not safe on the road after dark. There's moose everywhere around here. I told Samira that any time she needs a bed, she's got one at my house."

"Well, thank you, both," said Windflower as Tizzard came out of his office and handed the slips back to Betsy.

"All done," he said. "None of them super happy, but they all have a quote for the evening news. And all of them will be there tonight."

"I figured as much," said Windflower. "I'm ready to head back," said Tizzard.

"I'm staying, Corporal," said Gupta. "You can take my car if you'll bring it back tomorrow."

"Somebody will," said Tizzard. "See ya."

Tizzard drove off, and Windflower invited Gupta to come back to his office.

"I haven't really had a chance to really meet you and find out about you," he said. "Plus, we should talk about how best we can work together."

"That would be good," said Gupta. "It's been a bit of a whirlwind."

"It's not always like this, let me tell you,"said Windflower. "Grand Bank is a quiet, safe, and mostly retirement community now. There's the fish plant and the fabricating facility, so everyone who wants a job has one. But it's mostly seniors, and now they're leaving their houses and moving into retirement homes."

"That explains all the vacant properties," said Gupta.

"You picked that up already," said Windflower. "Good. It helps explain a few things."

"The rash of fires?"

"That's a part of it, but like all crimes, that only leads us to opportunity," said Windflower. "We also may have means. But we still need a motive. That's what I'm struggling with."

"So, what's next?"

"Well, first up is the meeting tonight," said Windflower. "We have to get the public back on our side."

"I've done some media and community policing before," said Gupta. "Not with the Force. But back home in Mumbai when I was trying to find my career path. We worked inside one of the major impoverished areas, Dharavi, have you heard of it?"

"Is that near the airport?" asked Windflower. "I think I have. It's one of the biggest slums in India, isn't it?"

"Over a million people crammed in together. When we started the project, there was rampant crime of all sorts, most of it violent and gangrelated. There's still crime, but now the people trust the police a little more, and we are able to keep them a little safer. We also had to win over a skeptical media that were convinced we were all crooks."

"Pretty impressive," said Windflower. "I think we can use your skills here right now." Just then his cell phone rang. It was Sheila.

"Excuse me," said Windflower.

"There's been another Molly sighting," said Sheila. "On

the other side of the brook again, near an abandoned house. Can you come and help us?"

"Give me a second," said Windflower. He turned back to Gupta. "Do you have any experience in finding missing cats?"

"Not much, but I like cats," said Gupta. "Why?"

"Community relations, maybe more like family relations," said Windflower. "Our cat is missing but has been spotted. Can you help?"

"Absolutely, sir."

"Please don't call me sir," said Windflower. "Sarge?"

"That would be fine," said Windflower. "Do you mind if I call you by your first name?"

"I would prefer that," said Gupta. "It's Samira. Sam for short."

"Okay, Sam, we're on the case," said Windflower. He picked up his phone again. "The cavalry is on its way," he said.

Minutes later, he and Gupta were across the brook and following Sheila and the girls around the neighbourhood.

CHAPTER 15

"There's the house that Molly was seen at," said Sheila.

"Okay, everybody wait here," said Windflower. "Constable Gupta and I will go have a look around."

Windflower and Gupta tried the front door, but it was securely locked, so they walked around the back, fighting their way through the overgrown alders and weeds that had taken over what looked like to be a vegetable garden at one time in the past. The back door was locked, too, but Windflower managed to jiggle the lock enough to push it open.

The smell inside was damp and dank. Like dead air, thought Windflower as they walked through the kitchen, which was dusty but still relatively clean, except for the telltale signs of rodent activity, of the smaller sort by the signs of it. And a few larger clumps that looked relatively new.

"I'd say recent activity," said Gupta. "Too big for a mouse or even a rat. And I've seen plenty of rats."

They continued their walkabout through the vacant house that was bare of furniture and the adornments that make a house a home. But even in its bareness Windflower could see the raw beauty of what was once there. Exposed beams in the ceiling of the living room, a handcrafted staircase that anyone would love to have. Upstairs, three smallish bedrooms, with only the curtains on the windows to show that someone, some family once lived here.

But no cat. And no sign of her anywhere, except for the traces of her or some other animal in the kitchen. He and Gupta went out to give Shelia and the girls the bad news.

The girls were crestfallen but brightened a little when Sheila invited Constable Gupta to come have supper with them. "I'd like that," she said. "It isn't very restful," said Windflower as a way of warning her what to expect.

"That's okay," said Gupta. "I miss my nieces so much. This will be fun.

How would you girls like to ride in the police car with me?"

"Really?" said Stella.

"Daddy never lets us ride in his cruiser," said Amelia Louise.

"Is it okay?" asked Gupta.

"Fine with me," said Windflower. "Seems like you've already got a few admirers."

The girls got in the back of the RCMP cruiser and smiled and waved at Windflower and Sheila.

"She seems very nice," said Sheila. "Plus, you and I get five minutes alone. Anything new besides fires and murder? At least everyone says it was a murder."

Windflower didn't bite at that gentle nudge for intel about his case. "Ron Quigley called today."

"What devious plan does Superintendent Quigley have in mind for you now?"

"'Doubt is a thief that often makes us fear to tread where we might have won,'" said Windflower.

"What does that mean?" asked Sheila. "Did you win something?"

Windflower laughed. "Sometimes he has good things to offer. Like a trip to Halifax. Soon. Maybe sometime in the next little while. Before the end of the month, sounds like. He wants me to speak at a conference about community policing. I said I'd do it if I could mix in a few days of vacation."

"That would be great," said Sheila. "But let's not say anything to the girls yet. They get so excited."

Windflower nodded as they pulled into their driveway. Gupta was already there, and she had a girl on each side of her, talking away, but it looked like she was enjoying it.

"Why don't you help the girls with their homework while I get supper organized?" Sheila said to Windflower.

"I'll come help you," said Gupta as she peeled herself away from the girls and followed Sheila into the kitchen.

Windflower helped Stella practice her addition and subtraction homework, and while Amelia Louise didn't really have homework from kindergarten, they wanted to get her into the habit, so he laid out some colouring for her to do. Sheila and Gupta seemed to get along well in the kitchen as they made the salad and waited for their supper to warm in the oven. The aroma wafting out from the kitchen was driving Windflower crazy.

Finally, Sheila called them for supper. There was a nice green salad with a homemade honey mustard dressing and a delicious looking casserole in the middle of the table. Sheila ladled up a helping for everyone and passed them around. Windflower took a moment to savour the scent of ham and broccoli and cheese that rose from his plate.

"I love this," he said after his first bite. "Is this a new recipe?"

"It's an old family one," said Sheila. "I figured it was a good way to use up some of the ham we had left over from Sunday."

"It's delicious," said Gupta. "Is it hard to make?"

"Simple," said Sheila. "You can use any pasta you want and just combine the pasta, steamed broccoli and ham in a baking dish. Make your cheese sauce and then your topping with some breadcrumbs and parmesan cheese. Pop it in the oven for twenty-five minutes. Easy-peasy."

"I'll have to get the recipe," said Gupta.

"You obviously eat meat, then?" asked Windflower.

"Yes, we're from Mumbai, but my family was non-religious, so we ate whatever we wanted," said Gupta. "My father liked the Tagore quote about religion. 'Religion, like poetry, is not a mere idea, it is expression.' He said too many people took it too seriously. At least in India."

"Hard to disagree with that, even here," said Windflower, passing his plate for a second helping. "Doctor Sanjay is a big Tagore fan. He has shared many great quotations with me over the years."

"Yes, the Bengalis claim Tagore as their own, but many Indians cherish him and his words. He was our first Nobel laureate," said Gupta.

"I love many of his quotes and sayings, too," said Sheila. "'Let your life lightly dance on the edges of Time like dew on the tip of a leaf.'"

CHAPTER 16

There were date squares and tea for dessert, and while she wanted to help clean up, Gupta was seconded to play with the girls, who insisted on showing her their dance moves and figure skating routines.

Windflower loaded the dishwasher while Sheila cleaned up the leftovers.

"She is very nice, and intelligent, too," said Sheila. "You're lucky to have her."

"I am indeed. But luckier to have you."

"That's true, too," said Sheila as Windflower's cell phone rang. It was Tizzard.

"We've got a name to go with our dead person," said Tizzard. "Gian 'Coco' Meier."

"German, French?" asked Windflower.

"Swiss," said Tizzard. "From Outlaws MC Valais, based in

Wallis, Switzerland, but active throughout the continent. Our system nearly exploded with the hits we got from France, Germany, Belgium and, of course, Switzerland. He's wanted on any number of charges. Or I guess we should say he was wanted. Drugs, extortion, armed robbery."

"Why is he, or was he, over here?" asked Windflower.

"Good question," said Tizzard. "But the authorities over there tracked him to a flight from Paris to guess where? Saint Pierre."

"Why didn't they stop him over there? Or catch him when he landed?"

"More good questions," said Tizzard. "One possible guess on this side is that he bought his way through."

"It has happened before," said Windflower. "Okay, keep digging.

Maybe call Quigley and see if they have a gang expert who can help."

"Will do," said Tizzard. "Good luck tonight."

"Thanks," said Windflower, remembering that his hardest task of the day still awaited him. He finished his tea and went to get Gupta to go to the meeting.

The Lions Club was almost full by the time they got there, and the room was hot and sweaty already. "Let's talk to the media people first," said Windflower.

"You're not going to kick us out, are you?" asked the camera guy from NTV.

"Supposed to be a public meeting," said a woman that Windflower recognized as a reporter for the *Southern Gazette*.

"It's all good, folks," said Windflower. "You can stay, but we ask you to not interfere with the meeting in any way. People are anxious, and we want them to feel comfortable expressing their views. If you want, Constable Gupta will stage our walk in, and we'll be both available for a quick scrum afterwards. Okay?"

The assembled media people nodded their agreement, and Windflower and Gupta went back outside and walked in again so the cameras could get their shots. The pair walked to the front of the room. It was very noisy when they first came in, but you could hear a pin drop when Windflower walked to the podium with Gupta.

"Good evening, ladies and gentlemen, and thank you for coming," he began. "I know that recent days and recent events have disturbed many of you. We want to let you know that we are doing everything we can to find out who is causing these problems in our community. I see Fire Chief Pike here this evening. He is leading the arson investigation, and I want to thank him and his volunteer firefighters for their efforts. I'm sure you will join me in showing your appreciation." He paused and allowed the audience to applaud.

"I also want to introduce Constable Samira Gupta, who has been assigned as my permanent assistant here in Grand Bank. I hope that you will give her as warm a welcome as you have me in this beautiful little town." Once again, he paused while the audience applauded, although, he noted, not as loudly as they had for their own fire chief.

"What we know so far is that we have had three fires in a short period of time. And while Chief Pike is still investigating the latest fire, we do believe that they are linked. It looks like the same person or persons may be involved. That likely means that someone in this community has had a hand in these fires." He paused and noticed that the room had grown even more quiet. "It might even be someone we know." That caused people to move around, as if they were uncomfortable.

"That is why we will all need to be vigilant in the next little while, until we catch the people who are responsible. It seems like the fires are being started very early in the morning, and I know some of you are up early, so we need you to start looking for anything different, strange, or out of the ordinary. This is a small community, and if we all stick together, we will find a way out of this. If you see or hear anything, anything at all, let me or Constable Gupta know right away. Now, we'll take your questions."

There was a group murmur from the crowd, and finally Harold Bungay, a large, gruff older man with a loud, booming voice, stood up. He did not need a microphone.

"Well, b'y," said Bungay. "You can talk all yer wants about us helping you. But yer the police here. You should be fixin' dis right now. People are afraid dey'll be burnt in der beds.

And now we got a murder. Right here in Grand Bank. You got to do better than dat, b'y."

"I can confirm that we have had a murder," said Windflower. "I'm not permitted to release many more details at this time other than to say that it was not a resident of this community, and our investigation has just begun. We have already had the forensics team here, as many of you may have noticed, and medical examinations are still underway. As more information becomes known, we will release it to you and the media."

"Dat's all well and good b'y," said Bungay, who had remained standing while Windflower spoke. "But dat's like barring the barn door after the horse is gone. What are you going to do now to help keep us safe?"

The audience murmured again, and Windflower could sense that many in the room agreed with Bungay's assessment of the situation.

"You know what, Harold, I agree with you," said Windflower. "We should be doing a better job of protecting you and your family and every family in Grand Bank. But what I'm saying to you is that we cannot do it alone. We need your help and the help of everyone here if we are going to keep this community safe."

Now, Windflower could feel the crowd moving back towards him, but that didn't last long.

"Yes, we have to do our part," said Bungay. "But listen, Sergeant, I tinks dat the problem is not with dis community. But with people coming in from, from, from...over dere."

Now people didn't hold back. They applauded long and loud for the man's last comment.

Windflower waited for the noise to die down. "We don't know that," he started but almost got drowned out. He started to speak again. "But even if that was true, we'd still have to fix it ourselves. Because somehow, whoever is responsible for all this, did it on our watch. On my watch. Now, we have a choice. We can blame someone from outside. We can even blame each other. But where's that going to get us as a community? I've lived here for twelve years. I have two little girls going to school. I want them to be safe. I want all of you to be safe. To feel safe. But we can only do it to gether. We didn't cause these problems, but now it's up to us to fix them." Slowly, people started looking around, and then one person started clapping. It might have been Herb Stoodley or Chief Pike. Might have even been Betsy. It didn't matter to Windflower. Because once it started, it spread like a ripple and then became a wave.

Windflower rode that wave and simply said, "Thank you," as he stepped away from the front and went to the side, where he stood with Gupta to take questions from the media.

CHAPTER 17

"Has the RCMP lost the confidence of the community?" was the first question.

"I think that people are scared and want this situation resolved. And I think they're willing to work with us and cooperate with us to make sure that happens," said Windflower.

"Do you believe, as some here tonight do, that this is the work of people from outside Grand Bank?" asked the reporter from the newspaper.

"We follow the evidence," said Windflower. "Wherever that leads us."

"Can you tell us any more about the dead man?"

"We may have more information to provide at the media conference tomorrow," said Windflower as he felt Gupta move up closer to him.

"Last question," she said.

"We heard a rumour that a man wearing a beret was seen at the scene of the last fire," shouted someone at the back of the pack. "Can you confirm that?"

"No comment," said Windflower. "Our investigation is still underway.

See you tomorrow. Thank you."

He turned and led Gupta out of the hall, pausing a couple of times to say hello to some familiar faces. But soon they were outside, and they continued walking right to Windflower's vehicle.

"Thank you for your intervention at the end," he said.

"No problem," said Gupta. "They'd keep you there all night. You were great, by the way."

"Thanks," said Windflower. "But one thing is clear. We may have their support now, but we have to act fast to keep it. Do you want me to drop you off at Betsy's?"

"That would be great."

The pair were silent until they reached Betsy's small bungalow just off Main Street. "Goodnight, Sarge. See you in the morning."

"Good night, Sam," said Windflower. "Thank you again for your support."

Sheila was waiting for him when he got home. So was Lady. Sheila pushed the Collie aside. "You can wait for a few minutes." Lady made a circle of the living room and planted herself directly in front of Windflower's chair, just in case he decided to make any quick moves without her.

Sheila poured him a cup of tea and offered him a date square from a plate on the tea tray. He gratefully accepted both.

"I hear you were very good tonight," said Sheila. "You've talked to people already?"

"It's Grand Bank," said Sheila. "This was the event of the week. They liked how you handled Harold Bungay. He's always been a bit of a blow hard."

"He had a lot of support in that room," said Windflower.

"But people want to support you and the police," said Sheila. "They just want to be safe."

"I know. I'm just glad that's over, for now anyway."

"You bought yourself a little grace time," said Sheila. "But not much."

Windflower finished his tea, went to Sheila and kissed her. Lady was at his heels.

"Okay, girl, let's go," he said.

Fifteen minutes later, he and Lady were back from their evening stroll. He filled her bowl and looked at Molly's. "We'll find you," he said. "Wherever you are, we'll find you."

He turned off the lights and went upstairs to join Sheila. She was reading Louise Penny's latest book, *A World of Curiosities*, and barely acknowledged him.

"Must be good," he said as he snuggled in beside her.

"Very good, as always," said Sheila. "You can have it when I'm done."

"Thanks," said Windflower as he burrowed a little deeper beneath the covers. It didn't take him long to fall asleep. It had been a long, long day.

Then he woke up. In another dream, of course. This time he didn't have to travel very far at all. Right at the edge of the bed was a cat. A speaking cat. Molly.

"I've been here before, you know. Don't be acting all surprised," said the cat.

"I remember. In another dream," said Windflower. Sarcastic little creature, he thought.

"You forgot I can read your mind," said Molly. "Both in here and out in the other world."

"Is that really true?"

"Why do I always know when you have treats? Leftover salmon that you grudgingly give me a little piece of," said the cat. "Why do you think that dumb dog is afraid of me? She knows I know. Everything."

The cat smirked. At least it looked like a smirk to Windflower.

"You know the drill," said the cat, yawning as if to show her impatience with this whole dream thing."

"Oh yeah," said Windflower. He'd learned over the years of practicing his dream weaving that he was supposed to ask whomever or whatever showed up in his dream if they had something for him. "Do you have a gift for me? Please and thank you."

"Grovelling helps," said Molly. "Actually, I have a riddle. Before the darkness falls to dawn. Before the sky burns in madness. Before the crowds have disappeared. The saddest son returns. To witness its destruction. While underneath the mountain, the golden idol gleams."

"That's pretty sombre," said Windflower.

"This is a serious situation," said the cat.

"Where are you, by the way?" asked Windflower. "The girls are worried sick."

"And you'd be just as happy I'm gone," said Molly.

"Remember, I can see you thinking."

"I know we haven't always had the best relationship," said Windflower. "But you've kind of grown on me."

"I know," said the cat. "I have that effect on people." She smirked again. "I'll be around. I've got something to do. Stay tuned."

Then the cat curled up and went to sleep, and Windflower could feel himself being pulled somehow back to his own bed. He woke and sat up straight. The cat was gone. Sheila stirred beside him.

"Are you okay?" she asked.

"Fine," said Windflower. "Just a dream." Or was it? He tried to remember all the dream, but all he could recall was the riddle. He repeated that to himself a few times to keep it fresh in his mind. Then sleep took over again until he heard the patter of little feet in the room beside him.

When he got downstairs, he found Stella and Amelia Louise fully dressed and ready to go out the door.

"Where are you going?" he asked.

"We're going to look for Molly," said Amelia Louise.

"Maybe we can find her if we go out early in the morning," said Stella. "Let me come with you then," said Windflower. He grabbed his coat and Lady's leash, and soon the small search party was investigating a very quiet Grand Bank. The girls had started out very earnest and were trying to be serious cat detectors, but that gave way to their usual happy, playful selves by the time they turned the corner for home. They were tired and certainly disappointed, but to Windflower they seemed happy that they had tried.

CHAPTER 18

Sheila was up and had coffee on, for which Windflower was very grateful. She also had fruit and oatmeal ready for breakfast. Windflower didn't stay for the school bus this morning but was out the door early enough to get a little time for himself before the craziness of his workday began. He parked at the end of the road to the beach and started the climb up to the Cape, the large, rocky outreach that stretched above Grand Bank. He wouldn't go all the way up, but he felt like he needed to be a little apart from the town in order to get some perspective this morning.

He stopped about halfway up the nearest side of the Cape. That would allow him the vista of the town below and a peek at the Atlantic Ocean just off to his left. He loved this view. It felt like he had a foot in the safety of his adopted home community and still could see the possibility of the vast ocean. He didn't have his smudging kit this morning, but that wouldn't stop him from praying while sitting on a large rock that seemed like a perfect place to stop.

First, he offered gratitude for all that he had. All that he had ever received. Which was a lot when he started listing his blessings. In addition to the suggestion of always starting by giving thanks, Uncle Frank said that if we were grateful, we might get to keep our gifts. If all we did was ask for more, maybe all Creator would hear would be the asking. It was a good approach to praying and to life, thought Windflower as he remembered his aunt and uncle and other ancestors.

He then prayed for strength and guidance throughout the day to do what was right and to practice kindness, even when it was difficult. As he felt the wind blow through his hair and the sun start to warm, he took one long breath in and held it for a moment before blowing it out slowly, like he was letting go of his stress and worries and making room for good energy to enter his body and spirit. Wide awake and ready to face the world, he walked down the hill and back to his car.

His phone rang as soon as he started up his vehicle. He looked down at the screen. "B. Thibault," he read.

"Good morning, Bernard, what's up?"

"Morning, Sarge," said Thibault. "It may be nothing, but I heard something that you might be interested in."

"Go ahead."

"An old friend of mine, associate I'd guess you'd call him, came by my apartment last night. He was high and wanted to sell me some dope. When I said no, he wanted to borrow money. I said no to that, too," said Thibault.

"That was good."

"Well, like I said he was pretty high, and he started yammering on about gold. Gold bars or something that was being melted down. Said the bikers were involved. All hush-hush. I don't know what it all means but thought you might be interested," said Thibault.

"Is this guy okay?" asked Windflower. "Maybe he was just super high or something."

"He was pretty stoned, but I'd say he's not crazy. I'm not sure what the story is, but there's likely something to it."

"Can you give me this guy's name?"

"I can, if you leave me out of it," said Thibault. "I don't want no trouble."

"Sure," said Windflower. "I can do that."

"Corey Osmond," said Thibault. "Have you got everything lined up over there for painting?"

"I think Levi is working on it. See you next week." Windflower hung up and called Tizzard in Marystown.

"Good morning, boss," said Tizzard. "I was just going to call you. We got a report from Interpol via RCMP Headquarters that our man, Coco Meier, was spotted on surveillance tapes in the airport in Saint Pierre."

"Good," said Windflower. "Can you check with Customs

in Fortune to see if they have any record of him coming into Canada, and if there was anyone with him? And can you send me Meier's official mug shot so we can release it to the media?"

"Will do," said Tizzard. "But I've got something even better. Both our guys and the Europeans were looking at Meier and his gang around a series of robberies in and around airports in Europe. One on an Air Canada flight from Switzerland."

"That's the gold heist," said Windflower. "Twenty million dollars' worth. Stolen from a hangar at Pearson Airport in Toronto after the flight had landed."

"Exactly," said Tizzard.

"Here's something even stranger," said Windflower. He told Tizzard about the call from Bernard Thibault.

"Wow," said Tizzard. "They still haven't arrested anyone for that. One theory I heard from an expert on these types of crimes said that it was likely the thieves would melt the gold bars and then ship it back to Europe, where it could be more easily disposed of."

"Better talk to Quigley," said Windflower. "And pick up that Osmond guy. Just hold him for now. If we're right, somebody bigger than us will want to talk to him."

"Will do," said Tizzard. "Listen, can you and Gupta do without her car today? I don't have anyone to bring it over, and I just can't get away myself."

"We can manage for a day. It's Grand Bank. We could walk anywhere we needed if we had to."

Tizzard laughed. "Hey, I saw you on the news last night. You were great but didn't tell them anything."

"You know the score, Eddie," said Windflower. "Be brave when you step in front of the cameras. 'Cowards die many times before their deaths; the valiant never taste of death but once.'"

"My dad always says, 'Two people can keep a secret if one of them is dead,'" replied Tizzard.

"That's harsh, true, and Mark Twain."

"And my dad," said Tizzard.

"Give me updates as you get them." Windflower was still smiling to himself when he walked into his office, where Betsy and Gupta were having a tea and a treat.

Betsy offered Windflower a blueberry muffin, which he was very happy to take. "Tizzard can't come over today, so we're riding together," said Windflower.

"That's great," said Gupta. "Riding shotgun with the famous Sergeant Windflower."

Windflower and Betsy laughed.

"Corporal Tizzard sent over a picture of the dead man," said Betsy. "I've printed up some copies for the media. They're coming at eleven."

Windflower took a look at the photo and the detail underneath. Gian "Coco" Meier, Caucasian, age thirtyeight.

Dual SwissFrench citizen. Scruffy beard and a scowl. Almost a caricature of an outlaw biker, he thought.

"He looked older," said Gupta.

"A sudden, violent death will do that to a person," said Windflower. "I try not to wish any evil on anybody, but I suspect that our friend here has likely done many violent things in his past. Not my form of justice, but..."

"You were very good last night," said Betsy. "My Bob said that we were very lucky to have you."

"Thank you, Betsy. Let's go in back before things get too hectic. I want to bring you up to speed on some things," he said to Gupta.

He ran through with her what he had heard from Tizzard about Meier and the phone call from Bernard Thibault.

"Wow," she said. "Do you think that gold might have made it here?"

"It's possible," said Windflower. "If they were sending it back to Europe, they would most likely send it by boat. Maybe in a shipping container of some sort."

"Maybe concealed inside a shipment of fish or something else," said Gupta. "Certainly plausible. But what was Meier doing in Grand Bank?"

"That's what we need to find out," said Windflower. "And who his connections were in the area. Hopefully Corey Osmond can help with that."

CHAPTER 19

"So, what's the plan for today?" asked Gupta.

Windflower opened his computer. "Here's a list of our informants in Grand Bank. Print it off and then guard it with your life. Some are willing, and some need a little encouragement. Track down as many as you can and ask them if they know anything about Meier. Don't mention the gold yet. We need some more confirmation on that, and we don't want to scare anybody off."

"Can I take the car? Your car?"

"Sure," said Windflower. "I have to get ready for the media, and there's a few things I need to do around here this morning. Come back for lunch, and we'll go over to the café."

Windflower took a look at the media release that Betsy had prepared. She had already added the demographic information about Meier. He thought about what else he could tell the media and if he should mention the biker gang connections. Not yet, he thought. Might spook the locals even more. They would have the general information from the media release and the mugshot. That would be enough for most of them.

While he was wading through the rest of his in-basket and email inbox, Betsy came in to tell him he had a visitor. "Chief Pike is here."

"Send him in."

"Thanks for seeing me," said Pike.

"No worries," said Windflower. "Want some coffee?"

"No, I'm good," said the fire chief. "Well, as good as can be. I'm worried that somebody on my crew might be involved."

"What do you mean, involved?"

"Have you ever heard about firefighter arson?"

"You mean when a firefighter starts the fire?" asked Windflower. "Our fires?"

"It's not that common, and we don't talk about it very often, for obvious reasons," said Pike. "But there has always been a small minority of firefighters who intentionally start fires."

"Why?" asked Windflower. "Isn't that the opposite of what firefighters are supposed to do?"

"Agreed," said Pike. "I don't know too much about it, but from what I've read about the issue in the United States, their motives could range from boredom and wanting excitement to be wanting to be seen as a hero when they show up to fight the fire."

"And you think one of your people might be doing this?"

"It is a possibility," said Pike. "I have little evidence but my suspicions.

That's why I'm bringing it to you."

"What makes you suspicious?"

"For the last two fires, one volunteer firefighter was first on the scene, even before me," said Pike. "I don't know about the first fire, since I was on vacation when that one happened."

"Maybe they just live closer," said Windflower.

"No, there's one who lives some of the farthest away."

"You must have more than that, though," said Windflower. "Who are you thinking about?"

"Greg Rose," said Pike. "The guy who was with me the other day. At first, I thought he was just upset about seeing a dead body. That would shake anybody up. But now I think he may have been disturbed because he thought someone might have died in a fire that he started."

Or maybe he even killed the guy, thought Windflower, but he kept that to himself for now. "Anything else?"

"Yeah," said the fire chief. "Now he's all happy and cheerful, making jokes and everything. That's a pretty rapid turnaround in a day or so. I'm thinking that if it was him, that now he believes he's gotten away with it."

"I guess that's a possibility. We could bring him in and talk to him."

"That might scare him off," said Pike. "Right now, I'd like to throttle him. I can't believe one of our own would do this. But I don't have any hard evidence."

"Okay, we can see him when he gets off work," said Windflower. "Great," said Pike. "He works at the fish plant and lives almost out at the T. The new bungalow just off the highway."

"I know that place," said Windflower. "I think it might be better to see him at home. We'll take a run out there later on."

"Okay, I'll leave it with you," said the fire chief. "I hope I'm wrong, but I've got a bad feeling about all of this."

Windflower stood and shook his hand before leading him out.

Betsy paused from her phone calls to say goodbye to the fire chief. "We're expecting a full house," she whispered to Windflower. He wasn't surprised. There was already a camera crew getting some outside shots, and another van was pulling up as Chief Pike drove away. He went back into his office and closed the door. He needed to clear his mind of everything that had happened so far today so that he could concentrate on get ting through the media conference.

By the time everything was set up, he was ready too.

This morning's event was a lot tougher than the previous evening. It seemed like the media people knew that they were being managed, which they hated, and that Windflower knew more than he would tell them. They were right on both counts, but Windflower was happy to listen to their questions and give them his pat responses. At the end he did a short walk outside so that they would have an action shot for their newscast and then smiled and walked back in.

"That went well," said Betsy.

"We survived," said Windflower. "But unless we start getting some results to tell them and everyone at the meeting last night, we're going to be in big trouble."

"My Bob says, 'It is better to keep your mouth closed and let people think you are a fool than to open it and remove all doubt.'"

"I've heard that somewhere before," said Windflower. "Good advice, though."

He went back to his office, expecting to have a few minutes of relative peace on this crazy morning, but that was not to be. There was good news, and maybe not surprisingly, more bad news as well. Windflower was very happy about the good news.

"We found Molly," said Sheila. "She was over near where the last fire was. One of the young firefighters saw her, recognized the picture and got her to come with an offer of a piece of his tuna fish sandwich."

"Which no cat could refuse," said Windflower. "What was she doing over there?"

"I have no idea," said Sheila. "But I can't wait until the

girls get home. I've given her a bath, which she did not like at all, and a whole can of salmon that she devoured. God knows what she's been eating. She looks a little scrawny and thinner, but we can fatten her up."

"That is excellent news," said Windflower. "I'm looking forward to seeing her, too."

CHAPTER 20

He hung up the phone and allowed himself to savour this pleasant moment a little longer. But he did have a nagging question that came back to him as he thought about Molly and remembered his dream. What was she doing at that house? And what was that riddle again? "Before the darkness falls to dawn. Before the sky burns in madness. Before the crowds have disappeared. The saddest son returns. To witness its destruction. While underneath the mountain, the golden idol gleams." What the heck did that mean?

He didn't have much more time to enjoy his good news because his phone rang. It was Eddie Tizzard.

"Corey Osmond is dead," said Tizzard. "I went to his apartment and knocked but no answer. I got the super to open the door, and he was dead on the floor, a needle still in his arm. No pulse. I tried naloxone and CPR, and so did the paramedics, but he's gone. We'll have to wait for an autopsy, but it looks like an overdose. I've got a team tracking back through his known contacts, but that will take time, too."

"Talk to Bernard Thibault," said Windflower. "He might know more about who Osmond was hanging around with. Plus, he still has an ear on the street. But be careful with him. He doesn't want to get pulled into anything right now."

"Okay," said Tizzard. "I'll see Thibault. Oh, and Quigley called me. He said that there's a lot of interest in Meier. He wants all the details. I suggested he call you."

"Thanks," said Windflower. "Call me after you talk with Thibault."

He hung up and was hoping nothing else would happen. He could barely keep up with what was going on. But sometimes it was like this with investigations. One moment you had nothing and the next you had a halfdozen leads. He didn't have that many yet, but enough to make him think they were moving in the right direction. Someone else who was moving in the right direction was Constable Gupta, who had come to pick him up for lunch.

"Any luck this morning?" he asked as he got into the car.

"Not much," said Gupta. "Surprised a few of our friends. I didn't check, but I bet the ones I saw were likely in violation of any restrictions they may be under. Both in terms of alcohol and drugs and the company they keep."

"I never understood some of the release conditions they

put on people," said Windflower. "I mean, I get the drugs and booze stuff. That's likely why they ended up in jail in the first place. But who are they supposed to hang around with? Some of their prohibited contacts are their family."

"In any case, only one knew Corey Osmond, said some of his family lived over here in Grand Bank," said Gupta. "But nothing on gold or robberies or anything else. I guess they could be lying, but the message is consistent."

"We'll check with Betsy when we get back about Osmond's family connections," said Windflower. "But I think your intuition may be right. Keep plugging away."

Gupta nodded her agreement as they pulled up in front of the Mug-Up. Inside, the lunch crowd was busy eating soup and sandwiches, and Windflower and Gupta both ordered the same thing, turkey with dressing sandwiches and pea soup. The pair ate their lunch quietly, and when they were finished, Windflower gave Gupta an update on what he had heard from Tizzard.

"Wow, an overdose to go along with everything else," said Gupta. "And not to be too disrespectful of the dead, but we lost a potential crucial witness."

"I know," said Windflower. "We might have something moving on the arson, though." He told her about his conversation with Chief Pike. "I think the day shift gets out at the plant at four, so we can go over to Rose's house shortly afterwards."

"Sure," said Gupta. "That's a strange phenomenon.

Firefighters starting a fire so they can put them out. Like cops committing crimes so that they can look like they're solving them."

"It does happen," said Windflower. "I'm not sure how often, but it does occur. I hear that people who study this kind of thing call it a hero syndrome."

"Doesn't sound like much of a hero to me," said Gupta. "More like a mental illness."

"That's true, too," said Windflower as they went to the cash to pay their bill. He looked around the corner in the kitchen and waved to Moira. "No Herb today?" he called out.

"I gave him the day off," said Moira, laughing. "He was whining about only so many good days left for troutin' this year."

Windflower laughed, too. "Time off for good behaviour. I hope he gets some big ones."

"You'll find out tomorrow night," said Moira. "I talked to Sheila."

"Then I wish him double luck."

He headed back to the car, where Gupta was waiting for him. She handed him the keys, but he indicated she could continue. She seemed pleased by that. Another reminder that it doesn't take much to make people happy. She drove to the RCMP office and dropped him off. She was starting to drive off when he tapped on the window.

"Do you need to go back to Marystown tonight?" he asked. "I kinda need to get a change of clothes and stuff."

"Why don't you see how many more of our insiders you can talk to and then just take this car back to Marystown?"

"That would be great," said Gupta. "But don't you need a vehicle?"

"I can get by for one night," said Windflower. "Besides, I could use the exercise."

"Thank you," said Gupta, rolling up the window and driving away with a big smile plastered across her face. "See you at four."

As Windflower walked inside the building, Betsy was just getting off a call, and he stopped to talk to her.

"Do you know Corey Osmond?" he asked. "Someone said he had family in Grand Bank."

"Corey is Fred and Mildred's son," said Betsy. "Fred is from here. He moved over to Marystown when the shipyard opened. Mildred is from Ship Cove."

"I'm afraid that Corey is dead," said Windflower. "Oh no. Was he murdered?"

"Why would you say that?"

"He's been in trouble all his life," said Betsy. "Was even charged with manslaughter in a fight where he killed somebody. But somehow, he got off on that. My Bob used to say that he didn't make friends, he made enemies."

"I actually think it might have been a drug overdose," said Windflower. "But it's very recent and certainly not out in public yet."

"Don't worry about me," said Betsy. "I try never to share bad news.

People find that out quick enough on their own."

"Is any of Corey's family still in Grand Bank?"

"No, b'y," said Betsy. "All of Fred's siblings moved away years ago. Old Mister Osmond stayed in their house until he moved into the Blue Crest, where he died. His house was where the fire was the other day."

That got Windflower's attention. "Thank you, Betsy. You've been very helpful, as usual." He walked away leaving Betsy looking pleased as punch. Another satisfied customer, he thought.

Finally, he had a few moments alone to think. What he just heard was interesting. Very interesting. Now he was starting to find connections. The recent fire, Corey Osmond and Coco Meier. Somehow, they might all be connected. But how? His brief thinking time was interrupted by Betsy, who was back at his door. "Superintendent Quigley on Line 1."

CHAPTER 21

"Looks like you've put Grand Bank on the map again," said Quigley. "Multiple arsons, drugs, diamonds, now gold? What's going on over there?"

"All outsiders, I would point out," said Windflower. "Most of it, anyway. How can I help you, Superintendent?"

"I like that degree of respect," said Quigley. "One must give the devil his due."

"Not the exact quote, but not bad," said Quigley. "Although I'm not sure I like being called the devil twice in one day. In any case, I talked to Tizzard, but he sent me over to you. I can't tell you how much interest you have generated from HQ on this. Tell me everything you know about Coco Meier and the gold."

"Well, we're still trying to figure all this out," said

Windflower. "And I don't think you've heard yet, but our main source of info is dead. Looks like an overdose."

"Is that the Osmond guy?"

"Corey Osmond," said Windflower. "We're following up on a few things over here, and Bernard Thibault has been helping us. I guess our big question is, what was Coco Meier doing in Grand Bank? Osmond has some family over here, but none of them are still alive."

"Anyone know or hear anything about gold?"

"Not so far," said Windflower. "Gupta is still tracking people down, but nothing and no connections to Osmond or Meier."

"Both the Europeans and our guys at Headquarters think that Meier and the Swiss Outlaws are involved in the gold heist in Toronto," said Quigley.

"They have some evidence of that on the ground in Zurich, but they also think that they were only players, and not the ringleaders. Someone had to orchestrate this on the ground at Pearson and then get the shipment out of there and somewhere else."

"I heard rumours that whoever took it was going to melt the gold bars and ship it back over to Europe," said Windflower.

"That's one theory," said Quigley. "And why people are so interested in Meier and what he was doing so far from home."

"We'll keep plugging away," said Windflower.

"Thank you, Winston. Once again, you have been thrust into the spotlight."

"I didn't seek it, that's for sure," said Windflower. "And I didn't expect it, in Grand Bank of all places."

"Ah, 'Some are born great, some achieve greatness, and some have greatness thrust upon them,'" said Quigley.

Windflower struggled to find a good response but was not quick enough. Again. He realized that he hadn't told Quigley about the possible connection of Corey Osmond to the house where Meier had died. He tried to call him back, but the line was busy already. He'd tell him later, he thought as he saw Sheila and the two girls show up outside his window.

"They wanted you to see Molly," said Sheila, holding a somewhat dazed Molly in her arms.

"She's back," said Amelia Louise.

"And she's never going away again," said Stella.

"We're all going to make sure of that, right?" asked Windflower. Both girls nodded vigorously.

"I'm happy she's back," said Windflower.

"Me too," said Sheila. "Me, too."

"Me three," said Stella.

"Me four," said Amelia Louise.

"I'll see you guys at home soon," said Windflower.

"And we're going to Herb and Moira's tomorrow night," said Sheila.

"That makes me happy, too," said Windflower. "I saw Moira today at lunch."

Sheila waved goodbye and loaded the cat and the girls back into the car.

Windflower went back inside.

"I see your lost cat has decided to come home," said Betsy.

"I think Sheila found her," said Windflower.

"Cats are only found when they want to be found," said Betsy. "I believe that cats choose us."

"I don't disagree," said Windflower. "Sometimes it feels like Molly barely tolerates me."

"'They allow us the pleasure of their company,'" said Betsy. "Anyway, I'm gone for the evening. Have a good night, Sergeant."

"Goodnight, Betsy," he replied. Soon after, his car with Gupta at the wheel pulled up in front of the building, and he jumped in.

"We're going out towards the T," he said. "Let's go see what Greg Rose has to say."

There were two vehicles in the driveway when they arrived, a beatup Honda Accord and a brandnew pickup. "Bet I know which one is his," said Gupta.

A large German Shepherd greeted them as they walked up the driveway. He had a fierce and ferocious sounding bark, but he was tied up and didn't cause them any trouble. Greg Rose came to the door. He looked surprised, thought Windflower. That wasn't a bad thing.

"Sergeant, what are you doing here?"

Windflower fibbed a little. "We're interviewing some of the volunteer firefighters about the recent fires. It should only take a few minutes."

"Okay," said Rose. "Let me tell the missus I'm talking with you. She's out back with the kids."

When he came back, he said, "We can sit here on the porch if you like." He seemed a little more comfortable with the situation.

"You've met Constable Gupta?" asked Windflower.

"Yes," said Rose, nodding to Gupta, who now had her notebook out. "So, did you notice anything suspicious about any of the fires?" asked

Windflower. "Anything seem out of the ordinary? You're from Grand Bank, right?" He asked that last question to make him even more comfortable.

"Yes, b'y, my whole life," said Rose. "Born and bred. But I don't know why you're talking to me. You should talk to the chief. I'm just a volunteer like everybody else."

"We have talked to Chief Pike a few times," said Windflower. "He said that you were one of the first on the scene of the last fire. How did you get there so fast?"

"Well, I monitor our chat, and I can get there pretty fast in this new rig," said Rose, pointing at his pickup.

"But you're almost the farthest away from town."

"Hard to admit to the Mounties, but I go pretty fast," said Rose.

He was still pretty calm, thought Windflower. He decided to shake it up a little. "Why were you so upset the other morning?"

That worked. Rose grew flushed and started to stammer. "It's hard to see a dead body like that," he said. "Never expected to see someone shot in Grand Bank. Is that all? I gotta go be with my kids."

"That's fine," said Windflower. "Thank you for your time."

CHAPTER 22

Back in the car, Gupta spoke first. "What did you think?"

"I'm not quite sure, but I have a feeling he's lying," said Windflower. "We haven't publicly released that Meier was shot. And he's a bit too smug for me."

"He could have just heard the rumours," said Gupta. "Or he could be involved."

"We don't really have much," said Gupta.

"True, but maybe he makes a mistake now. I'm sure he'll figure out that he's the only firefighter we're talking to beside the chief. If he thinks we're looking at him, he might try to cover up something. But unless he does something else, we haven't got much to go on."

"Unless he sets another fire," said Gupta as they neared Windflower's house.

"Let's hope not," said Windflower. "Have a good evening."

He waved goodbye and watched her drive away. Another fire, he thought. "I'm not sure anybody could go through that," he said out loud.

"Who are you talking to?" asked Sheila as she met him at the door. "Saying goodbye to Gupta," he said, trying to get in as quickly as he could.

"Why don't you get changed, and then I've got some fresh chicken breasts from Warren's that I hoped you could do something with for supper?"

"Absolutely," said Windflower, who first went to say hello to Stella and Amelia Louise, who were taking turns holding Molly and squeezing her. Despite this outpouring of love, Molly did not look pleased at all.

Windflower tried an intervention. "Maybe Molly needs a little break," he said gently. "She looks a little tired after all her adventures."

As if on cue, the cat closed her eyes.

"See?" he said, picking up the cat and starting to bring her into the kitchen.

"But she just got home," said Amelia Louise.

"And we missed her so much," said Stella.

"If we really love her and want to take care of her, then she needs to have some rest right now," said Windflower. "You can watch her sleep."

Both girls rolled their eyes, but Sheila came to his rescue.

"Your dad is right," she said. "Molly needs some rest.

Why don't you finish your homework before supper? Maybe he'll take us for ice cream for dessert."

That was enough incentive for the girls to forget about their cat for a few minutes and take out papers from their book bags.

Windflower kissed Sheila and went upstairs to have his shower and think about how he could cook the chicken for supper. He decided to barbeque it with some roasted small potatoes and steamed broccoli.

He didn't have time to marinate the chicken, so he first cut the breasts in half and then pounded the pieces with a kitchen mallet to make them even thinner. That would allow the chicken to cook faster. He washed some of the small potatoes and put them in the oven on high heat to get them started while he made his sauce.

A cup of ketchup with half a cup of brown sugar and half a cup of vinegar was the base. Then he added Dijon mustard, Worcestershire sauce and sriracha, along with garlic powder, onion powder and chili powder. He finished it off with his new trick addition, six drops of liquid smoke. He whisked the mixture and put it in the fridge to cool.

He went outside to light the barbeque with Lady at his heels and a suddenly attentive Molly watching his every move. While the grill heated up, he chopped the broccoli and put that in the steamer. He cut the potatoes in half, smothered them in butter and salt and pepper and put them tin foil. He went back out and brushed the hot side of the grill with olive oil and put the tin-foiled potatoes on the grill.

Now he was ready for the chicken. A couple of minutes on each side and then into the house for the sauce. He called to Sheila to put the broccoli on and set the table. A few minutes later he was back in with a delicious looking plate of grilled chicken coated in his sauce that had caramelized nicely all over the chicken.

It tasted as good as it looked. Everybody was very pleased with their meal, including Lady, who got a small piece of chicken in her bowl, and Molly, who got an even bigger portion.

"I love the bite at the end," said Sheila as they were finishing up.

"That's the liquid smoke," said Windflower. "If you don't have a smoker or just don't have time, it's a great way to get a hot and smoky flavour. I love it."

By now the girls had long past moved beyond chicken and were not too patiently waiting for the adults to clean up so they could go get ice cream. There was a large crowd surrounding the dairy bar, as if they knew this could be one of the last good nights for ice cream. He went inside and got their cones while Sheila, the girls, and Lady waited outside. Molly was safely and securely at home.

They took their softserve cones over to the children's playground and sat on a bench to enjoy them. They were nearly finished when a car came by and stopped next to them. The driver rolled down his window. It was Doctor Sanjay and his wife Repa. The Sanjays parked and came to join them in the park.

"Such a wonderful evening," said the doctor. "Are you enjoying your ice cream?" he asked the girls.

The girls nodded their approval, and Windflower got up so Repa could join Sheila on the bench. Soon after, the girls finished their treat and were off playing in the park.

"Do you have a moment to chat?" asked Sanjay, motioning for Windflower to come with him.

"Sure," said Windflower, following the diminutive doctor as he started walking around the track that circled the playground.

"I heard a rumble," said Sanjay. "More than a rumour, I think. You know how news travels quickly around here."

"What did you hear?"

"That someone from here might be involved in the fires," said Sanjay.

"Someone on the inside."

"That is disturbing," said Windflower. "Do you know who they are talking about?"

"That wasn't clear," said Sanjay. "At first, I thought it was the usual gossip. But now I have heard it a couple of times. Even if it is untrue, it does cause another level of concern."

"Agreed," said Windflower. "It's hard to know which is worse, having someone outside take these terrible actions, or someone you know."

"I will not ask you if it is true or not," said Sanjay. "I know I can trust you to take the appropriate actions."

"Thank you, Vijay, I appreciate your faith in me."

"'Faith is the bird that feels the light when the dawn is still dark,'" replied the doctor. "Now, enough business. Let us go see those beautiful girls of yours."

After fawning over them for a few more minutes, Sanjay reached into his wallet and pulled out two crisp ten-dollar bills. He handed one each to the girls. Their eyes grew big, and they looked to their mother for guidance.

"You shouldn't have," she said.

"I insist," said the doctor. "I am hoping to see your husband soon for some Scotch tasting, but I never see these two little darlings. It is my pleasure."

The girls smiled and said "thank you" over and over again. They gave both the Sanjays a hug goodbye and were soon happily skipping home, chattering incessantly about what they were going to buy with their new money.

CHAPTER 23

Windflower and Sheila said their goodbyes and caught up quickly to the girls before they reached the store.

"Not tonight," Sheila said firmly, much to the chagrin of her daughters. "We'll go to Dollarama after school tomorrow."

That was enough to buy peace and get everybody safely home. Lady had already been walked, but Windflower decided to take her for another round of the neighbourhood. It was such a nice evening that he stretched it to include a stroll on the wharf and a gaze out at the lighthouse, the white light of which was now blinking in the near darkness of the ocean. Satisfied that he had taken full pleasure from this evening, he walked back home and helped Sheila get two excited girls ready for bed.

They were still giggling and calling out to each other when Sheila and Windflower went back downstairs.

"The ice cream," he said. "And the money."

Windflower made them a pot of tea and brought it into the living room. The TV was on, but they weren't really watching anything, simply enjoying the tea and each other's company.

"I have to go to Marystown tomorrow," said Sheila. "I have a meeting, and then I'm having lunch with a friend. Do you need anything?"

"Not really," said Windflower. But then he remembered his car. "I do need something," he said. "My car. Gupta took it back with her. Maybe I can get a ride over with you. I need to see Terri Pilgrim, and I can have a quick staff meeting while I'm there."

"Perfect," said Sheila. "I was planning to leave around ten or ten-thirty.

Would that work for you?"

"That would be great," said Windflower. "I'll text Tizzard to get him to set things up."

"See you upstairs."

Windflower texted Tizzard and Terri Pilgrim. Terri was the admin assistant to the inspector position, but was really the office manager in Marys town. She looked after all the details over there so Windflower didn't have to worry about them. He would come over once a week or so to check in and meet with the leadership team, which now included Tizzard, a sergeant and two other corporals. Other than Tizzard, they were all relatively new, which made Terri's coordination role crucial.

Windflower also texted Gupta to tell her that he was picking up his car and to ask her to call him in the morning. Then he went to the kitchen for a pat on the head good night to Lady and a smile for a sleeping Molly, who did not stir as he walked past. She'd probably had a few rough days, he thought. Rougher than what she was used to, that's for sure. He turned out the lights, and minutes later he was in bed himself. Sheila was reading again, but that didn't stop him from falling asleep quickly.

Unfortunately, his nighttime reverie was aborted shortly afterwards.

He first heard a hissing, and then he sat up in bed to see Molly there, looking at him.

"C'mon," said the cat.

Windflower glanced at Sheila to see if she had woken up.

"It's a dream," said the cat. "She can't hear me. Only you. How many times do you have to do this to get it right? Geez."

"Okay, I'm coming," said Windflower. "Where are we going?"

"Upstairs," was all the cat replied.

Since they were on the top floor and the attic was quite small, Windflower was pretty sure they were going off on an adventure. Somewhere "up there." But all he could do was follow, and as they left the bedroom he could feel himself and the cat being lifted up, higher and higher. Not as high as before with his aunt and uncle, but high enough that Grand Bank was a simple string of lights on the ground below.

"I guess we're not going to Heaven," he said when they stopped rising and started to float around slowly.

"Nope," said the cat. "This is the end of the road. My job was to turn you over to my companion."

"Wait," said Windflower as he sensed the cat leaving. "Do you have anything for me?"

"I gave you the riddle," said Molly. "And thanks for the chicken, by the way. Not my favourite, but still good. Keep it up."

With that the cat was gone and another shape started appearing in the sky beside him. "That cat is something, isn't she?" said a voice, laughing.

"Who are you, and why can't I see you?" asked Windflower.

"You are a slow learner, aren't you?" said the voice. "I'm from the other side, obviously. I'm sorry I didn't dress for the occasion."

"Okay, now I get it," said Windflower. "You're dead." The voice simply sighed at that remark.

"So, who are you and why are you here?" asked Windflower. "And do you have anything for me?"

"Good questions," said the voice, which Windflower could now tell was male. "You don't really know me. But I've been watching you for years now. Even as we sometimes tease you from up here, you are a kind and gentle man."

"Thank you," said Windflower.

"I know you are struggling with some serious work right now. Things that are very important to the community," said the voice. "But ignore your head. 'Trust your instincts. Intuition doesn't lie.'"

"That's a quote, isn't it?" asked Windflower. "By someone famous?"

"Not me, obviously," said the voice. "The truth sometimes comes from strange places. That's Oprah Winfrey."

"So, you have advice for me. Is that why you came?"

"No, I need a favour," said the voice. "I know it's weird to be asked to do something. But my brother is in danger. I need you to trust your instincts and help him out."

Windflower had a thousand more questions now, but he felt himself falling downwards and soon after was back in his bed.

This time he couldn't go back to sleep. He had to process what had just happened in his dream. He went to the bathroom and washed his face. Then he went downstairs and took a peek in at the pets in the kitchen. Lady came to him immediately. Molly looked like she was solidly asleep in her bed and didn't move as much as an eyelid.

He had a glass of water and took a long, deep breath. Who was that person, and who was their brother? Then he remembered. Eddie Tizzard had a brother who was killed years ago in Afghanistan while serving in the Canadian military. Both Eddie and his father talked about him a lot. They still missed him today. What was his name? Windflower searched his memory but came up blank. Only after he got back in bed and was finally starting to fall asleep did it come to him. Sean. Sean Tizzard. Now, what kind of danger was his brother in, and what was Windflower supposed to do about it?

Those questions kept him awake a lot longer, until tiredness mercifully overtook him and he finally got back to sleep.

CHAPTER 24

He was still tired in the morning, so tired he didn't hear the first rounds of morning commotion. But perking coffee got his attention and got him out of bed and downstairs. Sheila had given the girls fruit and cold cereal, and Windflower plucked the last of the Rice Crispies out of the mini-packets on the counter.

"Thank goodness, there's one left," he said, kissing Sheila and grabbing a cup of coffee.

"No one eats them but you," said Amelia Louise.

"True," said Sheila. "They would much rather have Frosted Flakes or Cap'n Crunch."

"They'll all gone, Mommy," said Stella. "All that's left now is All-Bran, and not even Daddy will eat that one."

"That is true, too," said Windflower.

"Okay, girls, finish up and get your knapsacks organized," said Sheila. "Lunches are on the counter."

"I'll tidy up here if you want a break," said Windflower.

"Thanks," said Sheila. "I'll just text and confirm my meetings."

The school bus arrived as soon as the girls had their boots and coats on, and Windflower walked out with them and waved until they got safely on their way. Then he went back in and finished his own breakfast. Sheila came back to say her meetings were confirmed.

"Great, then I'll head over to the office and see you around ten thirty," said Windflower.

"See you then," said Sheila.

Betsy greeted Windflower with a smile and tin of home-made cookies.

"Hermit cookies. My favourite," said Windflower.

"Take a few then," said Betsy. "What's going on today?" she asked as Windflower bit into a cookie and stuffed another two into a napkin for his trip with Sheila later in the morning.

"I'm going over to Marystown to meet with the folks over there, but I'll be back this afternoon sometime."

"Well, take the whole tin over," she said. "I'm sure Corporal Tizzard would like one."

"Or several," said Windflower. "That's very kind."

"My Bob says it's good to be kind. And you can always be kind."

"That sounds like the Dalai Lama," said Windflower.

"I'll tell Bob," said Betsy. "He'll be pleased."

Windflower thanked Betsy again for the treat, got himself a coffee and went to his office to make his calls. First up was Gupta. She was happy to hear from him and even more pleased that she didn't have to figure out how to get his car back over to him in Grand Bank.

"Don't worry about that," said Windflower. "I've got a ride. And why don't you work from Marystown today? There's not much more to do over here. Come back on Thursday or Friday."

"That's great," said Gupta. "I do have a few things to do here and might even get a chance to do laundry."

Windflower laughed and hung up with his young constable. Next was Eddie Tizzard.

"We're all set up for your meeting," said Tizzard. "Terri has ordered some sandwiches so we can do it over lunch. I also talked to Bernard Thibault. He was pretty upset."

"What's Bernard upset about?"

"He says there's no way that Corey Osmond overdosed. Says he was much too careful and never used alone," said Tizzard.

"What does he think happened?"

"He thinks somebody killed him," said Tizzard.

"Can you set up a meeting with me and Bernard?" asked Windflower. "He won't want to come to the RCMP building, so we should arrange to meet him somewhere he's comfortable."

"Okay, will do," said Tizzard. "Anything else?"

Windflower hesitated. Did he want to tell him about his dream? Might be uncomfortable, he thought. Best to do it in person, he decided. "No, that's it for now," he said. Then he added, "'Be wary then; best safety lies in fear.'"

"What's there to be afraid of?" asked Tizzard. "It's Marystown." Then he laughed.

Windflower laughed too, a little less heartily, and hung up. He didn't have much time to think about that interaction as Betsy came in to tell him that Superintendent Quigley was on the phone and that he had a visitor.

"Ask them to wait," he said to Betsy. "I'll talk to the superintendent first... Good morning, Ron."

"Good morning, Winston. No formalities this morning?"

"Too busy for that stuff," said Windflower. "Besides, we've known each other too long for that. And it does feel like 'hell is empty and all the devils are here right now.'"

"My condolences," said Quigley. "But 'let me embrace thee, sour adversity, for wise men say it is the wisest course.'"

"Easy for you to say. So, how can I help you this morning, Superintendent?"

"Ah, I like that," said Quigley. "I have some news for you from my friend in Saint Pierre. Apparently, the late Coco Meier had some associates with him over there. He's managed to get some footage from a closed-circuit camera at the airport. He's going to try to pull some stills and send them over. He didn't recognize the other two men."

"That would be good," said Windflower. "I'm guessing that the same trio would show up on the CCTV over here in Fortune, too. I thought we checked on that, but I will follow up. You always wonder how criminals just move through airports and border points so easily."

"Lack of attention, wilful ignorance, and straight-up being in bed with the bad guys," said Quigley. "Eddie knows they have a problem on their end. Their security changes hands every so often, but the crooks seem to be able to buy their way through. I'd be more worried if anything like that is happening on our end."

"Like I said, we'll check out the situation in Fortune," said Windflower.

"Okay, I'll leave it with you," said Quigley. "'Boldness be your friend.'"

"'Virtue is bold, and goodness never fearful,'" replied Windflower.

"Touché," said Quigley. "Have a good day, my friend."

Windflower walked out to see Betsy after his call and to refresh his coffee. He was surprised to see Chief Pike waiting for him.

"Coffee?" he asked.

"Sure, why not?" said the fire chief. He followed Windflower to the back, and they sat in the small coffee room.

"What's up?"

"Two things," said Pike. "Greg Rose is not pleased that he was interviewed by you and your constable. He checked around and now knows that he was the only firefighter you talked to."

Windflower shrugged. "Just doing our job."

"I know," said the chief. "But the other thing I found out is that Rose has a number of weapons in his house. One of the other men told me about them. I mean, everybody's got a rifle for moose hunting and some likes shooting birds, but he's got more than that."

"What kind of guns?"

"Two rifles, a sawed-off shotgun and a number of pistols and handguns," said Pike. "Now, I haven't seen them, but my guy says he has a cabinet in the basement. I don't know if it's important. I just thought you should know."

"Thank you very much," said Windflower. "We'll check that out."

CHAPTER 25

He walked Pike out to the front and stopped to talk to Betsy.

"I need you to do a couple of things," he said. "Can you check the gun registry and see what, if any, guns may be registered to Greg Rose, one of the volunteer firefighters? And can you also see if the Fortune Customs office can review their tapes and see if they can see a picture of the dead man, Meier?"

"I have already asked them about that," said Betsy. "But I'll go back and see what they have to say. And we did receive some pictures from Saint Pierre. I've printed them out, or you can look at them on the computer."

He reached for the pictures in her hand. They were black-and-white and grainy, but he could clearly make out Coco Meier standing with two other men. One was a large man with a bushy beard. The second was slighter in girth and stature. He didn't recognize either of them.

Betsy stood next to him as if she was expecting something. "Yes?"

"I don't know both of them, but the smaller man is Todd Osmond," she said.

"Is he related to Corey Osmond?"

"His older brother," said Betsy. "If Corey was a problem child, then Todd was the devil's spawn."

"Can you send these pictures to Corporal Tizzard to see if he knows the other man? Have him send it up the line to Quigley and HQ as well," said Windflower. "Also, ask him if he knows where Todd Osmond is and if he can find him to bring him in. And when you talk to Fortune, see if any of these three men show up on their cameras."

"Will do," said Betsy, taking notes. "I think your ride is here," she added, pointing out the window.

Windflower grabbed his tin of biscuits and ran out to meet Sheila. "I'll call you," he shouted back to Betsy.

"Cookie?" he asked Sheila.

"Thank you," she said. "I love hermit cookies. Aren't you having any?"

"I've had a couple and more coffee than I can handle," said Windflower.

"So much happening, my head is spinning."

"Well, there's not much you can do for the next forty

minutes or so. You might as well sit back and enjoy the ride," said Sheila.

"That, my dear, is an excellent idea."

Windflower had done the drive back and forth to Marystown so much that he knew every hill and every bend in the road. Coming out of Grand Bank, they first passed the road to the L'Anse au Loup T and the collection of cabins across the way.

"More like houses than cabins now," said Sheila. "At one time these really were small cabins that people used when they lived up here during the summer. They all had large gardens and grew vegetables for the winter."

"It must have been nice for the women to get a break," said Windflower.

"They still had to cook and clean and helped harvest the crops and look after the animals," said Sheila. "But at least they got away from those big iron wood stoves when the weather got hot."

They drove past Molliers and Grand Beach, communities that had existed independently for years but were now greatly diminished as people chose to live in more established and better serviced areas closer to schools and clinics. Next was the turnoff to Frenchman's Cove.

"Did French people settle this place?" asked Windflower.

"Frenchman's Cove has been around a long time," said Sheila. "I heard people say that a family of Cluetts were the first settlers back in the 1830s and that they may have been French-speaking."

"All I really know about it is the provincial park and golf course," said Windflower as they continued to drive along the highway until they came to the entrance to Garnish. "Now, Garnish I love," he said. "Especially the Bakeapple Festival every August."

"There's more to Garnish than that," said Sheila, although she had to admit to herself that she enjoyed the week-long activities and meals sponsored by community groups that featured the treasured bakeapple. "Garnish was a crucial part of the old Banks fishery, and it was here that they cut the lumber for the schooners and then shipped it back over to Grand Bank for finishing,"

"I still like the Bakeapple Festival," said Windflower. He smiled as he thought of the peach-coloured jam and pie filling that came from these small berries that grew in marshy areas all over this part of the world. "But why do they call them bakeapples?"

"I guess it's because when you cook them, they kind of smell like apples," said Sheila. "But whatever the reason, they're sum good, b'y."

Windflower laughed and heartily agreed.

The couple spent the last few minutes together talking about the kids and their activities, and before they knew it they were passing the turnoff to Creston North and the beginning of Marystown. Sheila dropped Windflower off at the RCMP building.

"Don't forget, we have supper at the Stoodleys tonight," she called out to him.

He waved and walked into the building and up to the second floor, where Tizzard and Terri Pilgrim were chatting.

"Good morning to you both," said Windflower. "How is everybody? I come bearing gifts." He handed the tin of cookies to Pilgrim. "From Betsy," he added.

"Great," said Tizzard. "I have a few things to talk to you about before the meeting. But I bet Terri has some stuff for you, too."

"I do," said the admin assistant as Tizzard wandered back into his of fice. "It's nice to see you. How are things at home?"

"Things are well," said Windflower. "The girls are thriving at school and in their activities, and we even found our lost cat."

"Congratulations," said Pilgrim. "Corporal Tizzard has prepared the schedule for the month for your approval, and there are a number of leave forms to approve. Plus, it's time for employee evaluations."

If there was anything that Windflower hated more than paperwork, it was employee evaluations. "Is there any way out of that?"

"Well, if Superintendent Quigley approves, you could delegate the responsibility for all of the evaluations, except his and mine, to Corporal Tizzard," said Pilgrim.

"You are brilliant," said Windflower as he signed the leave forms and approved the schedule.

"Would you like me to draft that memo to Superintendent Quigley?" asked Pilgrim.

"Yes, please," said Windflower, handing back the papers and walking inside to see Tizzard.

"I guess this is technically your office as inspector," said Tizzard. "I could move out."

"No, no, it's fine," said Windflower. "You can ably assist me from in here. So, what have you got for me?"

"We're set up to meet Bernard Thibault right after our meeting here," said Tizzard. "He was pretty nervous about it, though. We'll meet up with him behind the Canadian Tire."

"Great," said Windflower. "Did you see the pictures from Saint Pierre that Betsy sent over? And what about Todd Osmond? Betsy says he has a bad reputation."

"Well deserved," said Tizzard. "He's well connected to a number of biker gangs, including the Outlaws and Bacchus. It appears from what we can tell that he drifts in and out of here periodically. But he's been in serious trouble in at least four Canadian provinces so far. Career criminal. Not a biker, but a certified one-percenter."

"Is he around here now?"

"We're looking," said Tizzard. "But somebody who is around here is the other guy in the pictures. His name is Robert 'Snake' Gibbons." He opened a file that was sitting on his desk. "He has major connections to the outlaw bikers. He was originally part of the Loners motorcycle club, but when there was the big biker war in Ontario, he refused to be patched over into the Hells Angels and linked up with the Outlaws. But that was a dangerous move, and he had to get out of Ontario. That's when he moved east and got involved with some of the local gangs in Nova Scotia and eventually connected with Bacchus."

"Wow," said Windflower. "He's heavyduty. Where is he now?"

"He has been over here a few times in the past as part of their annual rides, but we think he's in Nova Scotia," said Tizzard. "But we've got our antennae up."

"Okay," said Windflower. "Now we have three known bad guys operating right in front of our eyes and nobody, including Customs in Fortune, seeing anything until one of them shows up dead."

"I guess we have to figure out how they managed that," said Tizzard.

"And to find the other two, if they are still around here," said Windflower.

"We're on it, boss," said Tizzard as Pilgrim came in to tell them every one was in the boardroom.

CHAPTER 26

Windflower and Tizzard walked in behind Pilgrim. They both grabbed a drink and a couple of sandwiches from the tray. Windflower looked around the room and realized that there really had been a changing of the guard in Marystown. The only people he really knew were Tizzard and Terri Pilgrim.

"Okay, let's get started," he said. "Maybe we can do introductions first. I'm Winston Windflower, Acting Inspector. I've worked in this area for a long time, but only recently in this position. Welcome to all of you. Corporal Tizzard is my eyes and ears over here, so go to him for any operational issues, but if you need me, I'm here. You all know him and Terri, so why don't we go around and you can introduce yourselves."

"Sergeant Matt Williams. Originally from Edmonton. I've

been all over. Prairies and New Brunswick. Even did a tour in Haiti. Nice to meet you."

"Wow, how was Haiti?" asked Windflower.

"It was tough," said Williams. "People there have nothing, and the gangs are running the cities. They would behave when we were around. But I'm not sure we made any real difference."

Windflower nodded and pointed to the next person.

"Corporal Harvey Andrei from Longueil, Quebec. Been on the Force for six years. After training I was in B.C. and then a stint at HQ. Looking forward to working here."

"Nice," said Windflower. "Where were you in B.C.? I was stationed in Smithers."

"Not that far north," said Andrei. "Prince George."

"Next," said Windflower.

"Corporal Len Davies from Swift Current, Saskatchewan," said the last officer. "I was originally in the Personal Protection Group, but when the chance came to get out here, I jumped at it. There's not much ocean in Saskatchewan."

Everybody laughed at the comment.

"Glad you're here," said Windflower. "Isn't the PPG looking after the governor general? That must have been exciting."

"It was fun, for a while," said Davies. "But most of the time you are sitting around waiting for the big shots to finish their meetings or events."

"Well, thanks, everybody, and nice to meet you all," said Windflower.

"Tizzard, has everybody got their core assignments?"

"Yes, sir," said Tizzard. "Williams is on traffic, which is a big part of what we do. Davies is lead investigator, and Andrei has got internal security and the jail."

"Any issues so far?"

"We need more staff," said Williams. "If one guy is down, we all have to work overtime. And I'm guessing things don't get any better in the wintertime."

"Getting more resources is tough," said Windflower. "I know we are stretched thin. I'll make the case to Superintendent Quigley, but don't hold your breath."

"We also have major overcrowding in the jail, especially on weekends," said Andrei. "I don't know what the answer is to that. But we all know what happens when we have too many people in there."

"Not sure what we can do about that," said Windflower. "Too many people stuck in the revolving doors of parole violations and bail revocations. Is there any room in Whitbourne?"

"I think they have the same problem," said Tizzard.

"Can we look at another temporary facility, just for weekends?" asked Andrei. "That's when people convicted of less serious crimes like impaired driving are showing up. It's actually not safe for them, or our officers, when it gets too crowded."

"Take a look around," said Windflower. "There are a couple of vacant schools that might be a possibility. As long as they can be secure, we might be able to use them. Very short-term."

"Exactly," said Tizzard. "We don't want to build capacity in the system that will only keep getting filled up."

"Tizzard? Terri? Anything from you?" asked Windflower.

Tizzard ran through the duty roster and the leave arrangements while Pilgrim gave them the latest administrative updates and changes to procedures. Major sighs all around to those announcements. Windflower could relate but did not intervene. That was above his pay grade.

"Thank you, everybody," he said to close the meeting. "Be careful out there."

Tizzard and Windflower took another sandwich from the tray on the way out as they went to meet up with Bernard Thibault.

"That's a good team we have," said Windflower. "Lots of experience and skills."

"And they haven't been burnt out yet by the grind," said Tizzard. They parked behind the store and waited for Thibault to show up.

Windflower decided this was as good a time as any to tell Tizzard about his dream. "I had a dream last night," he started. "And your brother was in it."

"Sean? What was he doing in your dream?"

"I'm not really sure," said Windflower. "It takes a while to make sense of dreams, and it only happened last night."

"Did he talk to you? What did he say?"

"He said you might be in danger," said Windflower, thinking it was better to blurt it out rather than dance around it.

"What kind of danger?"

"He didn't say," said Windflower. "Just that you were in danger and that I should keep an eye on you."

"Okay," said Tizzard. "But I'm not in any danger right now, and I have very little at home unless Hughie tries to bite me or something."

"Just be careful," said Windflower. "These messages shouldn't be taken lightly."

They didn't have any more time to discuss the dream as Bernard Thibault tapped on the window. Tizzard opened the back door. Thibault slid in and ducked his head behind the headrest.

"How are you, Bernard?" asked Windflower.

"Nervous. There's some heavy stuff going on around here right now."

"What do you mean?" asked Windflower.

"The Bacchus supporters are pushing their weight around, and there's all this talk about gold and secrets. It's crazy. The word on the street is to say nothing, talk to nobody. People are going to get killed over this. I think Corey Osmond was just the first."

"You don't think Osmond died from an overdose?" asked Windflower.

"Not a chance," said Thibault. "He was a hardcore user, but he knew the score. How much tainted supply is out there. He was killed."

"Do you think that was connected to the story he told you about the gold?" asked Tizzard.

"I don't know too much about that," said Thibault. "Not too many guys will talk to me about anything. That's fine with me, by the way. But I've heard more than a few rumbles about gold and bikers. Where there's smoke, there's fire, my old man used to say."

"Who do you think might have done it? Corey Osmond?" asked Windflower.

"I dunno," said Thibault. "But I heard there was a big-wig biker around. And rumours that Corey's brother was back in town, too. He's bad news."

"Have you seen his brother?" asked Tizzard.

"No," said Thibault. "Nor do I want to see Todd Osmond. The last time I saw him about four years ago, I ended up in hospital with two broken ribs."

"What was that about?" asked Windflower.

"He was sent down by his 'bosses' to push out some of the small guys so that Bacchus could move in. I was one of the small fish. I survived, but only because I knew enough to lay low for a while. Some other guys weren't as fortunate."

"But he wouldn't hurt his own brother," said Tizzard.

"Blood didn't mean anything to Todd Osmond," said Thibault. "Money was his only interest. Anyway, I gotta go. I've taken enough risks just talking to you."

Thibault slunk out of the back seat and disappeared quickly up towards the mall.

CHAPTER 27

"Let's have forensics take another look around Corey Osmond's place," said Windflower. "Tell them we're looking for prints. Whatever they can find."

"I'm going to double our search for Todd Osmond," said Tizzard. "I still can't believe he would hurt his own brother."

"I know it's difficult for you to comprehend, but evil really has no bounds," said Windflower. "Do you still miss your brother?"

"I was a little kid when he went away. He was my idol when I was growing up, but he was so young when he went away. I didn't understand when they said he wouldn't be coming back. I guess I still don't."

Windflower nodded sympathetically. "Okay, give me a ride back to get my car. I'm going to head back."

He took his cruiser from the parking lot, stopped at Tim Hortons to get a coffee for the road and was on his way home soon after. He was outside Marystown when his car radio lit up. He answered the call.

"I have a few things to report," Betsy said. "First of all, Greg Rose has a long gun permit, issued five years ago."

"That's it?"

"That's all that's in the records," said Betsy. "I've also talked to the Customs people in Fortune. I sent over the pictures, and they have a match. But only for Todd Osmond."

"What about the other two men?"

"No sign of them and no record of them coming off the ferry from Saint Pierre," said Betsy. "Only Todd Osmond. And his vehicle."

"Do you have a description of the vehicle?"

"Black Chrysler 300 with the sports package and tinted windows," said Betsy. "Ontario plates. I have the license plate number, too, if you want it."

"Can you send all this information to Corporal Tizzard and tell him what you've found out? Ask him to follow up and let me know if he finds anything. Also, can you put that vehicle on the system with a note saying to advise me if it is spotted anywhere on the island? Send it Atlanticwide. Thanks, Betsy."

Now the picture was getting a little clearer. At least on who was involved with Coco Meier and how they got over to this side of the water. Todd Osmond was driving, and the others were hidden somewhere in the vehicle. It may not have been corruption, but it sure sounded like incompetence. Windflower wasn't surprised. Ever since they contracted out the security services at Fortune, there'd been a problem. And Customs was only interested in collecting duties from the Canadian and American tourists who liked the day trips to a slice of Europe so close to North America. Ah, well, more issues well above my pay grade, thought Windflower.

He was about to turn on the radio when he remembered the music that Herb Stoodley had given him. He reached over to the glove compartment, pulled out the CD and took a look at the liner notes. He was pleased to see comments from the artist, Rafał Blechacz, on his latest work.

Blechacz noted that while he had played many of the works in this recording since his teens, he was now looking to give them greater freedom and to add his artistic interpretation. Windflower liked that, too. The pianist talked particularly about the Funeral March piece and how he thought it had particular relevance to today's global and social events. Then Windflower pushed the CD in and pressed play.

He was amazed, not just at the high level of musicianship, but also at how Blechacz could use a moment of silence in parts of the sonatas to give lis teners a break from his flawless finger work and delightful technique. Windflower listened for fifteen minutes and then stopped to enjoy the feelings of calm and serenity the music had inspired in him. He felt full and allowed himself that golden reflection time until he saw the first exit to Grand Bank.

Betsy gave him his messages, and he went back to his office to take a look at them. A few from the media that he would have Betsy return with a simple "no further information available at this time." One from Gupta and one from Quigley. He took a look at his phone to find two text messages there as well. One was from Sheila saying she and the girls would meet him at the Stoodleys' at five o'clock. The other was from Tizzard, and all it said was, **Thank You, Funny not Funn**y. Windflower smiled. That was probably about the performance appraisals. He knew Tizzard hated them as much as he did.

He called Quigley and left a message. Then he phoned Gupta.

"How was your day?" she asked. "I was hoping to catch up with you, but you didn't stick around."

"I had to get back," said Windflower. "We have early supper plans. But I'm glad you called. Chief Pike came by today to tell me that Greg Rose has a number of guns on his property. I got Betsy to check the registry, and he has a long-gun permit, but no other guns registered. I'd like you to go check that out tomorrow. See what Rose has to say and if he would let you look around, especially downstairs."

"Sure, I can do that," said Gupta. "Anything else new?"

"Too much to try to catch up with you right now. Why

don't you talk to Tizzard? He can fill you in. See you in the morning."

His cell phone buzzed as he was ending his call with Gupta. It was Ron Quigley.

Windflower ran through what they had learned from Saint Pierre and their research so far.

"Send me the info on Gibbons," said Quigley. "I'm sure we have a file, and we may have some intel to offer. Might even know where he is, if he's on our radar. What about the other Osmond brother?"

"Tizzard is on that. And I've put a tracker out on the car. If it's in this area, it should be fairly easy to find."

"Maybe check the ferry terminals in Argentia and Port aux Basques as well," said Quigley. "They track license plates, and you can see if it's moved off the island. We're also getting some more information about the gold robbery. It looks like somebody had inside information about the shipment. They managed to get into the secure warehouse and produced a fake waybill. That was accepted without verifying it, and they simply backed a truck up to the door and drove away with twenty million dollars' worth of gold bars and another two million in American cash."

"Wow," said Windflower. "That's pretty brazen stuff. Are there witnesses who can identify the people who took the shipment? CCTV?"

"I don't know anything else," said Quigley. "But I've been asked to be on a call with HQ and Toronto police tomorrow morning, and I'd like you to join in. I'll send you the Zoom link."

"Okay, sounds good," said Windflower. "Oh, and I don't think I told you, but we have a person of interest in the arsons in Grand Bank. One of the volunteer firefighters."

"Really?" said Quigley. "I've heard about that, but it's pretty rare. But one thing I also heard is that if they are doing it now, they may have been doing it before."

"That makes sense," said Windflower. "We haven't bothered going back and looking at other suspicious fires, but that might be worth it. If there were any, they would have been oneoffs."

"That's why you didn't follow up," said Quigley. "But it sounds like your person is getting more serious. Good luck with that."

"'It is not in the stars to hold our destiny but in ourselves,'" said Windflower.

"True," said Quigley. "But 'fortune brings in some boats that are not steered.'"

After hanging up, Windflower asked Betsy to check on their mystery vehicle with Marine Atlantic. He closed off his computer and was packing to go when she came back in.

"No record of that vehicle crossing over to Nova Scotia," she said. "But they do have a record of it coming in through Argentia two weeks ago. There were two passengers, T. Osmond and R. Gibbons. The car is registered to R. Gibbons, Mississauga, Ontario."

"That was fast," said Windflower. "I have my connections."

"Great. Can you send that to Corporal Tizzard and copy Superintendent Quigley?"

He said goodnight to Betsy and drove directly to the Stoodleys'. His tummy started growling as he thought about his supper. He hoped that Herb would fulfil his promise of sea trout.

CHAPTER 28

Herb and Moira lived in one of the older homes in Grand Bank, right on the shore of the Atlantic Ocean. Their view, when it wasn't foggy, was simply magnificent. Tonight was one of those nights, and instead of going directly inside, Windflower strolled around the side of the house and stared at the magic of the ocean below. It was vast and powerful as the waves crashed against the rocky coast below, and he felt himself hypnotized by its magic.

"It's spectacular, isn't it?" said Herb as he came out the back door with a tray and the barbeque tools. "It's like going to church, at least for me."

"I agree," said Windflower. "I feel its power, but I also feel the peace underneath it all."

Stoodley opened the barbeque, cleaned it off and lit it. He

laid two tinfoil packages on the grill and closed it. "Veggies. I've got the trout marinating. Come on inside, and I'll get you a beer."

"That's an offer I would never refuse," said Windflower.

Inside, the girls were colouring at the kitchen table, and Sheila and Moira were having a glass of wine. The girls briefly interrupted their activities to say hello to their dad, and Herb brought the promised beer to Windflower, who joined the ladies in the living room.

"Just like home," said Windflower.

"Even better," said Sheila. "We don't have to cook."

He sat and chatted with Moira and Sheila, who were polite enough not to ask him about his police work or the investigations while Herb went back out with his plate of fish. Windflower could smell the fish on the barbeque, and his mouth was watering as he inspected his daughters' drawings and pronounced them excellent. Soon, Herb came back in with a heaping platter of food.

"Supper's ready," he called, and everyone was happy to join him at the table. Moira had made a nice kale salad with an apple cider and balsamic vinegar dressing. And Herb opened the foil packets to reveal steaming green beans with a strong aroma of garlic and the other with roasted baby potatoes with a hint of rosemary rising in the air. But the star of the show was the full plate of sea trout with a goldenbrown crust that Herb passed around.

Windflower had to stop himself from drooling as he

forked his trout open, revealing a perfect pink hue inside. He took a taste. "Oh, my goodness," he said. "This is just like candy from Heaven."

There was little conversation as everyone enjoyed their meal, and even after he had eaten two trout, Herb offered him a couple to take home. Windflower could not, would not, refuse that offer either.

Dessert was a delicious pineapple upsidedown cake that Windflower thoroughly enjoyed, and while Moira and Sheila and the girls cleaned up, he took his coffee out on the back deck with Herb as he cleaned the barbeque. Herb wasn't as circumspect as the women; he came right out with his questions for Windflower. The latter didn't mind, since he appreciated having an experienced mind to bounce ideas off.

"So, how's the investigation going?" Herb asked.

"Which one?"

"Start with the fires," said Herb.

"Well, we might have an inside job. A volunteer firefighter."

"Really?" said Herb. "That's a strange thing, isn't it? I've heard of rotten cops before, but never a firefighter who starts fires."

"Some kind of mental illness, I suspect," said Windflower. "We're no where close to an arrest, so keep that under your hat."

"Absolutely. What about the dead guy?"

"That keeps getting more interesting all the time," said

Windflower. "I guess he's some kind of heavy biker gang guy from Europe. We still don't know exactly what he was doing here. But there are whispers that he was involved in the gold robbery in Toronto."

"The twenty-million-dollar job?"

"The gold came in on a flight from Switzerland where our guy is located, and some people think that the gold bars are being melted down and shipped back to Europe," said Windflower.

"Interesting. But if anything like that was happening around here, somebody would be talking about it, no?"

"Yes, we did hear from one person," said Windflower. "But he's not available to talk anymore. Looked like an overdose, but we're taking an other look at it."

"They say that gold drives some men mad. Many to an early grave as well," said Herb. "Let me know if I can help in any way."

"I will, and thank you again for the CD. I listened to some of it on the way back from Marystown yesterday. The only reason I stopped was that I wanted to save some for later."

"I thought you'd like it," said Herb. "I want to show you something else while you're here. If you have time."

"Sure," said Windflower as he followed Herb to the sunporch at the side of the house.

There on an easel was a painting. Herb had taken up landscape painting in his retirement, and by the looks of his latest work, he was no longer a beginner.

"This is outstanding," said Windflower as he gazed at the picture of the iconic Grand Bank lighthouse as the sun set behind it and the fish plant crept out of the shadows beside it. "You are really good."

"Practice," said Herb. "It's like Bach once said about music: 'There's nothing really remarkable. All one has to do is hit the right keys at the right time, and the instrument plays itself.'"

"I've heard that some authors write like that," said Windflower. "They call it the creative flow or something."

"Exactly. And lots of practice."

Windflower and Herb went back into the main house, where Sheila and the girls were putting on their coats and ready to go home.

"And we got cookies," said Stella.

"Nanny Moira made them for us," said Amelia Louise. "Chocolate chip."

"Good work," said Windflower. "Thank you so much for a wonderful supper," he added as they said their goodbyes. "You're very welcome," said Moira.

"Oh, and don't forget your trout," said Herb. He ran to the kitchen and came back with a grocery bag with a tinfoil packet inside.

"Thank you again," said Windflower. He carried the bag out to his car and waited until Sheila and the girls were loaded in before following them home.

Homework was already done, so the girls went upstairs to

get ready for bed while Windflower took Lady out for a walk. But as he grabbed the Collie's leash, he could feel a set of beady little eyes following him around the kitchen.

"Okay, okay," he said. He went to the fridge and pulled out the tin foil with the trout inside. He broke off a medium-sized chunk of fish and placed it in Molly's bowl. There were no immediate signs of gratitude as the cat bent herself to the task. The best Windflower got was a sigh that sounded like satisfaction as she licked the bowl and settled back into her bed. That would have to do.

"You're welcome," said Windflower as he and Lady headed out into the evening.

CHAPTER 29

The wind had picked up since suppertime. But it was a mild, summer-like wind that was starting to gush. Windflower hadn't been paying much attention to the weather lately. Quite frankly, it had been too good. But he checked the weather app on his phone and saw the big red warning for all of the south and east coasts of Newfoundland. A tropical storm, maybe a hurricane, was on their way, maybe on Sunday or Monday.

Sometimes it was just a warning and the locals around Grand Bank would brush it off as just another "big blow." But it had to be taken seriously because if it was a hurricane, or even a tropical storm, and if it came ashore in this neck of the woods, the potential for danger to people and property was severe. Windflower had been through one of these before. Hurricane Igor had stormed its way through the Burin

Peninsula a few years ago, bringing washedout roads and power outages that cut them off from the rest of the world. It was scary, even for him.

One could only hope that wouldn't happen this time. But it was some thing else that he would have to prepare for. He only wished he'd been paying more attention or that someone had given him a heads-up. That frustration eased when he checked his text messages and saw one from Terri Pilgrim from earlier today. Weather warning issued. Storm watch protocol in place. Please advise next steps.

He quickly texted her back to proceed as usual and call him in the morning. That was all he had time for, since Lady was now almost dragging him down the road to the wharf. This time he pulled back and took them across the way towards the fish plant. He wanted to see the wharf from the other side the way that seafarers might approach the town of Grand Bank.

It was another magnificent view, and even Lady seemed content to stop and enjoy it for a moment. Windflower walked out towards the stone walkway that led to the light-house but had to stop because the concrete was uneven and broken in places. As he neared the lighthouse, he could see that its foundation was crumbling, too, and that its paint was chipped and peeling all over the place. He made a mental note to talk to the town manager about the lighthouse. Hopefully, someone had a plan to fix up and preserve this iconic landmark.

By this time, Lady had lost interest and was incessantly pulling on Windflower in the direction of home. He allowed himself to follow along, and soon they were back in their snug house. He heard Sheila trying to settle the girls down, which wouldn't be easy with their bellies full of chocolate chip cookies. He filled his four-legged friends' bowls and put the kettle on for tea.

When Sheila came down, they sat in the living room and talked about their day and plans for the weekend.

"Tomorrow, we're clear, so maybe our usual pizza and movie night," said Sheila. "But Saturday is a bit of a scramble. Stella has figure skating, Amelia Louise is at dance class in the morning in Marystown, and I have to be here to receive some supplies."

"I can take them over and back," said Windflower. "But I'll have to take your car, if that's okay."

"That works. I can walk over to the Mug-Up, and you can meet me there for pea soup and por' cakes for lunch."

"Perfect," said Windflower. He gathered up their cups and the teapot and dropped them off in the kitchen while Sheila went upstairs. Lady raised her eyes hopefully, looking for a treat, and was rewarded with a Milk Bone. Molly came over to see what the fuss was about and stared up at Windflower. He offered her a cat treat that she simply ignored as he laid it on the floor in front of her.

He thought about ignoring the cat in return but thought back to his recent dreams. He didn't say anything but walked back to fridge, got another piece of trout and put it in Molly's bowl. "You're welcome," he said again. As he said goodnight to Molly and Lady, he thought about the cat and his dreams with her in it. And the riddle that she had told him. "Before the darkness falls to dawn. Before the sky burns in madness. Before the crowds have disappeared. The saddest son returns. To witness its destruction. While underneath the mountain, the golden idol gleams."

Some of it was starting to make sense now. Maybe the first part of the riddle was about whoever set the fire. Maybe Greg Rose. But what was the last part about? "While underneath the mountain, the golden idol gleams." He thought a little more about this as he put on his pajamas, but by the time he got into bed it had fortunately begun slipping off into the darkness. That let Windflower have a peaceful and gentle night. No dreams, no disruptions. Nothing but a quiet and gentle sleep. He woke refreshed and ready for another day of policing Grand Bank.

He helped Sheila organize the girls and get them fed and on the bus to school. Shortly afterwards, he was in his office, chatting with Betsy.

"Looks like we might have a storm coming," he said.

"I saw the note from Terri," she said. "Although there's not much we can do with just you and me. When we had a full detachment, we could put our own storm watch in operation."

"We'll do what we can," said Windflower. "Stay on top of the alerts and let me know if they think it's coming our way."

"I'll do that. They say it might be Sunday or Monday. Sure hope it's nothing like that bad one we had a few years ago."

"For sure," said Windflower. "Betsy, do you know who is responsible for the lighthouse here in Grand Bank? It's starting to look pretty run down. And the concrete at its base is falling apart, too."

"You know, me and my Bob were talking about that the other day. He says he think it's the responsibility of the coast guard, since it's an aid to navigation or something. But I think the Harbour Authority might be sup posed to keep the area around it maintained."

"Well, whoever is responsible needs to get a move on before it's too late. At least give it a fresh coat of paint," said Windflower. "To me, that lighthouse is a symbol of Grand Bank."

"Agreed," said Betsy. "There's been a lighthouse there for as long as people can remember. We used to have a light-house keeper one time, but that was years ago. People say the last keeper was Bert Riggs, but that was in the 1930s. Now it's all solar power and automation."

Samira Gupta came in while they were finishing their chat. "What were you talking about?" she asked as she got herself a cup of coffee and joined them.

"The lighthouse," said Windflower.

"The Grand Old Lady," said Betsy. "That's what people call her."

"I love that lighthouse," said Gupta. "They're not talking about tearing it down, are they?"

"No, but maybe letting it fall into the Atlantic," said Windflower.

"That won't happen," said Betsy. "We'll make sure of that."

"Good," said Windflower and motioned Gupta to follow him into his office. "Did you get your update from Tizzard?"

"I did," said Gupta. "Everybody in Marystown is trying to find that biker and Todd Osmond. If he's around, they'll get him."

"We have some more information on Greg Rose," said Windflower. "There's a report that he has a number of guns at his house. And none of them are registered."

"What kind of guns?"

"The usual shotgun, but some other rifles and maybe handguns as well."

"I know they're illegal, but what's that got to do with our arson investigation?" asked Gupta.

"Not sure yet," said Windflower. "But it might have something to do with a murder investigation. In any case, we don't really want those types of guns in our community."

"Yes, sir," said Gupta. "Should I go over now or wait until he gets home from work?"

"Why don't you go over now?" said Windflower. "Ask his

wife about the guns and see if you can suss anything out. I've got a Zoom call with Quigley and some HQ guys, but I can go with you again later on."

Gupta left to go to Greg Rose's house, and Windflower realized he had a few minutes before the Zoom call with Quigley. He decided to take ad vantage of the opportunity to do a quick tour of Grand Bank.

CHAPTER 30

E ven though he lived there and spent what seemed like half his life walking the dog or chasing his children around town, he knew it was im portant for him to be seen by the community as their local police officer. It was also good for him to take another look around and see if there was anything unusual or out of the ordinary. It might not be a problem or any thing illegal, but it gave him a sense of what was happening, good and bad, in his little town.

This morning, nothing seemed really different, and he was about to circle back around to the office when he noticed a large dump truck at the scene of the recent fire and a crane backing up into the driveway. Chief Pike's vehicle was there as well, so Windflower decided to stop and say hello.

"Good morning," he called out, and Pike came over to his car.

"'Morning," said the fire chief. "We're getting ready to take down the severely damaged side." He pointed to the crane and the dump truck.

Windflower looked over as the equipment started to get into place. "Before you do, can I take one more look around the area where we found the body?"

"Sure," said Pike. "Let's go." He waved at the crane operator to stay in place and led Windflower inside.

The kitchen felt cold and empty, Windflower thought, as he had a careful look around. He took a peek again in the cupboards and below the sink, but there was nothing out of place. Nothing very interesting. He took a look at Pike, who was watching him survey the scene. "Okay," he said. "I'm good."

He started to follow the fire chief out when his shoe caught something on the floor. He stopped and looked down. Just a protruding nail, he thought. He reached down to touch it, and when he did, the floorboard moved a little. He pushed a bit harder, and it moved some more. He got down on his hands and knees and discovered if he wiggled the nail that was sticking out, the whole section moved up and down. He yanked on the nail and the board came completely up. The other nearby floorboards could come up as well.

"Can I borrow your flashlight?" said Windflower.

Pike took the flashlight from his belt and handed it over.

Windflower shone the light down into the hole he had created. There wasn't much down there, or at least he couldn't see very much. He was about to close the hole up when the light beam flashed against something. He wasn't sure that wasn't just a trick of the eye, so he passed the light over the area again. It was a gleam or a glint, like the sparkles that his daughters used for dressup.

"Tell me if you see anything," he said to Pike, who was now hovering just above him. He waved the flashlight back and forth as the other man knelt beside him.

"Nothing."

"Look carefully," said Windflower, moving the beam of light more slowly over the area.

"Oh, yeah," said the fire chief. "Something shiny. Like dust or some thing. Could just be dirt."

"Could be," said Windflower. "But given this is a murder scene, I don't want to leave it to chance. I'll need to get forensics back here to take a look."

"That's going to delay the demolition," said Pike. "It's fine by me, but the town will have to pay for the guys outside to sit around. And they're not cheap."

"I'll take responsibility for that," said Windflower, not really knowing what that meant or who he would have to answer to. "Better to be sure."

"Okay," said the fire chief. "I'll tell them to stand down for now."

"Great," said Windflower. "I'll get forensics over as soon as possible." He left Pike to talk with the crane operator and truck driver and drove back to the office. He wasn't sure what he'd just seen under the floor boards of the fire scene, but it was something. Molly's riddle somehow came to mind as he raced back to make it on time for the Zoom meeting. Maybe that something was a gleam. A gleam of gold.

He only had time to ask Betsy to call forensics before the Zoom call started. In addition to Ron Quigley, there were representatives from Inter pol, RCMP HQ, Toronto Police, Peel Regional Police, who were respon sible for the airport, and the Ontario Provincial Police. The call was a bit tedious and boring for Windflower, and he had few answers to the many questions everybody seemed to have. It seemed to him that all sides were blaming each other for not moving fast enough. That was not unusual in an investigation that involved so many players.

The most interesting presentation was from the Interpol representative who provided footage of a man that he recognized as Coco Meier at the Zurich airport. Meier was in a parking lot near the industrial shipping area, surrounded by several of his associates. Interpol had nothing from inside the secure area, but they were still working on that. They had also some wiretap evidence that Meier had been in contact with people in Canada, specifically Ontario, in the days just before and the days after the robbery. Unfortunately, they were unable to trace the calls to their source. "Likely a burner phone," said the Interpol rep.

Quigley gave them as much as he had on Todd Osmond and the biker, Gibbons. And after that, there wasn't much more to the call. Everyone agreed, Windflower included, that the priority was to find Todd Osmond and the biker, and he assured them that everything possible was being done on that from their end. After an hour, he finally got off the call.

He realized after the call as Gupta was coming into his office that he hadn't said anything about what he uncovered this morning. He had thought about it at a couple of points. But one thing you realize in investigations is that everyone jumps on the first possibility. And he didn't want all those other police forces falling all over him and his little part of the world before he had something substantial to report. They were already overwhelmed.

"How did you make out over at Greg Rose's?"

"Not surprising, he wasn't there," said Gupta. "And his wife would not voluntarily let me in to take a look around. She looked terrified."

"Of you?"

"No," said Gupta. "Of her husband. I noticed that she had multiple bruises on both her arms. I asked her what happened. She said she had an accident."

"You don't think so," said Windflower.

"No, sir," said Gupta. "I asked her if she wanted help, and she said no. But her eyes said something else."

"We better make sure that he doesn't hurt her again before we go back. Pick him up and bring him in for questioning about the guns."

"Can I call the Sparkes House?" asked Gupta. "They have

outreach people. I think there's one in Grand Bank. They could do a check-in."

"Okay," said Windflower. "Can they get over there today while we talk to Rose?"

"I'll make the call. Then I'll go over to the fish plant."

"I'll be here," said Windflower. Gupta left, and Windflower picked up the phone to check in with Tizzard, but before he could, he had a visitor.

"Good morning, Doc. This is indeed a pleasure."

"Good morning, Winston," said Doctor Sanjay. "I decided to fish where the fish are. 'You can't cross the sea merely by standing and staring at the water.' I came to see if you might be available tomorrow evening to come and sample my fine new whiskey."

"Thank you for the kind offer, but I will have to check with my wife."

"Not to worry, my friend," said the doctor. "Repa has already extended an invitation to Sheila and your children to join us for a meal on Saturday as well."

"I think you win," said Windflower, laughing. "I gratefully accept."

"Good," said Sanjay. "I know you are a busy man, but we have to make time to enjoy life as well as to work. 'The butterfly counts not months but moments and has time enough.'"

With that, his friend was gone, and Windflower picked up the phone to call Eddie Tizzard.

"They've got the pressure put right on us to find Todd Osmond and that Snake fellow," said Windflower.

"On it," said Tizzard. "Everybody with a badge in Marystown is out on the search. And we're tracking back through all our contacts. I saw Brownie from forensics this morning. They were over at Corey Osmond's place. Says they have some prints to check on. Why are they going back over to Grand Bank?"

"Just a hunch," said Windflower, still not willing to fully commit to what he thought he saw at the house this morning. "I want them to check out the fire scene one more time before the building goes down. Let me know if and when anything happens on the search."

His tummy was starting to growl when he saw Gupta's cruiser pull up in front of the building. He was hoping she was back and ready for lunch. But judging by the speed with which she was racing, she had more than food on her mind.

"He's gone," she said when she finally got inside. "He wasn't at work. I think his wife may have called him and told him I was there."

"Why would she warn him?"

"Partly because she's terrified that he'll find out we were there and she didn't tell him. And also because abused women often protect their abusers," said Gupta. "I know it doesn't make sense, but it's like why they don't leave them. In any case, he wasn't at home, and his pickup truck is gone."

"So, too, are the guns likely," said Windflower. "Can you

go over to the courthouse and get a warrant to search his house?"

Gupta left, and Betsy came in.

"Forensics will be here this afternoon," she said. "And Bruce Rideout called from the town. He wants to know why you've slowed down the demolition over by the cemetery."

"I'll call him," said Windflower. He picked up the phone and called the town manager.

CHAPTER 31

"Well, b'y, it's costing the town about $2,000 a day to have that crane and dump truck sitting around," said Bruce Rideout. "How long is it going to be?"

"We don't know for sure, but forensics will be over this afternoon," said Windflower. "We'll know more then. By the way, have you seen the shape of the lighthouse?"

"Oh my God," said Rideout. "I get more calls about that every day than anything else. The town wouldn't mind helping out. It is part of our tourism strategy, along with the development corporation, but it's not our jurisdiction."

"Well, somebody better do something soon or the foundation under neath it will be gone, and she'll be in the Atlantic."

"I hear you," said Rideout. "Let me know about the

demolition crew. If it's going to take longer, we'll send them home."

"Will do."

Before anyone else could call, he grabbed his coat and headed out the door. "I'm gone for lunch," he said to Betsy. "Tell Constable Gupta I'm at the Mug-Up."

The café was bustling today with locals and the last of the tourists who were coming in for a snack and maybe a piece of cheesecake before trav elling on the ferry from Fortune to visit Saint Pierre. Herb Stoodley was there but by himself at the counter, so he only had time for a quick hello and to take his order. Cod au gratin today. Windflower was hungry.

He was sipping his coffee and waiting for his food when Gupta came in.

She went to the counter and ordered and then came to sit with him.

"You know the drill," said Windflower.

"Get your order in first," said Gupta. "Corporal Tizzard told me that."

"He knows his food and how to get it fast. Did you get the order?"

"Got it, it's in the car," said Gupta. "Do you want to see it? I can go get it."

"No, no, sit down and have your lunch," said Windflower. "We spend too much time rushing around. Sometimes we just need to be patient and things come to us."

Gupta smiled. "That reminds me of the Maya Angelou quote: 'Seek patience and passion in equal amounts. Patience alone will not build the temple. Passion alone will destroy its walls.'"

"That's very good," said Windflower as Herb dropped off his food. He wanted to dig right in, but when he poked a fork in, the steam rising let him know that he would have to wait. He broke open his homemade roll and buttered it while he was waiting.

"How was Rose's wife when you went back?" he asked.

"Terrified, as usual," said Gupta. "These women live in perpetual terror. They're always trying to find the right recipe to stop their partner from getting mad with them. But there is no recipe. It's not about them or what they do."

"Will she talk to the woman from Sparkes House?" he asked, tempting fate by taking a forkful of fish from his casserole dish.

"I don't know," said Gupta as her lunch of turkey soup arrived. "But I'm worried about her."

"We can both talk to her when we go over," said Windflower. The next few minutes were quiet as Windflower savoured his cod au gratin, big chunks of cod in a creamy white sauce with cheese and breadcrumbs baked on top. There was a lot, but he managed to finish it off.

"Dessert?" asked Gupta.

"Not today," said Windflower. "I'm going to have to get a run in this weekend just to get rid of today's lunch. Never mind all the other stuff I've been eating lately. You seem pretty fit. What do you do?"

"I find that walking is the best activity for me. I also do a little yoga and meditation. I have some tapes you could borrow if you are interested."

"My yoga days are over," said Windflower. "And I've tried meditation, but my mind always wanders off. The only things that really quiet my mind are sitting by the ocean and smudging."

"I have never tried smudging," said Gupta. "Can only Indigenous people do that?"

"No, anyone can smudge," said Windflower. "Even if it does not come from your culture. Like yoga. It may have come from India, but anyone can practice it as long they are respectful."

"That's an interesting comparison."

"I can give you a package of my sacred medicines. And I have an extra smudge bowl you can borrow. Then all you need are some wooden matches to light the smudge."

"Don't I need a special feather or something?"

"No, you can use your hands to spread the smoke around your head and body," said Windflower. "I'll have the stuff ready for you on Monday."

"Great," said Gupta.

They paid their bills, left the café and drove directly to Greg Rose's house. His wife, Marsha, greeted them at the door. She wasn't very happy when Gupta produced the search warrant but allowed the RCMP officers to enter without protest. Windflower sat with the woman while Gupta went through the house. She started with the kitchen and then went through the bedrooms before going downstairs.

Marsha was sitting still, but Windflower could feel her nervous energy from across the room. Gupta was right. She was terrified.

Windflower saw the pictures on the fireplace and walked over to take a look. Two children, a boy of about eight, and a girl, maybe ten.

"Beautiful kids," he said.

"Thank you," mumbled Marsha.

"I have two little girls," he said. "I love them dearly, but they're a handful to keep up with."

The woman smiled at that comment despite herself.

"Are you okay?" asked Windflower.

At first, she nodded. Windflower didn't say anything but tried to look sympathetic. By the time Gupta came back up from the basement, she had her head in her hands and was openly sobbing.

"Nothing," whispered Gupta. "The cabinet was bare. Two empty gun cases."

Windflower grimaced. That wasn't good news. An unstable and probably angry man on the loose in town or nearby with at least two weapons.

"Ammunition?" he asked. Gupta shook her head.

It wasn't clear if the other woman had heard any of this, but all of a sudden she started talking. "Greg hasn't been okay for a while. Awake at night and out of the house early in the morning. I begged him not to leave. He said he didn't have any choice." Then she just crumpled and started crying again.

"We can help you," said Gupta. She went over and put her arms around her. "There's a woman coming who knows about a safe house. A place where you and the kids can go until we straighten out this mess with your husband."

Marsha shook her head and kept crying.

"You stay here with Marsha, and I'll start the process on our end," said Windflower. "Okay?"

Gupta nodded, and Windflower went out to his vehicle to call Tizzard in Marystown.

CHAPTER 32

"Eddie, we're going to need backup over here," he said when Tizzard answered the phone. "Greg Rose, the firefighter we're looking at, is gone and he's armed. He might feel trapped, so that makes this a very dangerous situation. Send me somebody good. Andrei or Davies, and I think at least two more."

"I'll get Davies. Andrei has his hands full downstairs," said Tizzard. "And I'll come as well."

"Full body armour, and bring some of the bigger weapons," said Windflower. "Check in at the office when you get here."

"Okay," said Tizzard. "We've also had a reported sighting of our mystery car down in Mooring Cove. Williams is heading out to take a look."

"Great," said Windflower. "Come over as quick as you

can." Next, he called Betsy. "We need to put out a public alert about an individual who is at large in the community. This individual is likely armed and should not be approached under any circumstances. Tell them to call the RCMP."

"Oh dear," said Betsy.

"It's Greg Rose," said Windflower. "Can you get his description and maybe a picture? Chief Pike might have that. And he has a new black F150 pickup. Can you see if you can get the license plate number for that as well?"

"Yes, sir."

"But first, put out the public notice," said Windflower. "We can add details later. Can you also get me the C8 from the back and a box of am munition? I will stop by to pick it up."

Windflower hung up and sat quietly in the car for a moment. He needed to slow his heart and his brain down a little. He had his service weapon in the holster at his side, but they might need more firepower to resolve this situation. That was a sobering thought and another reminder that police work, even in little Grand Bank, could always turn dangerous. He hoped he wouldn't need the extra protection and force that the C8 patrol carbine could provide, but better safe than sorry.

By the time he got back to the office, Betsy had already prepared the draft notice, and his rifle was sitting on a chair next to her desk with a box of ammunition. There was also a lightweight hard body armour and one of the new portable ballistic shields. Windflower wasn't that confident about either of these in the case of fire from a highpowered rifle, but he took all of the equipment and the weapon and carried them out to the trunk of his cruiser.

"I hope you never have to use all of that," said Betsy. "It chills me just to look at it."

It had the same effect on Windflower, but he tried to keep his emotions in check. "Tizzard is on his way with reinforcements," was all he said as he approved the notice and went back into his office to call Ron Quigley. He left a message, and while he was waiting, Gupta called.

"The woman from Sparkes House is here," said Gupta. "Marsha didn't want to talk to her, but I agreed that we would go together to pick up her kids if she agreed. They're on some kind of field trip and are getting dropped off over at the high school."

"Okay," said Windflower. "Wait for me there. I'll hang around near the Rose house in case he tries to come back around. You drive Marsha and then go back to the house. I'll bring you some equipment."

Gupta hung up, and Windflower went to talk to Betsy to get Gupta's rifle and gear out of the back. As he was leaving to go to the Rose house, Quigley called.

Windflower ran through the details of Rose being on the loose in the community with his weapons.

"That's not good," said Quigley.

"No, and it feels like we need to get to Rose before it gets any worse."

"You need anything from me?" asked Quigley.

"Not yet. Tizzard says they have a sighting of our missing car."

"Still around Marystown?"

"Mooring Cove," said Windflower. "If I remember right, that's where the old fish plant is."

"Probably a good place to hide out," said Quigley. "Okay, let me know about both situations."

"Will do," said Windflower. "One more thing, although it may be nothing. I thought I saw something at the house that burned down the other day. I went by just as they were getting ready to knock it down."

"What did you see?"

"There is a storage area of some sort underneath the kitchen floor boards," said Windflower. "When I shone my light down there, it looked like something gleamed back at me. Like I said, it may be nothing. But I've asked forensics to take a look. And that is delaying the demolition."

"I don't understand," said Quigley. "Like a knife or something you couldn't reach?"

"No, more like gold shavings, if that's even a thing."

"Maybe a place where gold had been stored, is that what you were thinking?" asked Quigley. "If it is, it could be really big."

"Or it could be nothing. In which case the town will

likely be screaming at you because I've got a crane and dump truck sitting idle."

"Given the stakes involved, I'm not worried about that," said Quigley. "This I want to hear about right away, okay?"

"Okay."

"And Winston, be careful," said Quigley. "Sheila would kill me if any thing happens to you."

Windflower left his office and called Sheila on the way out to the Rose's. He didn't want to, but he had to. "I wanted you to know before you hear it from somebody else."

"Oh, my goodness," said Sheila. "It sounds like he's dangerous. Be careful, Winston. Don't take any chances, that's all I ask."

"Fair enough," said Windflower. "I just wanted you to know."

"Thank you for telling me," said Sheila. "I love you."

"I love you, too."

He hated making that call, because he knew that Sheila would not be okay until she knew he was. And right now, he was heading into possible danger. That was the life of a police officer.

He took both rifles, put them in the back of his cruiser and drove to the Rose house. While he was waiting for Gupta to come back with Marsha Rose and her children, Chief Pike pulled up in his truck.

"I heard the message on the radio," he said. "Is there anything I can do?"

"Maybe check around with the rest of your crew. Maybe one of them knows where he might go. If he's going anywhere."

"He has a cabin," said the fire chief. "It's his family's cabin. Way up a small road at the back of Molliers."

"Okay, we'll check that out," said Windflower. "Let me know if any of your men hear anything."

"I will," said Pike. "It's strange, you know. He's not a bad man. Even with all the stuff he might have done."

"Sometimes good people do bad things. Especially if they're not well." Pike shook his head and walked back to his truck.

Windflower sat quietly and waited for Gupta to return. He saw the Honda Accord come up the driveway, and two children jumped out immediately. But Gupta and Marsha Rose stayed in the vehicle. He walked over to the car. He could see that the woman had been crying, and Gupta was trying to comfort her.

"What's going on?" he asked Gupta. She got out of the car.

"Her husband called her," said Gupta. "Threatened her if she talked to the police. She's pretty shook up."

"Does she have any family here?" asked Windflower.

"No, her family is from Little Harbour East," said Gupta. "And there's no one there who can help her."

"Well, I don't think she can stay here," said Windflower.

"That's what I was talking to her about," said Gupta. "But

she doesn't want to go to Marystown. I've got a call in to the woman from Sparkes House to see if they have anything, even temporary, in this area."

"Okay, we've got a lead to check on," said Windflower. "Apparently, Rose has a cabin in Molliers. Once Tizzard gets here, we'll go over as a team to check it out."

Gupta made her call and then helped Marsha back into her house. Windflower's phone rang. It was Betsy.

CHAPTER 33

"Forensics are here," said Betsy. "Do you want to talk to Corporal Brown?"

"Put him on," said Windflower.

"I hear we're going back to the fire scene. What are we looking for?" asked Brown.

"I think there may be traces of something in the kitchen. Under the floorboards," said Windflower. "I'll meet you over there. Put Betsy on again."

After Brown was off the phone, Windflower said, "Betsy, send Tizzard and whoever else comes with him over to meet me at the fire scene."

Gupta came out of the house as he was about to leave.

"There's a safe house in Grand Bank. Only for a night or two," said Gupta. "But Marsha has agreed to go. Guess whose house it is?"

"Whose?" asked Windflower.

"Betsy's," said Gupta.

"Why am I not surprised?" said Windflower. "Okay, you stay with them until they get straightened away and safe. I'm going to meet forensics. Call me when you're free here. And you should get your stuff out of the back." He walked around the back of the car, opened the trunk and passed Gupta her gear and carbine.

She half-smiled to show she was okay, and he half-smiled back to acknowledge the seriousness of the situation that was unfolding. He drove to the burnt-out house by the cemetery and parked behind the forensics truck. Brown nodded, and the Forensics team followed Windflower into the house. Everyone had heard the news of the gunman. No place for joking around today.

Under Brown's direction, his team got to work quickly, and Windflower left them to take their samples while he waited outside. The forensics van had drawn another crowd of onlookers, including the dump truck driver and the crane operator. More people came to join them when the two other RCMP vehicles with Tizzard and the officers from Marystown arrived. There was a gasp from the crowd as they saw them with their body armour on.

Windflower waved Tizzard over. "We're going out to Molliers."

"Is that where he is?" asked Tizzard.

"Maybe," said Windflower. Then he realized he didn't

know exactly where the cabin was in Molliers. "Hang on a sec." He called the fire chief. "Can you come with us and show us where the cabin is? We're at the fire scene. Thanks."

He went inside to double check with Brown that they didn't need him. "No, I think we're good. Shouldn't take us too much longer," said Brown.

"If you find anything, let me know right away," said Windflower. "And if you find gold, call Superintendent Quigley."

Back outside, Chief Pike had arrived and was talking with Tizzard. "We're ready," he said. "We'll follow Chief Pike."

The crowd watched the procession of the fire chief's truck followed by three RCMP officers with a degree of surprise and awe. They had all heard the news about Greg Rose, and after the vehicles left, most of them scat tered to tell their friends and neighbours what they had witnessed. Some thing big was about to happen. Nobody knew what that might be. But it was almost certainly going to be big.

Windflower hoped it wouldn't be big at all. Part of him hoped that Greg Rose wouldn't even be at that cabin in Molliers. Maybe that was his heart. His head told him he should be prepared for the worst. He took a long breath and tried to enjoy the brief trip to Molliers. At one time, like many of the smaller settlements in this area, Molliers had been a thriving, if small community. Now, there was an ATV trail and a handful of cabins that people from Grand Bank used to get away from the citified town life. They took the turnoff from the highway and followed Chief Pike to the end of the main road. He stopped and got out near the start of a narrow gravel pathway.

"Up there." He pointed.

"Is there any other way in or out?" asked Windflower.

"Not by car or truck," said Pike. "He may have a bike up there, though.

There's a trail that winds its way around the back."

"Thanks. You stay here," he said to Pike.

He got one of the constables to go back to the highway and use his cruiser to block any other access to this area while Davies stayed with Tizzard and the other constable and Windflower. Windflower indicated the pair should stay behind while he and Tizzard went ahead by foot. "Stay close to your radio and wait for instructions."

Windflower put on his protective vest, and he and Tizzard got their weapons out of their cars and crept slowly up the pathway. It was a lit tle slippery from the rain showers earlier in the day, but that meant they wouldn't crunch the leaves on the ground as they moved forward. Tizzard saw the pickup truck first and pointed it out to Windflower. Slowly, they moved ahead a little farther, trying to stay shielded within the canopy. And out of sight of Rose, if he was in the cabin. Windflower smelled the smoke before he saw it coming out of the chimney.

It was a onestorey wooden structure that had expanded over the years by the looks of it. It was clean and wellmaintained, as was the property around the cabin. They came to the top of the path but still almost out of sight and Windflower motioned to Tizzard to stop. They paused for a second, and then Windflower called out, "Greg, we know you're in there. Come out with your hands up. We can figure this thing out."

The two Mounties heard a scramble from inside the cabin, and the next thing they heard was a gunshot. It came from the cabin but didn't seem to be aimed directly at them. Still, both of them jumped back, and while their first inclination was to run, they simply moved back a little and stayed perfectly quiet. They could see the cabin from their vantage point, but now that was quiet too.

"I don't think he was shooting at us," said Windflower. "Just a warning shot."

"But he's armed and ready to shoot," said Tizzard. "Not a good sign."

Windflower and Tizzard were very surprised to hear noises coming up the path. "I tried to stop him, but he insisted," said Davies. "After we heard the shot."

"I think I can talk to him," said Chief Pike. "He might listen to me." Tizzard looked at Windflower as if to say that he might be right.

"As long as you stay behind me and Tizzard," said Windflower. "Go ahead and try."

Pike paused for a second. Then he yelled out. "Greg, it's me. Chief Pike."

There was no response. To Windflower that was good news. Rose hadn't shot again. He nodded to Pike to continue.

"It doesn't have to be this way," said Pike. "I know you're a good man. You're just mixed up right now. We can get you some help."

There was more silence from the cabin. Then they heard another noise: a motor starting and the squealing of tires. Windflower and Tizzard ran towards the cabin, but all they saw was a flash of metal through the woods as a fourwheeler sped into the distance.

"Davies, you secure the cabin. Check it for weapons," said Windflower. "Where does this trail go, Chief?"

"It goes all the way back through the barrens and then comes out in Grand Bank," said Pike. "But there's a hundred of side trails that come off it to cabins and ponds and places where people like to hunt or pick berries."

"And I guess a few cabins along the way?" asked Windflower.

"About a dozen or so, I'd say," said Pike.

"Tizzard, can you call Betsy and see if there's a map of this trail online? And get copies of it printed off for all of us," said Windflower. "Then go and have the Grand Bank end of the trail secured. We may not be able to track him easily in there, but we sure don't want him back in town."

Davies came back out with empty hands. "Nothing, at least in plain sight."

"That means he's got all his weapons with him," said

Windflower. "Okay, let's leave one person behind here in case he comes back. Davies, can you follow Chief Pike? He can show you where the trail comes out in Grand Bank. We'll have to monitor that. Keep everybody else off it, for starters. Everyone else, meet me at the office."

Windflower went to talk to Chief Pike before he left. "I know you want to help, but I have to ask you to stand back and let us do our jobs."

"I know," said Pike. "I was just trying—"

Windflower cut him off. "We may be able to use you along the way. If we have another opening, I will call you, okay?"

The fire chief nodded and got in his truck.

CHAPTER 34

Windflower drove back to Grand Bank in silence. He needed to come down from the adrenaline high of the last few minutes. He took a couple of long breaths and felt his heartbeat come back to something like normal. When he got back to the office, Tizzard and the other officer were going over a printout of the trail that Betsy had found.

"So, basically the trail runs along the coastline and then circles back into Grand Bank, avoiding the many small ponds and brooks along the way," said Tizzard. "There are lots of offshoots, by the looks of it, but only two main ways in and out. And we've got them both covered."

"We'll need to get in there," said Windflower. "Betsy, can you get us a couple of ATVs on loan?"

"My Bob has one you can borrow, and I bet he can scrounge up another one," she said.

"Great," said Windflower. "Tizzard, can you go in and check things out along the way? Make sure that there's no one in any of the cabins along the way. When Betsy comes back, we'll set the radios up. What's your name, son?" he asked the other officer.

"Avery, sir," said the constable. "Marcus Avery."

"Okay, Marcus," said Windflower. "You will be with Corporal Tizzard.

Take the second ATV and follow behind him. Be careful, okay?" Constable Avery looked terrified but nodded.

Tizzard called Avery to come with him to the back. "Let's make some coffee. We're going to need it."

Windflower's phone was buzzing constantly now as he went to his of fice. He checked his texts: Sheila, Gupta, Quigley and Bruce Rideout from the Town of Grand Bank. He called Gupta first. Rideout would have to wait.

"Everything is good here," said Gupta. "I was just checking to see if you wanted me to do anything."

"No, just stay there and make sure Marsha and her family are okay. Rose was at a cabin in Molliers, but he got away on an ATV. He has his weapons with him."

"Okay, I'll stay until we can make the transfer to Betsy's," said Gupta.

"Get your carbine out and have it ready," said Windflower. "Just in case."

Next, he called Sheila.

"Everybody's talking about it," she said. "Are you okay?"

"We're fine," said Windflower. "Just stay home and don't go out until we know it's clear. I have to go. You reminded me of something." He called Betsy.

"We need to move to the next level," he said.

"Shelter-in-place? I have the text ready for you to look at."

"I love you, Betsy," said Windflower as he scanned the message.

She read it out loud:

> "Attention all residents of the area from Grand Bank to Molliers. Please be advised that we have an active shooter situation underway. Residents are advised to shelter in place until the police advise that the situation has been resolved. Residents are also requested to stay off the ATV trails in the area until further notice."

"Perfect," he said. "Put it on the emergency channel."

"Oh, and Bob and his friend are on their way over with the ATVs."

"Thank you, Betsy, and thank Bob for me as well."

He was about to call Quigley when Corporal Ted Brown came into his office.

"This is a busy place," said Brown. "You need us?"

"Maybe, if you could hang around until this becomes a

little clearer. That would be good. What did you find at the house?"

"In that area you exposed, we found several more fragments like the one you saw. We checked the rest of the kitchen, even took up the floor boards, but only that area," said Brown.

"And?"

"Can't be a hundred percent positive 'til we get to the lab, but the fragments are not magnetic, and they don't float," said Brown. "Two signs that they might be gold. I was just about to call Quigley."

"Let's talk to him together," said Windflower. He got Quigley on the line and put him on speaker.

"I saw the alert," said Quigley. "Is everybody okay over there?"

"Yeah, we're good," said Windflower. "The shooter is loose on an ATV trail. We're trying to contain him. Ted Brown is here with me."

"Brownie, what did you find?" asked Quigley.

"Some fragments, shavings is more like it. Looks like gold," said Brown. "Have to confirm, but that's the initial finding."

"Is there much of it?" asked Quigley.

"That's hard to say," said Brown. "But I'd guess not too much. If it was gold bars, they're a little over seven inches, just less than twenty centime tres, maybe a couple. Max, four or five."

"Okay, get me the info on the samples as soon as you can confirm," said Quigley. "Good work. Let me talk to Windflower alone."

"I think Tizzard's got coffee in the back," Windflower said to Brown as he picked up the receiver.

"What do you think?" asked Quigley.

"It wasn't likely the full shipment, if that's what this turns out to be," said Windflower. "There must be hundreds of kilos of gold from that robbery."

"Four hundred kilograms of gold bars was what I heard," said Quigley. "I'm thinking that maybe somebody was taking an early slice of the pie. Anyway, you got bigger fish to fry. Do you need any more help?"

"We have a good crew, and Brown and his team will hang around in case we need them," said Windflower. "I'm hoping we find our guy soon. Once it gets dark it will be near impossible."

"I'm going to see where our chopper is," said Quigley. "He can't get there before dark but might be able to help in the morning."

"Okay, that would be good," said Windflower. "But I'm hoping we don't have to wait that long. Thanks."

"Okay, good luck," said Quigley.

Tizzard, Brown and Avery came back into his office once they saw he was off the phone. Tizzard brought him a cup of coffee, and he was carrying a tin. Inside was an assortment of homemade cookies and squares. "Thanks," sad Windflower, taking a shortbread with icing. "From Betsy?"

"No," said Tizzard. "She said a neighbour dropped them off. They're sum good, b'y."

Windflower had to smile, even with the dire situation they were en gaged in. They were all enjoying another cookie when they heard a rum bling noise outside: two men on ATVs. Both men got off and handed the keys to Betsy as the RCMP officers watched.

"Brownie, do you and your guys have equipment?" asked Windflower.

"We have vests, always carry them. It's mandatory. We never know where we'll end up," said Brown. "And we have service weapons, but no carbines."

"Betsy can fix you up on that end," said Windflower. "Brownie, you and one of your guys take one of the ATVs, and the other can go with Tizzard. You are trying to find our guy, Rose, but also to secure the trail and make sure we get anybody who's in there out safely. Tizzard will be your lead. Avery, you stay with me. I have another assignment for you."

CHAPTER 35

Tizzard and Brown and their companions were soon off to the trail, and Windflower took Avery to Marsha Rose's house. "I'm going to get you to relieve Constable Gupta," said Windflower. "You don't need to do any thing but stand guard, and don't let anybody in. Rose may somehow try to get back here, but that's unlikely. I need you to stay vigilant until we can move the family, okay?"

"Yes, sir," said Avery.

There was nothing else said on the way to Rose's house. When they arrived, he introduced Avery and pulled Gupta outside.

"How are things here?" he asked.

"Not good," said Gupta. "She's a mess and the kids are upset, wondering where their dad is. Maybe you should talk to her. You seem to have a calming influence on people."

Windflower half-smiled at that remark and walked back inside. Marsha was in the kitchen, and he went to join her. Gupta followed behind him.

"How are the kids?" he asked softly.

"Oh, they're so upset. I don't know what to tell them." She started crying and put her head in her hands.

"This is a very difficult situation," said Windflower. "For everybody, but especially them. I can tell you that we are doing everything we can to resolve this peacefully with nobody getting hurt."

"Please don't shoot Greg," she said. "I know he's in big trouble, but he's just confused in the head. He's not a bad man. I don't know what we're going to do after this."

Windflower nodded. "First, we have to keep you and your children safe. That's the important thing. We'll be moving you to Betsy Molloy's house. Just for tonight, while we sort this out. Then, there'll be help for whatever comes next. Do your kids like pizza?"

"Who doesn't like pizza?" said the woman, managing to stop crying for a moment.

"Constable Gupta will take their orders," he said, looking at Gupta. "She's coming with me right now but will be back to get you. Constable Avery is going to be just outside if you need anything."

He and Gupta drove back to the RCMP office. There was no traffic on the roads at all, not even kids riding their bicycles. That was good, thought Windflower. People seemed to have gotten the message.

"You were very good back there," she said as they arrived at the office. There, they were greeted by a horde of media people who started coming towards their car.

"I was trying to be kind," said Windflower. "And not to tell her the truth. We don't know how this will end up, but there's no point in getting upset about things that haven't happened yet."

"That sounds like a great philosophy," said Gupta. "Yours?"

"My Uncle Frank," said Windflower. "He would always say don't worry about the future, it hasn't come yet. Don't worry about the past because it's already happened. Focus on today. Today is a gift. That's why they call it the present."

"Good advice," said Gupta. "What do you want to do about this?" She pointed to the news people who were starting to gather around their car.

"Can you tell them we'll have something to say in thirty minutes?" said Windflower. "After you tell them that, I will follow behind you inside."

"What are you going to tell them in thirty minutes?"

"That's what we have to figure out," said Windflower.

Gupta got out and made her announcement. The media sea parted, and Windflower slowly walked behind Gupta into the office.

Betsy had set up the small board room as a kind of

command centre. She had blown up copies of the trail map on the table and had moved the coffee pot into the room.

"Thank you, Betsy," said Windflower.

"We have done this before. What are you going to do about them?" she asked, looking out the window.

"Well, we need them to get our message out," said Windflower. "I just have to figure out what that is. But we've bought thirty minutes."

He checked in with Tizzard and Brown, but there wasn't much to report. Yet.

"We've spotted a couple of people in cabins and got them to move out," said Tizzard. "But this is going to take a while. We split up every time there's a side trail, but even then, this will take hours."

"Keep at it," said Windflower. "Make sure you mark off the areas that you've searched so we don't have to go over them again. I think we probably have two, max three hours of light left."

Gupta had gotten herself a snack and a cup of coffee. She brought one to Windflower.

"Thanks," he said. "I guess we should think about food. Can you orga nize that with Betsy? Maybe soup and sandwiches from the café. And after that, can you go out to Molliers and relieve Davies? Thanks."

Windflower had a few brief moments to compose himself before he saw the parade of people and cameras go down the hallway into the large boardroom. He closed the door of his new command centre and made a few notes for himself. Finally ready, he walked out of the room and into the glare of the lights.

Blinded at first, he got his bearings and slowly walked down the hallway into the very crowded boardroom. He noticed Grand Bank Mayor Jacqueline Wilson in the audience. He called her to the front and whispered to her. "Do you want to say anything? Or stand up here with me?"

"I'll stay in the audience but say a few words when you're done," said the mayor.

"Okay," said Windflower. He stepped to the podium. He ran through what they knew and the fact that reinforcements had already been brought in from Marystown. And that more were available as required. He gave a brief description of Greg Rose and that he was last seen on the ATV trail near Molliers, but that his exact whereabouts could not be confirmed. That was why it was important for everyone to stay indoors and safe until he could be apprehended.

He took a few questions and tried not to be too specific about the type of weaponry that Rose might have. He didn't want to scare people any more than was necessary. Then he asked Mayor Wilson to say a few words.

The mayor talked about how the town was nervous about the situation but that she had great faith in Sergeant Windflower and the RCMP. She urged residents to stay vigilant and to report anything suspicious to the RCMP. With that, Windflower thanked the media and left the podium. He waited while the reporters asked the mayor some followup questions and then walked out with her so that they could get their closing shots.

He invited Mayor Wilson into his office, and Betsy came in with coffee for them both. Windflower had had his fill of coffee for the day but sipped on his while he listened to the mayor chat about things going on in the town. Finally, Betsy came in to give them the all-clear. The media had all left the premises. He followed Mayor Wilson out.

"Well, at least there's one piece of good news," said the mayor. "The storm has shifted out to the Atlantic. We'll get wind and lots of rain, but no hurricane."

"That is good news," said Windflower. "Thanks for being here today. We really appreciate your support."

"We're partners," said the mayor as they went outside. "And here comes the rain."

It was pouring now and starting to grow dark. That meant they wouldn't have as much daylight as they had thought for the search. But it would also make it uncomfortable for Greg Rose to stay outside. He would have to find shelter, if he hadn't already. Windflower went back inside and called Tizzard.

"How's it going?" asked Windflower.

"It's wet," said Tizzard. "But it's not cold. Nothing really to report. We have a long way to go to get through this trail. It must be five or six kilometres long by the looks of it. I'd say we may only be a klick in right now."

"That's good," said Windflower. "It looks like we may have less time to search today. It's too dangerous to be out there in the dark with Rose still on the loose. Focus on cabins and shelters as fast as you can. I'm thinking that Rose will be looking for shelter."

"Good point," said Tizzard. "I'll go ahead a kilometre or so and let Brown come in behind me. You're right about the light. It's fading fast inside the woods. I'd say we only have an hour or so left."

CHAPTER 36

G upta was back soon after with the order from the Mug-Up.

"Have something to eat and then go relieve Davies," he said, grabbing a sandwich from the tray. "Can you also see if Betsy has a pot to put the soup in to keep it warm?"

He tried to eat his sandwich slowly but ended up gulping it in two bites. He took another one and closed up the cellophane wrap. Betsy came in with a pot to look after the soup.

"Any news?" she asked.

"Not much yet. Betsy, can Marsha and her kids come over to your house now? I think I'd feel better knowing they were safe before it got dark."

"Sure," said Betsy. "I can go with them if you'd like."

"That would be great," said Windflower. "Before you go

out to Molliers, can you go over to the house and bring them to Betsy's? And don't forget the pizza."

"Next thing on my list," said Gupta, finishing her soup. "Whenever you are ready, Mrs. Molloy."

The next hour was tense but rather uneventful. Then Windflower got the radio call he was hoping for.

"We've got Rose trapped," said Tizzard. "He came out of a trail between me and Brown, but we chased him down a side trail. He's in an abandoned cabin by the looks of it. A shanty, really."

Everybody in the control room stood up to listen.

"There's no way out of the back," said Brown, who came on the radio. "He's not making any noise right now. But we're pretty sure he's in there."

"Is there any way he could walk out the back?" asked Windflower.

"It's pretty thick bush back there," said Tizzard, coming back on. "We brought one of the ATVs as close as we could and left the lights on. We can see pretty well anything that moves on the outside."

"Okay," said Windflower. "You guys stay there and make sure he doesn't move in any direction. If he does or there's any sign of life, let me know. Davies, call Betsy and see if we can get two more ATVs. Better yet, go to her house. Here's the address." Davies took the paper and raced out the door.

"Tizzard and Brown, we're arranging additional ATVs," said Windflower. "Hold tight and I'll get back to you." He called Gupta and the other officers and gave them an update. "Hold your positions and wait for further directions." Then he and everyone else waited for what seemed like an eternity. But fifteen minutes later, they heard a noise.

Windflower heard and saw Davies first, then the welcome roar of the ATVs behind him. He ran out into the rain and thanked the ATV drivers and then quickly went back in to get ready to go.

"Avery, you stay here and man the control room. Can you do that?"

The young constable nodded. "Yes, sir."

"Davies, you're with me." Windflower and Davies put on their protective gear and then their rain gear. They checked their weapons and loaded them into the storage box on the ATV. The last thing Windflower grabbed on the way out was a megaphone. Maybe the most important piece of equipment they would need. At least he hoped so.

They drove as fast as they could through Grand Bank, noticing that almost every window had their curtains drawn open to see the Mounties in action. They got to the trail, and Windflower took the lead, driving as quickly as they could through the dim light of the forest until they could see lights ahead. Davies pulled up alongside him.

"I want you to go about half a kilometre up ahead," said Windflower, "to make sure he doesn't get far if he tries to make a run for it that way. But keep your radio on and come if we call you."

Davies jumped on his ATV and drove off as directed.

"Everybody else, full armour up and be ready for anything," said Windflower. He put on his face shield and made sure his rifle was fully loaded and ready to go. He checked with everyone to make sure they had done the same. Then he took the megaphone out of his ATV and walked towards the cabin, careful to stay out of line of sight. He motioned Tizzard to follow and for the others to come along behind him.

Windflower walked close enough to the cabin to make sure that Greg Rose could hear him. He could almost see right into the cabin with the lights of the ATV shining ahead of him. He stopped behind a tree and held a hand high in the air to stop everyone behind him. He turned on the megaphone.

"Greg, it's Sergeant Windflower. We need to talk." He thought he heard a rustling from inside the cabin and ducked down, just in case. But there was nothing else. So quiet he could hear his own heartbeat. He tried again. "Greg, we need to talk. We can work this out."

No sound at all from inside this time. One more try, thought Windflower. "Greg, we have the place surrounded. There's nothing else to do but for you to surrender. Come out with your hands in the air."

This time he heard more scrambling around from the cabin and then a deathly quiet. Windflower looked behind him and waved for Tizzard and the others to move back. He backed away slowly with careful eyes trained for any movement from the cabin.

When they were safely away from danger, he called Tizzard over to him.

"This may take some time," he said, looking around at the area. They were all completely soaked, but their rain gear had diminished most of the damage. And it felt like the rain was easing up.

"Sounds like it," said Tizzard. "I don't think there's much point in trying to go in. Maybe we wait him out. He'll have a long, cold night in that cabin. He might feel more cooperative in the morning."

"He might," said Windflower. "But I'm actually more worried about his current mental state. That he might harm himself if he can't see a way out."

"Who would he listen to?" asked Tizzard. "His wife?"

"We can't bring her into this," said Windflower. "Spousal abuse. That's why we're putting her and her kids into a safe house. But maybe Chief Pike. He wouldn't talk to him earlier, but he might now. I think we have to give it a shot."

Tizzard nodded. "I'll call him and get him to meet me at the start of the trail."

"Okay, we're not going anywhere."

"There is one other piece of information you should have," said Tizzard. "Avery is a bit of a marksman. Had the highest scores in the academy."

"Good to know," said Windflower. Tizzard sped off back

down the slip pery trail, and Windflower called Ron Quigley to give him an update.

"We got the situation contained but not resolved. He won't talk to me.

Not yet anyway. We're bringing in the fire chief to see if that works."

"Good plan," said Quigley. "I'll cancel the chopper. Sounds like you won't need that. You can probably lift the shelter-in-place order now. Unless you really need them, those things cause more anxiety in the community than anything."

"Will do," said Windflower.

He hung up from Quigley and called Gupta. "Can you go back over and relieve Avery? Get him to go meet Tizzard and the fire chief at the start of the ATV trail." Then he phoned Betsy. She was home with Marsha Rose and the kids. "Is everything okay there?"

"Yes, we're all good. The children are downstairs watching a movie.

Marsha fell asleep in her chair. She must be exhausted."

"Gupta is coming to take over, and I need you to go back to the office," he said. "We need to rescind the shelter-in-place order. Can you look after that? You can say that we have located the suspect but that a police operation is still underway. People must stay off all ATV trails until further notice."

"That shouldn't be too hard, given the weather," said Betsy. "How is everybody over there?"

"We're all good right now. Can you do me a favour, Betsy? After you finish getting this stuff done, would you mind calling Sheila? Just to tell her I'm okay. She'll hear the news and be worried."

"I will certainly do that," said Betsy.

Windflower hung up and went back to join the other officers who remained. There was not much to do but wait until Tizzard arrived back with the fire chief.

CHAPTER 37

There was little activity from inside the cabin, at least from their vantage point. Every so often Windflower would see what he thought was Rose moving around a little, but that might just have been shadows or the wind.

After what seemed like forever, Tizzard arrived back with Chief Pike sitting beside him and Avery hanging on to the back of the ATV. He was also holding a large pot in his arms.

"Supper," said Tizzard. "In case we're here for a while."

"Great. Put all that aside for now," Windflower said to Avery. "Thanks for coming," he said to the fire chief.

"I'm glad you called for me," said Pike.

"Tizzard, give Chief Pike your vest and shield. And give Avery your rifle." While Pike was putting on his gear, Windflower pulled Avery aside.

"I hear you're a bit of a shooter."

"I can shoot," said Avery. "My family were skeet shooters, so I kind of grew up with it. With the weapons now and the sights, almost anybody can do it."

"I don't know about that," said Windflower. "I want you to get into position with a direct line of sight into the cabin. Don't do anything else unless I give you the order to shoot. Is that understood?"

"Yes, sir," said Avery. "I wait for your order."

"No one else, just me," said Windflower. "I will only give that order if our lives are in danger. Understood?"

Avery nodded.

"Get into position and stay calm," said Windflower. He walked back to Pike and Tizzard. "Corporal, you stay behind. Avery is giving us cover." Tizzard stayed put while Windflower and Pike edged closer to the cabin.

As they got within earshot, Windflower turned the megaphone on again. "Greg, I've got someone who wants to talk with you." Silence from inside the cabin.

"Go ahead," he whispered to Pike.

"Greg, it's me. Roy Pike," said the fire chief. Still no response.

"Keep going," Windflower said encouragingly.

"Greg, we need to talk," said Pike. "This can still turn out okay. You may have made some mistakes, but maybe you're not okay. We can get you some help."

Still nothing.

"Greg, please talk to me. You're a young man. You still have lots of life ahead of you. Think about your kids."

"I want to see my kids," came a voice from the cabin.

Pike looked at Windflower. "If he puts down his weapons and comes out, he can see his children," Windflower whispered.

"Your kids are safe," said Pike. "Come out with your hands up and you can see them real soon."

"I don't believe you," said Rose. "It's a trick."

"No trick," said the fire chief. "You have my word."

"I don't know," said Rose. "It's no use. I might as well finish it off now."

"It's never too late," said Pike. "I didn't become a fire-fighter until my forties, and now I'm the chief. Good things can still happen. Don't give up, Greg. I promise you that I will stick by you and help you. But you have to come out and end this thing now."

There was a minute of silence that felt like an hour to Windflower. He knew that they were at the make-or-break point. Either Rose would come out peacefully. Or... He didn't even want to think about that. He took a peek around him and saw Avery in a crouched position with his rifle pointed directly at the cabin.

Finally, they heard the cabin door open. Windflower held his breath, ready for anything. Then into the blinding lights of the ATV walked Greg Rose with his hands empty and held high above his head. Windflower ran towards him and tackled him to the ground. Tizzard, Avery and Chief Pike were close behind. Rose lay passive in Windflower's arms, and he released him so that Tizzard could put cuffs on him.

Greg was openly weeping, and Pike was trying to console him. "It's going to be okay now," said Pike.

"My kids, my kids."

Tizzard looked at Windflower.

"You and Avery take him back, and I'll follow behind you. Chief Pike can come with me."

Windflower got on the radio and gave the all-clear. He phoned Betsy. "Suspect is in custody."

"Thank God," said Betsy. "Is everyone okay?"

"Everyone is fine," said Windflower. "Can you put the word out? We will be bringing Greg Rose back to our offices. We haven't used the cells for a while. Are they okay?"

"Clean as a whistle," said Betsy. "I've got a pot of soup on. Should I bring that over with me?"

"That would be great," said Windflower. "When we get straightened away, we are going to bring his kids over to see him. I'll get Gupta to look after that."

Windflower went inside the cabin and retrieved Rose's weapons and ammunition. He put them in the storage container and drove back with Pike, following closely behind Tizzard and the prisoner. It had started raining again, but he could hardly feel it. All he could feel was relief.

Back at the RCMP offices, there was a great congregation of ATVs and police officers waiting for them. They all went inside and started taking off the rain gear. Tizzard took Greg Rose into the back and put him in a cell. Betsy came in with her soup and started dishing up bowls to the wet and hungry officers. Avery had managed to salvage some of the sandwiches, and they disappeared very quickly. But soon after, they were replaced by a package of food from the Mug-Up, including more sandwiches and a large white box.

"Is that what I think it is?" asked Tizzard as Herb Stoodley laid the box on the table in the control room where the officers had gathered.

"It is indeed, Corporal. Freshly made coconut cream cheesecake."

"My favourite," said Tizzard, and everyone laughed.

Before they could get a chance to sample the cheesecake, Betsy came in.

"It's Superintendent Quigley," she said to Windflower. "He wants to talk to you and Corporal Tizzard."

"I'll take it in my office," said Windflower. He left the control room with Tizzard behind him.

"Great work on resolving the situation," said Quigley.

"We had help from the fire chief," said Windflower. "He convinced Rose to give himself up."

"Anyway, I'm happy with the way it turned out," said Quigley. "Good job all around. We do have some new information on the other case. Tizzard knows about this. Williams found a body in the car out at Mooring Cove. It's Snake Gibbons."

Windflower looked at Tizzard. "I didn't want to bother you. Looked like you had enough on your hands."

"We'll need forensics back over to Marystown," said Quigley.

"No worries," said Windflower. "They'll be back tonight. Anything from the scene so far?"

"Just a lot of blood, according to Williams," said Quigley. "Looks like he was stabbed."

"Are you thinking that it might be Todd Osmond involved in this?" asked Windflower.

"Well, they were together, along with Meier. But until we get prints, we won't know for sure. I'm in St. John's, coming to Marystown tomorrow, by the way. Any chance we could meet up? There's a lot of loose ends right now."

"Could do it for a few minutes," said Windflower. "I'm on kiddie duty. Stella has figure skating and Amelia Louise has dance. Luckily, both are in Marystown."

"Super," said Quigley. "I'm driving over tonight, so call me in the morning."

"Will do," said Windflower.

"And Winston, congratulations again on resolving this peacefully. I know this stuff is really hard. Thank you," said Quigley.

"'All's well that ends well,'" said Windflower. "It seems like we have a lot of problems right now."

"But you're getting through them," said Quigley

"Remember, 'When sorrows come, they come not single spies, but in battalions.'"

"Okay, have a safe drive," said Windflower. "We have cheesecake," said Tizzard.

"What kind?" asked Quigley.

"Coconut cream," said Tizzard.

"That's my favourite," said Quigley.

"Mine, too," said Tizzard.

Windflower rolled his eyes. "Goodnight, Ron. See you tomorrow."

CHAPTER 38

He and Tizzard went back out to the control room, where there were two pieces of cheesecake left. "It's a good thing you came back soon," said Brown.

Windflower took up a piece and handed the other to Tizzard. He laid his on the table and stood up.

"I want to thank you all for coming and helping out," he said. "A special thanks to Chief Pike, who managed to talk Rose into surrendering." All of the officers applauded. "Thank you again to Brownie and the forensics crew for hanging around. You're needed back in Marystown, but we really appreciate your help." Another round of applause.

"And here's to our leader, Sergeant Windflower," said Tizzard, who'd finished his cheesecake. Loud applause from everybody.

"I almost forgot," said Windflower as he noticed Betsy at the back of the room. "Thank you to Betsy and her husband, Bob, and all the neighbours who helped us out by loaning us their ATVs."

Betsy blushed as the assembled Mounties cheered.

The room cleared out shortly after that. Avery was sent with Tizzard to bring Rose's children over to see him. Once that visit was over, they would take them and Marsha back home. Their imminent danger had cleared. Gupta would stay overnight at the offices and sleep in one of the cells near Greg Rose.

"Why don't you take him with you back to Marystown tomorrow?" he said to Gupta. "I'll follow behind as an escort. There are more facilities and more people over there to deal with him. We'll need to get him in front of a judge so that we can get a psychiatric assessment going."

"Sounds good," said Gupta. Windflower stayed for a few more minutes to help Betsy and Gupta clean up and then went home. Sheila was waiting for him and rushed to the door to greet him.

"I'm so glad you're okay," she said, hugging him closely. She knew better than to ask for details. He almost never talked about the difficult parts of his police work. He said that he didn't want to bring that home with him. "The girls were really worried about you. They wanted to stay up until you got home, but I told them they had skating and dance in the morning. I can take them if you need me to."

"No, I'm okay," said Windflower. "Quigley is going to be in Marystown, so I can see him while the girls' activities are going on."

"Okay," said Sheila. "Are you hungry? There's some left-over pizza I can warm up."

"That would be great," said Windflower. "I can't remember what I ate today. I had a piece of cheesecake for my supper."

Sheila laughed and went to put on the tea and get his pizza heated up in the microwave.

"Nice," said Windflower when she came back in with it. "Homemade pepperoni pizza."

"Well, we had to make our own since some crazy RCMP guy told us we couldn't go out," said Sheila, laughing.

After his pizza and a cup of tea, Sheila went upstairs while Windflower went to see Lady and Molly. Lady was excited to see him, as if she had thought he was dead and now returned to life. Molly took a peek to see if there were any food offerings. Seeing none, she closed her eyes and drifted back to sleep.

Windflower got Lady's leash, and they went outside. The rain had started again, but this time it was gentler. Like a summer rain, thought Windflower. He and the Collie wandered the streets of quiet Grand Bank with every house seeming to blink a largescreen TV in the darkness of night. Everybody was safe at home, he thought. Just as it should be.

He wandered down around the wharf and then headed for home.

Minutes later, he was drying Lady off and heading upstairs. He could see the light on in their bedroom as he went into the bathroom to have a shower before going to bed. He let the water run long and hot. It seemed to wash away the worries of the day, and by the time he reached the bed he was relaxed and ready for sleep. Sheila turned out the light and came closer to him. He didn't stir until the morning light shone into his bedroom.

Saturday morning at his house was a much more relaxed affair. The children didn't get up until they were called, and that let Windflower and Sheila sleep in a little. They were both grateful for the extra rest. Windflower got up first and went downstairs to put the coffee on. While he was waiting for that, he got his smudging kit and went out in the back with Lady close behind. It was raining steadily now, a bit fiercer than last night but still with a warming breeze.

He got a chair and sat underneath the eaves to get out of the rain, lit his smudge, and started moving the smoke around his head and his body. When he was done, he did his prayers, first thanking Creator for his blessings. He started with being grateful for last night. That nobody, including Greg Rose, got hurt. He ended with prayers for all the RCMP officers in his command and of course Sheila and Stella and Amelia Louise.

By the time he got back in, the coffee was ready, and he

had a few moments by himself to sit and have a cup. Then he heard sounds from above, and soon both girls appeared at the bottom of the stairs.

"Good morning, sleepyheads," he said.

"'Morning, Daddy," said the girls.

"We're glad you're home," said Stella.

"But you missed the movie," said Amelia Louise.

"What was the movie?" asked Windflower.

"It was called *Gump*, and it was about a dog that had to find its way back home," said Stella.

"Maybe we can watch it again with you tonight," said Amelia Louise.

"Maybe," said Windflower. He had learned to try not to say yes or no.

Maybe meant he could back out if there was a better option. He remem bered about Sanjay and the invitation to supper. "We're going to the Sanjays for supper tonight."

The girls may have preferred to watch *Gump* again, but this wasn't a hill they intended to die on.

"Can we watch TV?" asked Amelia Louise.

"Sure," said Windflower. "I'll make us some breakfast, and then you'll have to get ready to go to Marystown." He turned on the TV and found a cartoon channel the girls agreed on and went to make breakfast. He quickly scrambled half a dozen eggs and made toast and fruit to go with it. He was starting to put it on their plates when Sheila came down-stairs to join them.

He gave Sheila a cup of coffee and called the girls. They were happy and giggling and in good spirits as they nibbled on their food until Windflower told them it was time to get ready. He and Sheila had a few minutes to chat, and then the girls were back and ready to go.

"We'll be back sometime after noon," said Windflower.

"Meet me over at the Mug-Up," said Sheila, coming to kiss all three of them before they left.

Windflower took Sheila's car, even though he was on semiofficial business escorting Gupta and Greg Rose this morning. He drove by the office and went inside.

"Everything okay?" he asked.

"All quiet over here," said Gupta. "Betsy came by with breakfast sand wiches for me and Rose."

"Did he say anything last night?" asked Windflower.

"Not a word. I think he's in shock."

"We'll talk to him when we get over to Marystown," said Windflower. "Ready to go?"

He went with Gupta to the back to get Rose. "You get his weapons from the evidence locker," he said, handing her the keys. "They should go with him to Marystown. I'll look after Rose." Greg Rose barely glanced at him as he got him to stand and put on the handcuffs. No struggle and no words as he put on the shackles.

CHAPTER 39

Gupta went out first and put Rose's guns in her trunk. She came back in and escorted Rose to the back seat of her vehicle. She waited until Windflower was in position and then slowly led them out of Grand Bank and onto the highway.

"Is that man a bad man?" asked Amelia Louise from his back seat. "Mommy said a bad man was in Grand Bank and that's why we couldn't go out and get pizza," said Stella.

"We had pizza anyway," said Amelia Louise. "Mommy made it. I had cheese pizza."

"He's not really a bad man," said Windflower. "Then why was he all tied up?" asked Stella.

"It was for his own protection," said Windflower. "He's a sick man. But we're going to get him some help."

That seemed to satisfy the girls, and they were mostly

quiet and chatted amongst themselves as Windflower drove to Marystown behind Gupta. He left her when she turned into the RCMP parking lot and continued on to take the girls to their activities. He dropped Stella at the arena for figure skating first, said hello to her coach and then went straight to the high school where dance classes were held. Amelia Louise danced her way into the school and Windflower left her with the dance instructor inside.

He called Quigley, who suggested they meet at Tim Hortons for coffee. That was perfect for Windflower. He pulled into the coffee shop parking lot and found a spot right in front of the building. The people behind the counter looked frantic, but the place was almost empty. He took a look at the drivethrough, which now stretched almost back to the road. People sure loved staying in their vehicles and getting their coffee served to them, he thought.

Right in the back corner next to the window, he spotted Quigley. He ordered his coffee and went to join him.

"Did you have a nice drive over?" asked Quigley. "It was pouring buckets last night."

"Pretty nice," said Windflower. "Seems to be clearing a bit again now. And it looks like we're going to miss the big storm. That's a good thing. We've had lots going on."

"Agreed," said Quigley. "How is Greg Rose?"

"Mostly incommunicative," said Windflower. "Gupta brought him over here this morning. I'm going to interview him later. Do you want to sit in?"

"Sure," said Quigley. "You never know. We might pick up something from him that helps us with the other case. How are you going to proceed with him?"

"We think he'll need a psychiatric assessment," said Windflower. "We'll tell the judge about the incident later and tell them we're worried about his mental health. That he is a threat to the community."

"That should be enough to get the judge to okay that."

"But we'll want to try to get him charged on the arson case as well," said Windflower. "The problem is that we haven't got a lot of evidence."

"So, you'll need a confession."

"We'll get one shot at it this morning," said Windflower. "As soon as we get him to court, he'll have representation, and if he follows their advice, he'll say nothing after that."

"Is he connected to the gold story?"

"Well, if he's our arsonist, he burned down the house where it looks like some of the gold was held," said Windflower.

"But did he know what was in there?"

"Good question," said Windflower. "He did have weapons. Shoot, I almost forgot. Forensics has the shell casings. We'll need to see if we can match them with his gun. Gupta brought them over. I'll get her to check that out."

"That would be good," said Quigley. "Some real evidence. You won't need it for the assessment, but if you bring charges..."

"Agreed," said Windflower. "Let's go interview Rose."

Greg Rose was waiting in an interview room when they arrived. Gupta was standing outside the door. "Good morning, Superintendent," she said when she saw Quigley.

"'Morning again, Sergeant."

Gupta and Quigley went to the adjoining room, where they could watch and hear from behind the twoway mirror. Windflower went inside and sat across from Rose.

"Good morning, Greg. How are you doing?" he started. Rose looked at him but did not respond. "I'm going to ask you a few questions." He paused, but there was little reaction from the other side of the table.

"Did you start the fire at the house by the cemetery?" No response. "Did that man find you at the house, and you got scared and shot him? Maybe by accident?" He knew it was a stretch, but he had to try something. Some times a prisoner would take an out like that to try to save themselves. It almost never worked, but they grabbed at the slender rope that was offered them by investigators. But still no response.

"I want to see my kids," said Rose.

"That's not going to happen unless you talk to me first."

Rose looked at him for a long time and finally spoke. "I'll talk to Chief Pike. But only him." With that he folded his arms and sat back in his chair. "Okay," said Windflower. "We'll get Chief Pike to come over and you can talk to him. But Constable Gupta will be in the room, too."

"And my kids?"

"We'll bring your kids to see you before you go anywhere else," said Windflower. "Deal?"

Rose nodded, and Windflower left the room and went next door to see Quigley and Gupta.

"Good work," said Quigley.

"He trusts the fire chief," said Windflower. "Must be a father figure thing or something. He probably wants to ask for his forgiveness."

"We don't care about his rationale," said Quigley. "As long as he talks."

"Gupta, can you call Chief Pike and see if he can come over as quickly as possible? We want to strike while the iron is hot," said Windflower. "And make sure you record the interview."

"Got it," said Gupta. "I'll take Rose downstairs and make the call."

Windflower stayed with Quigley while Gupta carried out her first task. "Anything else from Mooring Cove?" asked Windflower.

"Waiting for forensics results," said Quigley. "But you can leave if you have to. I know you have commitments. I'll let you know what we find out."

"Perfect," said Windflower. "Hope you find something."

"'The miserable have no other medicine but only hope,'" said Quigley. "My hope is that we find some hard evidence."

"Fair enough. I still wish you luck," said Windflower. "We

can all use some. 'But fare thee well; thou art a gallant youth.'"

"I'll take that compliment every day of the week," said Quigley. The men shook hands, and Windflower went to pick up the girls. Amelia Lou ise was waiting for him inside the gym, redfaced and very excited to tell and show him about her dance class. And to tell him that she was "so, so, thirsty."

"We'll get a drink at the arena," said Windflower. There, they retrieved Stella and got soft drinks for both girls, who chattered and laughed all the way back to Grand Bank. As they entered the town, the rain finally stopped, and Windflower and the girls admired the rainbow that hung over their little town as they drove right to the Mug-Up café.

CHAPTER 40

They found Sheila and sat down at the table she had been saving for them. The café was bright and busy this Saturday, and it seemed to Windflower that people were nicer to him than they had been for a while. It was probably because of last night, but he didn't question their motives. He was just glad to have their approval back.

They all ordered pea soup and por' cakes, a Grand Bank tradition that had been in place since Sheila was a little girl, creamy pea soup with lots of vegetables and a few specks of salt meat. The por' cakes were a kind of small potato pancake with pieces of minced pork baked into them. They were served with jam at the Mug-Up, but Windflower and the girls each ordered molasses, which came in their own small metal jug.

When they arrived, Windflower pronounced them to be

"sum good b'y," and the table was quiet for the few minutes it took to eat their meal. After their delicious lunch, the girls wanted to go to the store to spend the money they'd gotten from Doctor Sanjay. Sheila suggested going to Dollarama, which pleased them to no end.

"Let's go for a hike later, too," said Windflower. He didn't get as much of an enthusiastic response to that request. But Sheila made it a condition of shopping, so they reluctantly agreed.

"But only for an hour," said Stella.

"And no big hills, either," said Amelia Louise.

"They know you well," said Sheila as she dropped him off to pick up his cruiser. He thought about having a nap but didn't really have the time to do it justice, so he drove to the RCMP office instead.

He was surprised to see Betsy there.

"Just cleaning up after our guest," she said. "Got to keep the place spic and span."

"Thank you, Betsy. You're wonderful."

"Thank you very much, Sergeant," said Betsy. "My Bob said to thank you for the kind words about him loaning you his bike. He was some pleased, b'y."

Windflower smiled and went into his office. He had started rummaging through his papers when Gupta called.

"Corporal Dan Brown called me," she said. "He said that the casings from the fire scene are the same calibre as Greg Rose's gun. They'll have to examine things more carefully before they know if it's an exact match, but they're kind of busy with the other scene."

"Gotcha," said Windflower. "Has Chief Pike come over?"

"We've got a bit of a hiccup. Rose is prepared to talk with Chief Pike, but he wants a lawyer."

"Okay," said Windflower. "See who's on duty counsel and let him talk to Rose. We can't refuse him, since he's asked for representation. Let the lawyer talk to him this afternoon, and then get Chief Pike to come over tomorrow. Matter of fact, I'll come too. Set it up for the morning."

"Good," said Gupta.

Windflower played around a little with the papers on his desk, but his heart wasn't in that today. He said goodbye to Betsy and went home to get ready for his walk with the girls. He filled his water bottle, cut up an apple and then added a small plastic bag of cookies to his knapsack. Lady was all set to go and stood by the front door just in case he tried to make a run for it. Molly, not so much. She casually strolled to the living room and jumped up on the couch to see if there was anything more interesting outside. Before long, Sheila and the girls were back, and they just had to show their dad their purchases before they could go.

Stella had three small packets of candy, some gum, a necklace and a game in which you lined up the different coloured plastic circles. So like Stella, thought Windflower. Amelia Louise had two chocolate bars, two candy packs and some kind of blue plastic owl that lit up when you pressed a button. She squealed every time she hit the button.

"And believe it or not, they still have money left," said Sheila.

"Okay, let's go," said Windflower.

"Do you have the water?" asked Stella, the sensible one.

"Do you have any cookies?" asked Amelia Louise, certainly more frivolous than her sister.

"We're all set," said Windflower. He managed to separate the girls from their dollarstore loot and got them and Lady into the car. Today, they would do the shorter side of the walk up the Cape, starting from an area the locals called L'Anse au Paul. They drove towards Fortune and then took a narrow, rocky road, almost a path that led down near the ocean. There was space to park a few cars and a picnic bench, but today they were the only ones. Maybe because the rain has only stopped recently, thought Windflower.

Usually, there would be a couple of cars and families out having lunch or exploring the beach. The girls wanted to go do some beachcombing first, so Windflower watched as they picked up small pieces of sea glass and clam shells and a few small beach rocks each. He had learned his les son around beach rocks. They could only take back what they could carry themselves.

He put their beach treasure in the trunk, and they started their walk. First, over the little brook that ran down from the hillside. Actually, both girls and Lady walked through the water. Windflower didn't mind that. That's what their rubber boots were for. Then, up a series of open spaces with only rocks and a few lowhanging trees as big as shrubs clinging to the earth for dear life. They took one of the small footpaths that led them right next to the coast and got to look down into the greenblue ocean with the sea birds flapping and squawking in the wind.

Amelia Louise tried to bargain for stopping at the very first rise, but Windflower and Stella were prepared to do a bit farther. So, the younger daughter trudged along behind them with Lady at her heels to make sure she didn't get away from her flock. Finally, at about the third rising, which Windflower guessed was about halfway up this side of the Cape, they paused for a snack and a drink. Windflower liked this particular location because it was the first place you could see down into Grand Bank and still all the way out to Fortune Bay. It always filled him with a sense of wonder and humility. He thought about how small we humans were in the face of this majesty.

After snacks, the girls raced each other on the way down while Lady and Windflower ambled behind them. At the bottom, there was another small dip in the brook and more scavenging on the beach. Then it was time to go home and get ready to go over to the Sanjays' for supper. Windflower changed and had a quick shower before heading over early to see the good doctor and to sample the Scotch before everyone else arrived.

Vijay Sanjay greeted him at the door with a hearty welcome, and Windflower went into the kitchen to say hello to Repa. He gave her a hug but was surprised to find another cook in the kitchen. It was Gupta with an apron on.

Windflower obviously looked surprised, so Vijay took it upon himself to explain. "We hope you don't mind that we have invited Samira to join us," he said. "We South Asians stick together, you know. Besides, she is a wonderful cook who can make naan in a frying pan."

"That's a unique skill," said Windflower. "We're happy to have you join us," he said to Gupta. "Looking forward to sampling your cooking."

"She does much more than bread," said Repa. "You will see. Now get out of our kitchen while we are cooking."

Vijay laughed and guided Windflower by the arm to his study. On a side table was the Scotch. Windflower looked at the label. "Benriach: The Original Ten," he read out loud. There was also a carafe with water and four tasting glasses.

"It's a little unusual," said the doctor. "Benriach is one of the few distilleries that still does its own floor maltings. Most other whiskey distillers outsource that work. People say it adds an additional maltiness, so we shall see." He poured them about half an ounce each. They sipped their Scotch slowly to savour the experience.

"It's very nice," said Windflower. "Smooth. I like it. You can taste the malt, and it has a great smokiness to it."

"Yes, very nice," said Vijay. "I get a hint of fruit and

vanilla as well." They each took a small glass of water to cleanse their palate and repeated their experiment.

"Even better the second time," said Windflower. "I get the fruit and maybe some chocolate as well."

"Very refined," said Vijay as he finished his second tasting.

They sat there for a minute in the afterglow. If they stayed there much longer, Windflower felt he might have fallen asleep. No luck with that, though, as they heard the scampering of little feet that announced the presence of Sheila and his two daughters.

CHAPTER 41

After they visited for a little while, Repa announced that supper was ready. There were many dishes on the dining room table already. She announced that she had made the appetizers and small snacks while Samira had made the main dish and the naan. Everyone applauded the appealing buffet in front of them.

There were homemade veggie samosas with several dips and beguni, a dish consisting of deepfried eggplant slices served with a chutney on the side. There were also crispy onion bhajis with a cucumber dip that were absolutely delicious. In the centre of the table was a basket of golden brown naan that was still steaming and a pot of something that looked almost orange with pieces of fish swimming in it.

"What is that?" asked Windflower.

"It's Mumbai fish masala," said Samira. "You might have

heard of it as Bombay masala, but since the names have changed... You can use chicken, but I prefer fish. And cod is the perfect fish to absorb all of the ingredients."

"Is it hard to make?" asked Sheila as bowls of the masala and rice were passed around.

"It is not hard to make," said Repa. "But it is hard to make well. Samira has learned how to do that from her family."

Samira laughed. "My mother would tell you that I still have much to learn, but it's a relatively simple dish. I sauté some onions, ginger, garlic and spices and just add the marinated fish directly. Some people sear the fish, but I find it dries out cod too much. This way it's flaky and smooth."

"It is gorgeous," said Windflower after his first few bites. "It's sweet and tangy and not overly spiced. Perfect."

Everyone agreed that it was a great dish, and the naan went quickly when people discovered they could dip it into the broth. Windflower ate far more than he thought was possible and absolutely refused a third helping. That was good because there was still dessert.

"Come and help me," said Repa to Stella and Amelia Louise. They and Sheila followed their hostess to the kitchen and came back shortly afterwards with trays of cookies and cups and saucers. Samira brought the tea urn with Bengali chai tea, while Repa had small bowls that she handed to everybody.

"I know this," said Windflower. "We had it before one time. "It's called mishti doi," he announced proudly.

"Very good," said Repa. "Do you remember what's in it?"

"Hmmm," said Windflower, taking a taste to remind himself. "Yogurt with caramelized sugar and warm milk. I think you bake it and chill it."

"We will have to make you an honorary Bengali," said Vijay as every one laughed. "But do you remember our saying about our special tea?"

Windflower thought hard but could not.

"We call it doodh cha. They say back home, 'To have doodh cha not when you need it, but when you feel like you've deserved it.'"

Everyone laughed again. With full bellies and full hearts, Windflower and Sheila and the kids bid them goodnight with a hearty thankyou to Repa and Vijay. Windflower lingered a little afterwards, while the Sanjays fawned over the girls, to say goodnight to Samira.

"Thank you for a delicious supper," he said. "You are certainly a person of many talents."

"I am glad you enjoyed it," she said. "You must have been surprised to see me."

"Very pleasantly so," said Windflower. "Will you stay over tonight?"

"Yes, I've reserved my place at Betsy's," said Samira. "I'll go back early tomorrow."

"Great," said Windflower. "Well, enjoy the rest of your evening, and I'll see you in Marystown." He could see that Sheila was trying to get the girls in the car and went to help.

He waved goodbye again, and minutes later they were all back home.

It was way too early for bedtime, and it was Saturday night, so the girls begged, and their parents relented and allowed them to watch their movie again. Windflower made popcorn, and even he enjoyed Gump, a story they followed along through the eyes of a stray dog. He especially liked the devotion shown by a dog who would clearly do anything for his master.

"I wonder if Lady would do those things for me," he said at the end of the movie.

"Lady would do anything for a Milk Bone," said Stella.

"Okay, girls, time for bed," said Sheila. The girls groaned but went up stairs. "I'll settle them down and tuck them in if you take Lady," she said to Windflower.

"That's a fair deal," said Windflower. "Oh, by the way, I have to go to Marystown in the morning. We have to interview Greg Rose again."

"Okay," said Sheila. "Amelia Louise has shown a new interest in church, so she can come with me and Stella. Will you be gone all day?"

"I don't think so," said Windflower. "But I'll be back for supper, for sure."

"Good," said Sheila. "Maybe you can barbeque something for us. I'll see what they have at Warren's."

"Another good deal," said Windflower as he took Lady outside.

It was a fine, clear night with a brisk wind that was certainly cooling things down. More seasonable weather, thought Windflower. Cooler, but at least the storm had passed them by. He pushed his collar up and headed into the wind, tugging Lady around until they both had enough of the walk and the night.

Back at home, he gave Lady a Milk Bone and offered a cat treat to Molly. She took it but was clearly expecting something more. She turned her back to Windflower and curled up in a ball. "Sorry about that," said Windflower. "But hey, maybe tomorrow night you might get lucky." There was no response from the cat as Windflower turned out the lights and went upstairs.

He tried to read but found himself drowsing, so he gave up and cuddled up with Sheila. Very quickly, he was asleep. Almost as quickly, it seemed, he woke up. In a dream.

This time he was on solid ground. Somehow, he preferred that to floating around in the clouds. He was in the middle of a meadow, and it was summertime. He could see birds flittering around and hear bees buzzing above his head. In the middle of the meadow was a clearing, and sitting on a large rock was a young man in a military uniform.

"You're Sean," said Windflower. "Sean Tizzard."

"Well, I used to be," joked the soldier. "This is what I looked like when I left home."

"Well, nice to see you," said Windflower. "But why are you back?"

"Same message. I need you to let my brother know he's in great danger."

"I've told him that already," said Windflower.

"I know," said the other man. "But he's not listening. I've tried sending him other messages, too. He's not paying attention. Now it's very close. The danger. It's a man with a gun. I can't see his face because it hasn't happened yet. But you must warn him."

At that last word, a dark black cloud swept over the meadow, and it was like the young soldier was swept up in it. Seconds later he was gone, and so was the meadow. Windflower woke up in bed in a cold sweat. Sheila had fallen asleep too by now but woke when she felt her husband shaking behind her.

"Winston, what's going on?"

"I had a dream," he said. "I'm okay now."

"Tell me about it," said Sheila.

CHAPTER 42

Windflower did not often talk to Sheila about his dreams. Part of it was being kind of embarrassed to show just how much stock he put into them. Part of it was he wanted to protect her if it happened to be in any way threatening to him. He didn't want to worry her. But tonight, he needed to talk.

"I had a dream about Tizzard," he started. "His brother came to me to say that Eddie was in danger."

"His brother that's dead?"

"Sean," said Windflower. "It's the second time this has happened. He said that it could happen soon."

"Did you talk to Eddie? Did you tell him?"

"I did, and he laughed it off," said Windflower. "Now I'm really worried."

"Well, you'll just have to talk to him again then, won't

you?" Windflower was relieved that she didn't think he was crazy for believing in a dream. Or at least this dream.

"You can also talk to Richard, get him to help you," said Sheila. "That's a really good idea," said Windflower. "I'll talk to Richard before I go over to Marystown. I'll get him to call Eddie, and I'll try and see him, too, in Marystown. You are very smart, Sheila Hillier."

"Thank you, I know. Now, can we get some sleep?"

With a plan based on solid advice from Shelia, Windflower snuggled in and was soon off to sleep again.

The light from the window woke him in the morning. That meant it was probably a little after seven. Good timing, he thought. Lots of time to get ready. He wondered if Richard Tizzard might be up. He did say he was an early riser. Windflower and Lady could take a walk over and find out.

Lady was pleasantly surprised to see him and jumped at the chance to get out early with her master. Molly, on the other hand, barely stirred in her bed. "Good morning to you, too," said Windflower as he and the Collie left for their walk. Lady was happy to walk past their usual stopping points and over to Richard Tizzard's little house. Windflower was even happier when he saw a light on in the kitchen.

He knocked on the door and was greeted by some very roughsounding growling from inside. Both he and Lady instinctively moved back. Windflower could hear Richard moving around inside and talking to his dog. "Quiet down there, buddy," he heard him say as the door opened.

"Winston, it's you. Come on in," said Richard. "This old girl has more bark than bite. She wouldn't hurt a soul. Come in, come in."

Windflower came in, followed by Lady, who stood there to let the new dog inspect her. Once it was clear that there was no danger, both dogs did their sniff and greet, and the two men went into the kitchen. Richard got both dogs a treat and offered Windflower a cup of coffee.

"That would be great," said Windflower. "Sorry to bother you so early."

"No worries there, my friend. I'm up with the light. I don't know why. I got nothing to do and nowhere to go. Old habits, I guess. I'm glad for the visit."

Windflower didn't know where to start, so he just started talking. "I had a dream. About Eddie."

"That's funny," said Richard. "I had a dream too. Sean was in it."

Windflower was surprised but not shocked. It had happened before when someone close had similar dreams. But not like this. "Sean was in my dream, too."

"You know, people would think I'm a crazy old man, and some of that is true, but I talks to Sean and Mary, my wife, all the time, even though they've been dead for years," said Richard. "I thinks they might hear me, but I'm never sure. And sometimes they do come to me in dreams. Mary sometimes comes to visit, bless her soul. But Sean hardly ever comes. I was surprised to see and hear him."

"Sean told me that Eddie is in danger," said Windflower. "He came twice to warn me. He said he tried to give Eddie messages, too, but they didn't seem to get through. I told Eddie myself, but he didn't take it too seriously."

"Eddie is a fine boy, a good man," said Richard. "But he takes after his old man a bit too much. He's not much for listening or following advice. He likes to carve his own path. I called him and left him a message. I'll talk to him when he calls back. But he's pretty stubborn."

"I'll try to see him when I go over to Marystown."

"Thank you for caring about Eddie," said Richard. "He loves you like a brother."

"I love him, too," said Windflower. "Anyway, we've got to get going. Thank you for the coffee."

"Come back and see me any time," said Richard. "And remember, we can provide advice and suggestions, but we do have our own paths to fol low. 'Let us not pray to be sheltered from dangers but to be fearless when facing them.'"

Windflower had to rouse Lady to get her away from the fireplace and the other dog. She seemed quite comfortable there. But she came when called, and the pair retraced their steps until they were back home again.

Windflower put the coffee on and went outside to smudge. Lady fol lowed along, not wanting to miss any of the action. He mixed and lit his smudge and let the smoke encircle him. He stayed in that aroma and space for a few moments to let the sacred medicines penetrate his body and mind and heart. Then he offered prayers of gratitude for the many blessings he continued to enjoy. Prayers of thanks and acknowledgement to the people who had come before him and were still helping him on this journey.

He also had two specific prayers this morning, one for Greg Rose and his family. For Rose, that he be given the courage to ask for help. Because once he did that, his healing could begin. For Marsha and his two children, that they find the support and strength they would need to continue on without their father and husband. They, too, would need help to heal and recover.

Second, he prayed for his friend, Eddie. He knew he could not control fate or destiny and that he could not and would not interfere in another person's journey. But he prayed that even in danger he would be protected and that Eddie would be given every opportunity to move away from that danger. That was all he could ask for. Anything else was not up to him.

He finished smudging and went back inside. He could hear the girls get ting up and went to bring them downstairs so they wouldn't disturb Sheila. Maybe she could sleep in a little this morning. He placated the girls by letting them watch their movie again while he made waffles for breakfast.

By the time Sheila came down, the girls were eating their waffles and fruit on the floor of the living room and watching Gump.

"Again?" she asked as she took a cup of coffee from Windflower. "The fun never ends around here. Waffles?"

"Absolutely," said Sheila. "I think I might watch the last of the movie, too."

Windflower laughed, cooked them both their breakfast and brought it out to join Stella and Amelia Louise for breakfast. After cleaning up, he went to have his shower while Sheila and the girls got ready for church.

Amelia Louise was finished first and was waiting downstairs when Windflower came down.

"I hear you like going to church now," he said.

"Yes," said Amelia Louise. "My friend at school, Maggie, says that God will grant you anything you want if you are good and go to church."

"I don't think it works that way," said Windflower as Sheila came down the stairs.

"What are you talking about?" she asked.

"I was starting to explain to Amelia Louise that you can't just ask God for anything you want."

"Not everything," said Amelia Louise. "Just the important stuff."

"I think that's fair," said Sheila. "As long as you don't have expectations."

"What's spectations?" asked Amelia Louise.

"That's when you think you will absolutely get something just because you asked for it," said Sheila.

"Like an extra cookie? Or staying up late?" asked Amelia Louise.

"Exactly," said Sheila.

"We also have to be grateful for what we already have," said Windflower. "Like the delicious waffles you just ate."

"Those are gone," said Amelia Louise. "I like Mommy's splanation better."

"I give up," said Windflower. "Have fun at church, and we'll see you when I get back."

CHAPTER 43

He drove out of Grand Bank, most of which was still in bed by the looks of it, and turned onto the highway. He took his CD out of the glove compartment and put it into the player. He needed some Chopin this morning to soothe his brain and his spirit. Rafał Blechacz gave him exactly that.

The second half of the CD was as good as the first, and Windflower found himself entranced by the music and the pianist's artistry. It was smooth and almost silky, and he loved the gentle rocking rhythm and tenderness that Blechacz showed in his interpretation of the great artist. He was filled completely by the music and a little sad when it was over. The good news, he told himself, was that he could listen to this CD again and again.

With that pleasant thought, he put the CD back in the

glove compartment and concentrated on enjoying the rest of his ride into Marystown. When he arrived at the RCMP building, he checked in at the lockup first. Gupta was already there.

"Good morning," she said. "Nice drive over?" "Perfect. You didn't get much sleep."

"'I slept and dreamt that life was joy. I awoke and saw that life was service. I acted and behold, service was joy,'" said Gupta.

"Very good," said Windflower. "My second Tagore quote this morning. I dropped in to see Richard Tizzard."

"Rose seems okay this morning," she said. "A little agitated, but that's understandable. His lawyer is with him now. We're waiting on Chief Pike, but he called to say he was on his way."

"Who's the lawyer?"

"Gerald Templeton," said Gupta.

"Not the worst," said Windflower. "A bit full of himself, but he under stands the system. I'm going to run to Tim Hortons to get a coffee. Do you want one?"

"Small with milk," said Gupta. "Thanks."

Windflower drove to Tim Hortons and ordered their coffees at the drive through. Then he decided to get two more coffees, doubledouble. Maybe Rose and his lawyer would like one too. Couldn't hurt.

Back at the building, he parked outside the lockup area and carried his tray inside. The constable on duty directed him to an interview room down the hallway. Inside the room were Rose and his lawyer, Gerald Templeton, on one side of the table, while Gupta and Chief Pike were sitting on the other.

Windflower nodded to his side of the table and went around to shake Templeton's hand. He placed a coffee in front of Rose and his lawyer. Rose grabbed his right away. It was a good idea, thought Windflower.

He asked that the recording be turned on.

"My name is Acting Inspector Winston Windflower. In the room with me are Constable Samira Gupta, Chief Roy Pike from the Grand Bank Volunteer Fire Department, Gregory Wayne Rose and his solicitor, Gerald Templeton. We are here to interview Mr. Rose in connection with recent fires in the Grand Bank area."

"I would like to record my objection to this interview," said Templeton. "In my view, Mr. Rose is distressed, and I have advised him not to proceed."

"Mr. Rose, do you wish to proceed?" asked Windflower. "You said I could see my kids if I cooperated," said Rose.

"Yes," said Windflower. "We can accommodate that request. As we stated earlier, we will allow your children to visit you before you leave this facility."

"I want to see them today," said Rose.

"It won't be today," said Windflower. "We'll have to make arrangements to bring them here. Can we continue?"

"I guess so," said Rose.

"For the record, I am acknowledging that Gregory Wayne Rose is agreeing to this interview," said Windflower. "Greg, what time did you get to the house near the cemetery? The one that burned down?"

Rose sat there for a minute and didn't say a word. Windflower was going to ask him again when he spoke up, very quietly. "I was there early in the morning. It was still dark. I parked my truck downtown by the post office and walked over there."

"Did you start the fire?" asked Windflower.

Another long pause, and then Rose started talking again. "I started the fire in the other end of the house. There was nobody there."

"Then what happened?" asked Windflower.

"I heard a noise from the other side of the house. From the kitchen," said Rose. "I went out to see what was going on."

Rose stopped talking, and Windflower wasn't sure he would go on, but Rose gulped and continued. "There was two men in there arguing. One of them came at me. I didn't know what to do, so I pulled out my gun and told him to get back. He wouldn't stop and I–and I shot him. It wasn't my fault. He wouldn't stop." He put his head in his hands and started crying.

"Let's take a break," said Windflower. "Turning off recording." He made a note in the recording log of the date and time. "Fifteen minutes," he said to Templeton before leading Gupta and Chief Pike out into the hallway.

"I take no joy in being right," said Pike.

"No, but at least we've stopped him before anybody but the late Coco Meier got hurt," said Windflower.

"It'll be hard to explain to the other men," said Pike.

"It's clearly a mental illness," said Windflower. As they were speaking, Templeton came out of the interview room.

"A word if you don't mind, Sergeant," said the lawyer.

"He needs help," said Templeton once they had moved away from the others. "You can't be serious about charging him with anything."

"We will charge him with one count of arson, and maybe the others," said Windflower. "But if he continues to cooperate, we will be immediately moving for a psychiatric assessment. Charges will be held in abeyance until we get that back."

"Got it," said Templeton. "Give me two more minutes with my client."

A few minutes later they were all back in the interview room. "I wants to see my kids," said Rose.

"We're almost done here for today," said Windflower. He turned the tape recorder on. "Greg, what did the two men in the house look like? Were they tall or skinny or fat?"

"The guy I shot was bigger," said Rose. "I didn't get a good look at the other guy. He was smaller, but he took off as soon as me and the big guy started to struggle. When I looked up, he was gone."

"Anything distinctive about either of them?" asked Windflower.

"I think one of them was a Frenchman," said Rose. "He swore at me. I think it was French."

"Okay," said Windflower. "Just a couple of more questions. Greg, did you start the other two fires?"

Rose sat quietly for a few moments. "Yes," he finally said.

Roy Pike sat forward in his chair. He looked at Windflower, who knew what he was going to ask. He nodded to indicate that it was okay.

"Greg, why did you do it?"

Windflower shut off the recording. No one needed to hear this answer except for the people in the room.

"I don't really know," said Rose. "I guess it made me feel important. I only felt I had value when I was fighting fires. People looked happy to see me and would thank me for doing a good job. I never got any of that growing up. I was told I was a loser. That I'd never be anything. Now I was special. I was something."

"Have you been doing this long?" asked Pike.

Windflower turned the recording back on. "Sorry, Chief, can you ask that question again? It's for the record."

Pike repeated the question.

"For about four years," said Rose. "I started the brush fire down near the T, but that scared me 'cause it got out of control so fast." Windflower remembered that fire. It had begun in a meadow but had moved quickly in the wind and took out three cabins before the fire department could get it under control.

"I stuck to houses after that, only abandoned houses with nobody in them. I made sure of that," said Rose.

"How many in total?" asked Windflower.

"Two more, plus the three this year," said Rose, growing more visibly upset.

"I think that's enough," said Gerald Templeton.

CHAPTER 44

Windflower turned off the recording. "Greg, we're going to bring you to court and get the judge to send you for some tests."

"What about my kids? You said I could see them."

"First the judge, and then we'll bring the kids over," said Windflower. Windflower left the room with Gupta and Roy Pike.

"You okay?" he asked the fire chief, who looked as pale as a ghost. "Not really," said Pike. "I think I'll need to talk to somebody."

"You might want to bring in a trauma counsellor," said Gupta. "I know someone in Marystown. She usually does a group session and then hangs around for confidential sessions with people one-on-one."

"That's a good idea," said Pike. "I'll take her number."

Gupta wrote the number down and handed it to him. He tucked it in his pocket and left.

"Another talent," said Windflower. "How do you know the trauma counsellor?"

"Part of my work in community liaison," said Gupta. "You need to find and access all the community resources."

"Like the shelter and counsellors?"

"Exactly," said Gupta. "People don't know where to look, so I help connect them. There are many resources already here, not enough and all overworked, but they will always help when we ask."

"That's good to know," said Windflower. "I'm going to try to find Cor poral Tizzard. Will you look after getting Rose moving in the system?"

"He's on the docket for Judge Prowse, first thing in the morning."

"And we have to talk to Marsha Rose to see if she is agreeable to letting her children see Greg," said Windflower.

"I've talked to her once, but I'll follow up again," said Gupta. "She understands that it might be quite some time before they see him again. She won't come but is okay if we go pick the kids up and bring them over."

"Okay, I'll leave that with you," said Windflower. He was about to call Tizzard when Ron Quigley called.

"Working Sunday morning?" asked Windflower.

"No rest for the wicked," said Quigley. "Checking in to see how you're doing."

"And if we have anything on Todd Osmond."

"That would be good," said Quigley. "I tried Tizzard, but he's not answering. Must think he gets family time off or something."

"I'm going to track him down and see if he has anything," said Windflower. "We have confirmed our arsonist."

"The volunteer firefighter?"

"Greg Rose," said Windflower. "Confessed to the three recent fires, plus some others over the last few years. And he also says he shot Coco Meier. Claims it was self-defence."

"What else did he say?"

"He said there was another man. Him and the Frenchman, he called Meier, were arguing. Meier came at him, and the other guy ran away while they were struggling. Didn't get a good look at him."

"Well, you might have solved a murder, too, this morning," said Quigley.

"And it's not even noon yet."

"Good work," said Quigley. "'Make use of time, let not advantage slip.'"

"It's just good to start seeing some resolution," said Windflower. "Although this Greg Rose situation is going to unsettle some people. I guess 'what's done cannot be undone.'"

"I like how you slipped that one in there, Winston," said Quigley with a laugh. "Let me know any news about Todd

Osmond. Feels like he's the missing link to a lot more questions. And answers."

"Will do," said Windflower. Instead of calling Tizzard, he decided to drive over to his house. It wasn't far, and it was a good break from what he had just been through. He parked his car on the street. Tizzard's Jeep was in the driveway; that meant he was home.

Tizzard was surprised to see him. "Carrie, come see who's here. Come on in," he said to Windflower.

Carrie Evanchuk was also surprised but was happy to see him. She was carrying her baby but handed her to Eddie as she went to give Windflower a welcome hug.

"It is so nice to see you," said Carrie. "How are Sheila and the girls? I haven't seen them in forever."

"Everybody is good at home. You look good." Although the truth was that Carrie looked like she hadn't slept in days.

"You are very kind," said Carrie. "But I'm exhausted. Eddie helps when he can, but having two changes your life. Completely," she added as Hughie poked his head out between her legs.

"Hi, Hughie," said Windflower, but for now the boy scattered back towards his mother and hid behind her. The baby, on the other hand, seemed to be interested in Windflower, and when he held his arms out, she reached her little hands towards him.

Tizzard handed her over. "She's very friendly."

Windflower looked into the baby's eyes, and she stared

right back at him. "Curious, too," he said. "Hello, Sophie." She seemed to smile at her name. "Looks like you've got your hands full," he said to Carrie.

"It'll be a break to get back to work," she said. "After Christmas?"

"First thing in the new year, although I hear my replacement is pretty special," said Carrie.

"She is great," said Windflower. "But not as good as you," he added quickly.

"Good catch," said Tizzard. "You want coffee or tea?"

"I'd love a cup of tea," said Windflower. "I'm all coffee'd out." Tizzard went to put on the kettle while Windflower kept chatting with Carrie and then Hughie when he figured it was safe to come out of hiding. He and Windflower played a game of peekaboo until Eddie came back with the tea.

"I'm guessing you are not just here on a social call," said Tizzard. "Although we're glad of having visitors."

"I've got to change Sophie. Can I leave Hughie here with you?" asked Carrie.

"He'll be fine here," said Eddie.

Eddie bounced Hughie on his lap as Windflower told him about Greg Rose.

"It still shocks me," said Eddie. "How someone could do that. In their own community."

"I know," said Windflower. "It will take some time for everyone to get over it. Have you heard any more about Todd Osmond?"

"No sign of him yet," said Tizzard. "The only thing we're getting back is that he's not wellliked. Everybody is afraid of him."

"Anything on the prints from Mooring Cove?" asked Windflower. "Brown and his crew were over there last night. I'll text him to see if he has any news."

That pause gave Windflower a chance to bring up his dream. "I had another dream," he said.

"Not about me again, I hope," said Eddie. "People will start to think you're weird." He laughed, but Windflower didn't join in.

"It was Sean again," said Windflower. "He said the danger was close now. You have to be especially careful."

"My dad called me, too," said Eddie. "I'm going to be careful."

"That's a good thing," said Carrie, coming back in with a freshly cleaned baby. "Since that isn't your forte."

"What do you mean?" Eddie protested.

Now Windflower had to laugh, despite himself. "Take no chances," he said. "Now, I've got to get back. You have to come over with Sophie and Hughie," he said to Carrie.

"We will," she said. "I miss the girls."

Windflower gave them all a hug, even Hughie, who had accepted him into his circle. "Call me if you hear anything from Brown."

CHAPTER 45

Windflower got back in his car and was soon on the highway back to Grand Bank. He didn't bother putting on the radio or any music. He wanted to feel whatever was stirring inside of him. Right now, it was all mixed up. Some relief, obviously, at having stopped the person who was causing so much damage in their community. But sadness, too, that everyone had to go through so much pain. He felt especially sorry for Marsha Rose and her two children. He wondered if she could stay, or even want to, in Grand Bank after all of this. And he had this nagging sensation about Eddie. That something was going to happen. Something bad.

He drove in silence almost all the way back to Grand Bank. Then he took that narrow dirt road that led down to the L'Anse au Loup T. He needed that space today. He parked his car and walked right down to the end of the pathway. The wind was strong, but it did not deter him. He loved the feeling of being so close to the sea, and, as luck would have it, was all by himself. He stopped at the end and looked out into the ocean. He could barely make out the islands on the distant shore. One of them was Brunette Island.

Windflower had read about that island and heard the stories of the old days when people lived on Brunette Island and others had come for the summer to fish in the rich inshore fishing grounds nearby. In the late 1940s and early 1950s the population of the island was around three hundred. But then the fishing industry shifted to a fresh cod fishery, and processing plants were built in Burin, Fortune and Grand Bank. Many of the men from Brunette Island found work on trawlers, and their wives could get jobs at the plant, so they started to move off the island.

In a short period of time, most of the residents of Brunette Island had resettled in Grand Bank and Fortune. Some families tried to hang on, but they couldn't keep a teacher for the school, and in December 1957 the last eighteen families left for good. Their final act before finally departing was to burn their Anglican church to the ground to stop smugglers from using it as a storehouse for contraband liquor and cigarettes from Saint Pierre. That was a bitter ending for the residents of Brunette Island, which was now left completely deserted.

It was a sad story that seemed to fit Windflower's mood completely today. He walked down a little closer to the water and watched as the wa ter came in currents flowing in and then out again. Sometimes there were waves that crashed into the shoreline. Today, there was only the softest touch of the ocean onto the land. That was fitting, too, he thought. The ocean and nature can heal us but also remind us that we are only a small part of something much bigger. That seemed to comfort him as he walked back to his car. He wasn't at peace yet, but at least he had found some acceptance, and that was a great first step.

He had just started his car again when his cell phone rang.

"We got the print report from forensics," said Tizzard. "Snake Gibbons and Todd Osmond's prints from the car. And they discovered a bloody knife in the woods nearby. Todd Osmond again."

"I think you may have solved a murder," said Windflower. "Now, all we have to do is find him."

"I don't know why, but I think he's still around here some-where," said Tizzard.

"Maybe he's got a little hidey-hole."

"He doesn't have any family left here, but I wonder if he has a girlfriend or an ex who would put him up for a while," said Tizzard.

"Talk to Bernard Thibault," said Windflower. "He might know. Or know who to talk to."

"That's a good idea. I'll give him a call. I'll also put the word out and see if we can find a connection. Talk later."

Windflower hung up and started to drive back to Grand Bank. His phone rang again. He thought it might be Sheila, but it was Roy Pike.

"Chief, what can I do for you?"

"I'm not sure, but when I got back to the fire hall, almost all the crew was waiting here," said Pike. "They wanted to know what happened. I don't know what to tell them. I called that woman that Gupta suggested, and she can come over tomorrow, but I need to say something to them today."

"I agree," said Windflower. "But why are you calling me?"

"I don't really know," said the fire chief. "I was thinking that maybe you could come be with me when I talk to them. Maybe say something, I don't know."

Windflower really didn't want to have anything to do with this, but he heard the desperation in Pike's voice. "I'm not sure what I can say. But if you think I can help you, I'm happy to come over for a few minutes."

"That would be so great," said Roy Pike. "Come over when you can. I really appreciate it."

"I'm just leaving the T right now," said Windflower. "I'll be there in ten minutes or so." He put his phone on speaker and called Sheila along the way.

"How was church?" he asked.

"Church was good," said Sheila. "Stella was great, as usual, and even Amelia Louise behaved. I was impressed and surprised. Are you on your way back? We've finished lunch, but I can make you a sandwich."

"That would be nice," he said. "I'm on my way, but I have to stop at the fire hall."

"What are you doing there?"

"That's what I'm asking myself," said Windflower. "Greg Rose con fessed to the arsons this morning, and the chief doesn't want to be alone when talking to the men."

"And women," said Sheila. "There are two female volunteer firefighters now."

"True," said Windflower. "I guess I'm going for moral support."

"Okay. We'll be around here. I wasn't planning on going anywhere."

"See you soon," said Windflower as he drove past the "Welcome to Grand Bank" sign and headed towards the fire hall down near the brook.

There was a collection of vans and pickup trucks that filled the parking lot at the Grand Bank Volunteer Fire Department building. Windflower squeezed in beside the chief's truck and walked in. He could hear voices upstairs and walked up the staircase next to the two fire trucks that were parked inside.

The chief saw him and came towards him as the twenty or so firefighters turned to watch him enter the room. He waved awkwardly at them as Pike took him into the kitchen and poured him a cup of coffee. "I haven't said much yet.

They know we were talking to Greg, and some have suspicions, but nothing confirmed," said Pike.

"Okay," said Windflower. "Why don't you give them the basic information, and I'll say something afterwards? Then, maybe we can take questions, if that's okay with you."

"That would be great," said Pike. "If you're ready, we can begin. "Ready," said Windflower. He followed Pike out into the big room and stood beside him at the front.

CHAPTER 46

The chief ran through the events of the last few days as matter-of-factly as he could. He told them that Greg Rose had confessed to starting the fires in Grand Bank. There was a collective gasp when he said that. He paused and then introduced Windflower.

Windflower gulped and then started. "First of all, I want to thank you for your service." He looked around at the room and tried to look as many of them in the eye as possible. Some of them were starting to cry.

"Despite what he did, I don't believe that Greg is a bad man," said Windflower. "He is a sick man. Yes, he will be charged with arson." There was a definite murmur in the room at the mention of that word. "But we're also going to make sure he gets the help he needs."

At this last statement, one of the firefighters, a man,

simply got up and left the room. But everyone else, including the two women firefighters, stayed. But the room was eerily quiet. Windflower looked around and then spoke again. "We need you here in Grand Bank. We need you to help us keep us safe. I need you to keep my family, my wife and my two little girls safe." He stopped and moved a little behind Chief Pike.

"We're going to have somebody come and talk to us tomorrow," said Pike. "Right after work at five o'clock. Somebody who might be able to help us. I hope you can all come. We can get through this together. Does anybody have any questions for me or Sergeant Windflower?"

At first, nobody moved, and no one spoke. Finally, one of the men stood up. "What about his wife and kids? They can't be okay. Shouldn't we do something to help them?"

That was the moment that Windflower knew they might be okay them selves. As soon as they started thinking about Greg Rose's family, they stopped thinking about themselves. Plus, they were volunteers, helpers. Maybe they could find a way to help.

Windflower stayed for a few more minutes as the firefighters talked a little about how they helped but more about how they could help the other victims of this disaster. Then, he said his goodbyes to the chief and went outside. He was grateful for the brisk wind and a nice big breath of fresh air that he held a long time before releasing. What a day, he thought, and it was far from over.

He drove home to a much happier, if more hectic, scene at home. The girls were in the living room with Lady. They called it playing. To Windflower it looked more like torture. They had tied a hat on top of Lady's head and were trying to put other decorations on her. Lady saw Windflower and made her escape. He removed the bonnet, and Lady gratefully slunk away into the kitchen.

"What were you doing?" he asked.

"We were dressing her up for the dog show," said Stella.

"We saw it on TV," added Amelia Louise, trying to make their defence. "They watched a show where contestants dress up their dogs to see which one could be the cutest," said Sheila. "The hat was fine, but I think they went a little overboard. I think they need an activity. I was thinking about going to the supermarket in Marystown. I'm guessing you don't want to go."

"No thanks," said Windflower, getting his sandwich out of the fridge. "I've had my fill of Marystown for one day."

"Okay," said Sheila. "Girls, clean everything up out here, and let's get ready to go."

"Thanks for the sandwich," said Windflower, taking a large bite out of his ham and cheese sandwich. "I was starved."

"You're very welcome," said Sheila. "I got a nice roast at Warren's. It's on the counter. Do your magic with it."

Windflower finished his sandwich and waved goodbye to Sheila and the girls as they drove off on their errand. He went to the counter to inspect the meat. He opened the brown paper wrapper, which held a beautiful eye of round roast. One of the best of the inexpensive roasts, not that any meat was cheap these days. It was perfect for slow roasting on the barbeque.

Windflower liked to use a dry rub to marinate the beef, and rather than his usual dry rub, he found another recipe online that featured rosemary and thyme as key ingredients. He mixed up a lot of those herbs with garlic, salt and black and cayenne pepper in a bowl with olive oil. Then he rubbed it all over the meat and covered it with tin foil. He would let it sit in the fridge until it was almost time to barbeque, then clean the herbs off the meat before putting it on the grill. It smelled delicious already.

He thought about going outside and cleaning up the garden, but that remained a thought because as soon as he sat on the couch, he could feel tiredness overwhelm him. He laid back, just for a minute, he thought. He didn't wake until he heard Stella and Amelia Louise run into the house.

"I see you made the best use of your time," said Sheila.

"I did indeed," said Windflower, still groggy from his long nap. "Man, I was tired."

"Understandable. There's been a lot over the last few days."

"You forget how emotional things are," said Windflower. "In the moment you can be calm and collected. Just doing your job. But as soon as it's over, the feelings come flooding in."

"You should talk to someone to process all of this," said Sheila. "You don't want to carry it around with you."

"There's a woman coming over to talk with the fire-fighters tomorrow.

Maybe I can see her."

"That's an excellent idea," she said. "I'm proud of you for dealing with this."

"Well, I don't want to bring it home with me."

"So, what's the plan for the roast?"

"I have it marinating in the fridge," said Windflower. "I can probably put it on the cold side of the barbeque now. It'll take about two hours. Maybe I'll take the girls out too."

"You do that, and I'll look after the veggies," said Sheila.

Windflower took the roast out the fridge, cleaned it up and brought it outside. He lit the barbeque and put the roast on the cool side. It would cook slowly by convection heat and in a couple of hours would be tender and moist inside with a nice brown crust on the outside. He closed the barbeque and went back inside to round up the girls.

"Put your rubber boots on," he said. "We're going down to Point Crewe." He grabbed a knapsack and put a bottle of water and a small bag of cookies inside. A few minutes later, they were driving on the highway past Fortune until they came to the turnoff they were looking for. He parked the car, and the girls and Lady ran ahead on the trail that meandered through the forest before it came out into a clearing. A little farther on was one of the girls' favourite parts of the trail. That was where the water from a nearby pond flowed down and crossed the path near a side road that separated the trail from the ocean. There were large pools of water that the girls made sure to tramp through, and Lady had a drink from each one to make sure the quality was maintained. After the water, the path led directly into what was left of the abandoned community of Point Crewe.

It had been an active and vibrant fishing community at one time. But all there was left now were some markings on the ground and the remains of the foundation of what may have been a church and a school. He had heard that people left the little community when electricity came to this part of Newfoundland. They had petitioned to have a line sent down their way, but when that was rejected, they chose to leave rather than to stay in the dark.

Windflower and the girls had a cookie and a drink of water on the beach rocks down by the water and then retraced their steps back to the car.

CHAPTER 47

The girls were tired but happy when they got home and told their mom all about their adventure while Windflower went to check on their roast. He could smell it as soon as he opened the back door. The smell of roasting meat and rosemary and thyme almost made him weak. It looked fabulous, just as he hoped, blackened-brown on the outside. He used a meat ther mometer to check to see if it was cooked all the way through. "Perfect," he said as he saw the temperature on the thermometer.

"We're good to go," he announced when he came back inside. "Great," said Sheila. "I have been smelling it cook all the time you were gone. I'm starving. Carve it up while I steam some broccoli to go along with our baked potatoes."

He took a plate and a carving knife out to the deck, removed the meat from the grill and started cutting slices.

Some welldone pieces at the edges with that beautiful crust and then growing a little pinker as he went into the middle. Finally, a few rare slices for him and Sheila. He covered the rest of the roast beef and carried it all into the kitchen.

He put some meat on each of the girls' plates and cut the slices up. He put an outside piece and a pink slice on his and Sheila's. She came right behind with a baked potato and some of the steamed broccoli. After the potatoes were dressed, she called the girls, and they all sat at the kitchen table.

"This is so good," said Sheila. "You can really taste the herbs all the way through, but especially on this outside piece. Rosemary?"

"Rosemary and thyme," said Windflower. "Plus, the usual suspects. I love taking a piece of the pink meat along with the crust. Like heaven."

There was little more talking until after the meal was completed. Windflower sliced the rest of the roast beef and put it in a container in the fridge, saving two small pieces for his fourlegged friends. He went out and cleaned up the barbeque with Lady and now Molly paying close attention to his every move. They were rewarded when he came back in and put chopped up pieces of meat in both their bowls.

Since tonight was Sunday, it was homework first and then bath time. Windflower helped Stella do her multiplication tables in the kitchen while Sheila and Amelia Louise read a story together in the living room. Afterwards,

Windflower ran their bath as Sheila got them clean pajamas to start the new week. When the bath was ready, Sheila took over that chore. Windflower went downstairs and grabbed Lady's leash. Molly followed them all the way out. Windflower knew what she wanted and tried to think of something else so she couldn't read his mind. Finally, he gave up. "Maybe later," he said as he closed the door in her face.

Tonight was cool and the wind was a bit high, but no rain. That was good, he thought. Maybe Bernard Thibault could start on the painting to morrow. He decided to walk down along the wharf and then circle up around the B&B. He was pleased when he got close to see that the construction company had been by sometime on the weekend and put up the scaffolding on the front of the building. That meant the old girl could get her new coat of paint this week. He couldn't wait to get home to tell Sheila when his phone rang. It was Tizzard. "Eddie, what's up?"

"We've got a lead on Todd Osmond," said Tizzard. "Thibault told us about an old flame of Osmond's. We tracked her down to an apartment on Harris Drive. The landlord says he hasn't seen her in a few days. We've got that place staked out, and now we're reaching out to her friends."

"Okay, be careful, Eddie," said Windflower. "If you find him, don't engage until you have backup."

"I'll be careful," said Tizzard. "My dad gave me the same message."

"Good." Windflower hung up and headed for home. Lady was very happy to receive her additional piece of meat. Molly, while grateful enough to eat her treat, hung around Windflower until he went upstairs, just in case. Sheila had just got the girls settled away when he came up, so he grabbed Sheila's book off the nightstand and opened it.

"Hey, that's my book," she said, snatching it back. "I'm almost finished, too. You can have it when I'm done. It's very good."

All Windflower could do was to gaze longingly at Louise Penny's book. Then he remembered he had an unfinished book of his own. He went downstairs and found it in the living room. Operation Masonic was by Newfoundland author Helen Escott and was about the fictional murder of the Freemasons' Most Worshipful Grand Master. It was a fictional ac count but based on true stories and intrigue that surrounded the Masons in St. John's, the capital city. The detectives in the story followed clues that led them to a series of hidden tunnels under churches and buildings in the centre of old St. John's and, ultimately, Windflower hoped, to the killer. He read until his eyes started to fade and his body along with them. Even though he already had a long nap in the afternoon, he soon fell quickly and solidly to sleep.

He woke in the morning to the happy sounds of two little girls playing in one of the bedrooms next door. Sheila had already gotten up, so he snuck a peek at his playing daughters and went quickly to the bathroom to have his shower.

Freshly dressed and shaven, he went downstairs, where the girls were eating cereal and Sheila handed him a cup of coffee.

"Good morning, my love," he said. "Everyone seems in a good mood this morning."

"So far, so good," said Sheila. "Want some toast?"

"Thanks, but I need to go outside first this morning," he said. He took his coffee and got his smudge kit from the closet. With Lady at his side, he went out into the cool morning. It was a little chilly, but when he checked the forecast, it said that it would warm up throughout the day. That would make it a perfect day for painting, he thought.

He mixed his sacred medicines and smudged. Afterward, he sat there for a moment to allow the smoke to come into his body and spirit. This one act connected him, even if briefly, to himself and to what he believed was the spirit world. In that space he offered thanks to those who had come before him and asked for help in this world, not just for himself but for anyone who might be struggling this morning. He thought of Greg Rose and prayed that he would get the help he needed.

He prayed for all those affected by his actions, his wife and children and Chief Pike and all the other volunteer firefighters. That reminded him that he needed to talk to the person who was coming to meet them. He also prayed for all the people in Grand Bank who had been afraid or traumatized by what Greg did. And the feeling that they were not safe in their own homes in this tidy little community. He ended his prayers as he had begun, with thanks for his blessings and for the strength to be a good man in this world.

He placed the hot ashes on the ground and went back inside for break fast. After breakfast he helped Sheila get the girls' lunches and backpacks in order. He waited until the yellow school bus had left for Fortune before heading over to the RCMP offices.

Betsy was there with a cheery smile and a blueberry muffin for him. "Thank you so much, Betsy," he said, taking his muffin to his office with him. He opened his computer and amidst a flurry of new emails was one from Interpol that had been forwarded to him from Ron Quigley.

The subject line of the email was *Gold Robbery Update*. He read further:

> *Please be advised that Swiss police have arrested several members of the Outlaws Motorcycle Club and are questioning them regarding their appearance on surveillance video at or near Zurich Airport on the date of the gold shipment to Toronto, Canada. Also in the video was Gian "Coco" Meier, believed to be deceased.*

That was good news, thought Windflower, but if he knew the bikers, they wouldn't tell the authorities anything. They would rather go to jail. He read on:

In addition, we have received reports from several "under-ground" gold buyers that a large shipment is on its way to Europe from somewhere in Canada. We have advised the appropriate Canadian authorities but recom mend that member countries redouble their efforts to identify and locate any shipments from Canada that may seem out of the ordinary.

He called Quigley. "Looks like the Europeans have been busy."

"That just turns up the heat more on us," said Quigley. "But I can tell you that the Toronto people have managed to find CCTV footage from the area around the storage ware-house. They have Coco Meier presenting the fake waybill and what looks like Snake Gibbons driving the car he left in.

They have pictures of the truck that was used to carry off the shipment, but it was stolen, of course. They were able to put pictures of the license plate into their database and have picked it up on radar all the way from Ontario to Nova Scotia."

"What happened then?"

"It looks like the shipment may have come to Nova Scotia, and perhaps over there as well. Either way, the theory about it being melted down and shipped back to Europe seems to have some legs," said Quigley.

"But where would they melt down that much gold? It's not something you could do in your shed."

"No, would have to be a commercial operation of some sort. Maybe a mill or a mine that's been mothballed. We're going through a list in Nova Scotia," said Quigley. "So far, nothing."

Windflower paused for a minute. "There was a mine that just shut down around Long Harbour. It was a weird mineral, not gold or silver. Give me a sec." He punched in Long Harbour mine and watched as the results popped up.

CHAPTER 48

"It was an antimony mine," said Windflower. "Says it's used in flame retardants and combined with other metals to make leadacid batteries and in manufacturing paints and ceramics. Closed earlier this year because of market conditions, says the press release."

"Where's Long Harbour?" asked Quigley.

"I knew you were going to ask me that," said Windflower. "It's off the highway near Whitbourne. Not too far from Argentia."

"Where the ferry is."

"Exactly," said Windflower.

"I'll get the Whitbourne detachment to go take a look around," said Quigley. "What about Todd Osmond?"

"The last I heard from Tizzard, they were looking for an exgirlfriend. She hasn't been around for a few days. They've got her place staked out. And Greg Rose is being arraigned this morning. Hopefully, he'll get his thirty-day assessment."

"I'm still struck by what a strange situation that is," said Quigley. "It's hard to make sense of it."

"Everybody over here is pretty shook up. Especially his fellow firefighters. There's a trauma counsellor coming over this afternoon to talk with them."

"That will be good," said Quigley. "Are you okay? It's been a lot."

"I'm okay right now, but I'm going to see the lady, too," said Windflower.

"Good," said Quigley. "Let me know if you hear any more about Osmond. He feels like the missing link."

Windflower hung up and realized that neither of them had tried out a Shakespeare quote this morning. Maybe it just wasn't time for joking around. But it was time for more coffee. Instead of getting a cup from the back, he walked past Betsy, who was on the phone, and walked to the Mug-Up.

Usually, he would have driven, but he wanted to check in on the B&B first. And he did need the walk after all the eating the past weekend. He was pleased when he turned the corner to see Thibault up on the scaffolding scraping the front of the building.

"Good morning, Bernard," he called out.

"Morning, Sarge," said Thibault as he scampered nimbly down the ladder next to the scaffolding. "It's a great morning. A little cool to paint, but great for scraping."

"Good stuff," said Windflower. "Do you need anything?"

"No, b'y, I'm good. I got my thermos of coffee and my lunch."

"Okay, I'll let you get back to work."

"Listen," said Thibault, speaking a little quieter, "did you find Todd Osmond yet?"

"Still looking, I think," said Windflower.

"Well, I hope you gets him soon," said Thibault. "He's a dangerous man."

Windflower nodded. "I'll see you later."

He walked off towards the nearby café. Before he went inside, he called Eddie.

"Good morning, boss," said Tizzard. "Any news on Todd Osmond?"

"Nothing yet, but the troops are out scouring for information," said Tizzard.

"They're turning up the heat again. Quigley called me this morning. The Swiss have picked up Coco Meier's peeps in Europe, and they think the gold was melted down here or in Nova Scotia. Do you know what is out in Long Harbour?"

"There was a prosperous mine out there one time," said Tizzard. "And there's a big nickel processing plant that was built a few years ago. There are five hundred people working there. It processes nickel from Voisey's Bay in Labrador. But there was also a small mine that recently shut down. I forget what they were mining, though."

"Antimony," said Windflower. "It's used in batteries and other stuff."

"Are you guys thinking the gold was melted down there?"

"Maybe," said Windflower. "It wouldn't be at the big plant. Too much activity and security. But it could be that smaller mine that was just moth balled. Close to the ferry. Quigley is going to get the guys from Whit bourne to check it out."

"Interesting," said Tizzard. "Sounds like a well thought out plan, if that's what happened."

"Anyway, let's find Osmond before Interpol shows up," said Windflower. "And be careful, Eddie."

"I will," said Tizzard. "'We should be careful to get out of an experience only the wisdom that is in it and stop there lest we be like the cat that sits down on a hot stove lid.'"

"What the heck does that mean?" asked Windflower.

"I dunno," said Tizzard. "But my dad used to say that. I thought it was funny."

"Talk to you later," said Windflower, smiling despite himself.

"You're in a good mood for someone who's been ridden hard and put away wet," said Herb Stoodley as Windflower entered the Mug-Up.

"We just have to smile sometimes. 'A smile cures the wounding of a frown.'"

"Very nice," said Stoodley. "Go sit down, and I'll bring you a cup of coffee."

The café was relatively quiet right now in between the breakfast rush and the gang of men who came to chat and have their coffee break together a little later on. But the people who were there greeted Windflower with a smile and a friendly "good morning."

He found a spot to sit, and true to his word, Herb was over with two cups of coffee, one for each of them.

"You've had quite the weekend," said Herb. "How are you holding up?"

"I'm okay," said Windflower. "It was a lot. But we did a good job, and things should get back to normal pretty soon."

"I hope so," said Stoodley. "Chief Pike was in for breakfast earlier. He's pretty shook up. He said some of his people are in bad shape."

"Yeah, I was over there yesterday for a few minutes. It looks like every body else is pretty calm after what happened."

"Short attention span," said Herb. "Plus, most people just want to get on with their lives, raise their children, complain about their aches and pains. Grumble about the lighthouse."

"Well, somebody should do something about that," said Windflower. "Before it's too late."

"Already on it. You know I'm on the Grand Bank Historical Society board, and I have it on the agenda for our meeting tonight. I'm not sure what we can do, but I hope we can get the ball rolling in the right direction."

"Let me know if I can help."

"That's what I really wanted to talk to you about," said Herb. "You know the foundation and the walkway around the bottom of the lighthouse is rotting away?"

"Yes," said Windflower. "I've seen that."

"I think it's in unsafe condition," said Herb. "It's not safe to drive on.

Maybe not even safe to walk on."

"Agreed," said Windflower. "What does it have to do with me?"

"Well, you are the authority, and if you see something is unsafe, you should report it, shouldn't you?" asked Herb.

"I guess so," said Windflower. "But to whom?"

"Here's a list," said Herb. "Coast guard, harbour authority and town council. And you should protect the public, warn them about a potential danger."

"I'm not sure I want to go that far, but I could put some police warning tape around the area," said Windflower. "It is unsafe for motor vehicle traffic."

"That will be great," said Herb. "I knew you'd help."

CHAPTER 49

Before Windflower could say anything else, Herb jumped up and ran off to the back. Likely to draft up more letters, thought Windflower. He smiled again. Maybe this will take people's minds off everything else, he thought. He was about to leave when his cell phone rang.

"We've got the order for Greg Rose," said Gupta. "We were in and out in fifteen minutes. He has to go to the Waterford in St. John's."

"Good," said Windflower. "Will you come over to pick up the kids?"

"I was wondering if we could bring him over there," said Gupya. "Might be easier on the children. We could do the visit at our office."

"That's a good idea," said Windflower. "Bring someone

with you as an escort. I'll call Betsy to let her know if you call the mother."

"Will do," said Gupta. "I should be over right after lunch."

"Okay, I'll see you then," said Windflower.

He left the café, waving to Herb on the way out. He was already on the phone, plotting his next move. He drove down near the lighthouse, parking well away from the crumbling concrete near the base of the lighthouse. He got his roll of yellow police tape and marked off the entranceway. That might not keep everyone out, he thought, but it sure would get people talking. Maybe that was Herb's whole point.

Back at the office, Windflower told Betsy about Gupta's plan, and she tidied up one of the small interview rooms for the visit. She also ran home to get some treats for the children. "They might be hungry," she said. Windflower felt a little hungry himself and thought about going back to the café for lunch. Then he remembered that leftover roast beef.

He drove home, where Sheila was just finishing up a Zoom call.

"This is nice," she said. "You came home to see me. And to get some of that roast beef, too, I bet."

"I cannot lie," said Windflower. "But I'm really glad you're here. Why don't I make us both a sandwich?"

"That's an offer I can't refuse."

Windflower put mayo and lettuce and several slices of roast beef on some nice multigrain bread that Sheila had bought and put the kettle on to boil. When the tea was ready, he brought the tray with the sandwiches out to the living room.

"This is nice," said Sheila. "I know you've been busy, but have you heard anything else about maybe going to Halifax? I think it would be a great trip for the girls, and I would love to mix some shopping with business."

"I'll check with Ron the next time I talk to him," said Windflower, totally enjoying his sandwich. He was savouring the last bite when his phone beeped. He looked at his phone. "Chief Pike," he said. "The trauma presentation is starting soon. I'm going to text back and ask for a meeting with the counsellor." He sent his text and got a quick reply saying okay.

"I guess I should go back," he said. "Gupta is bringing Greg Rose over here to see his kids. He's been given a thirtyday assessment at the Water ford."

"That's nice for them," said Sheila. "They didn't do anything wrong, and yet they will pay a big price."

Windflower gave Sheila a kiss and drove back to the office. Betsy was back, too, and she had brought a tray of cookies that she had put into the meeting room. Soon after, Gupta and Constable Avery showed up with Greg Rose in the back of their cruiser. He was handcuffed but not shackled this time. They quickly brought him into the building and put him in a cell in the back. Avery stayed behind while Gupta went to pick up the children. Ten minutes later, she was back and led the children inside. They looked very confused and frightened. Betsy tried to calm them down and took them into the interview room and offered them a treat. Gupta sat with them while Windflower went to get their father from the back. He took off Rose's handcuffs and got Avery to stand outside the room while he brought Rose in.

The children were shy and held back when Rose first came in, but they seemed to warm up a little. The boy did, at least. The girl wouldn't even look at her father, even when he spoke directly to her. Windflower glanced at Gupta, and it seemed that she was thinking the same thing he was. She was super mad at her father, and it would take some time, if ever, to for give him.

After twenty minutes, Windflower told Rose he had five more minutes and went and stood outside the door. Gupta started to leave, too, but he motioned her to stay behind. Safety trumped privacy. After the five min utes were up, Windflower went back in and escorted Rose out. Avery and he took Rose back to the cell, where Avery put the cuffs back on.

Gupta was leading the children out as he came back, and he watched as Gupta took them to her car and drove off.

"How did that go?" asked Betsy.

"As well as could be expected," said Windflower.

"That little girl looked angry," said Betsy. "I can't say that I blame her."

"Me either," said Windflower. He went to his office to wait

for Gupta to come back. He closed the door and said a quiet prayer for the boy and the girl who would not see their dad for a long time. He got kind of lost thinking about them when he heard a knock on the door.

"We're ready to go back," she said. She and Avery brought Rose out to their vehicle and put him in the back seat. Gupta came back in to see him. "Unless you need me, I'll probably stay over in Marystown tomorrow," said Gupta.

"Sure, that should be fine," said Windflower. "Things have settled down considerably over here. Let's hope it stays that way. Maybe you can help Corporal Tizzard with the search for Todd Osmond."

Gupta waved goodbye, got in the cruiser and drove off, heading back to Marystown.

"What will happen to Greg Rose now?" asked Betsy.

"He will see a psychiatrist who will determine his mental health status," said Windflower. "They'll do some tests and observe him over a period of time. If they find him mentally competent, he'll come back to Marystown or Grand Bank and be charged with arson. If not, he'll be institutionalized, likely at the Waterford."

"Either way, he'll be gone to those children," said Betsy. "That's sad."

"It is, Betsy. Tragic." His phone beeped as he was standing with Betsy.

It was Roy Pike. You are on the list to see Tanya Janes in thirty minutes.

Thank you, he texted back.

"I have an appointment," he said to Betsy. Even though it was only five minutes to the fire hall, he wanted a few moments to collect himself before he saw the counsellor. He drove around Grand Bank, across the brook, down by the wharf and then circled back so he could check on Bernard Thibault's progress at the B&B.

Thibault was up there, working away, and Windflower didn't want to do anything to hinder his work, which looked like quite a lot for the first day. He had the top section of the front of the B&B almost done. He would have to get Levi Parsons and Levi's friend to help him shift the scaffolding, but that was a lot for one day. Feeling pretty pleased about that, he drove over to the fire hall and walked inside.

There were a couple of firefighters hanging around, but it looked like most had stayed for the main session and left. Windflower found Pike and said hello and was then escorted into his office, which was being used for the individual sessions.

"Welcome, Sergeant, I've heard a lot about you. I'm Tanya Janes."

"Nice to meet you, and thanks for making time to see me," said Windflower.

"No problem. I'm here until five o'clock. Most of the firefighters don't want to let the others see them come in to see me, so they go away for a while. That gives me a few free minutes."

"Thanks, again," said Windflower. "I don't know where to start."

"You must have some reason why you wanted to see me, talk with me," said Janes. "Why don't you tell me about the last couple of days?"

Windflower started talking, and much to his surprise he didn't stop for about fifteen minutes. He talked about Greg Rose and the incidents on the ATV trail and the fires and the meeting with the community. He ended with talking about Rose's kids. After that, he just started crying.

There was a box of Kleenex on the table, and Janes nudged it towards him. He took one but continued to cry.

"It's good to let it out," said Janes. "We're taught that we're supposed to hold all this stuff in and be strong and everything, but unless we can process what happens to us and how it makes us feel, it just goes inside and can cause us problems later on. How do you feel now?"

"I feel relieved somehow," said Windflower. "I didn't realize how much I was carrying around. Thank you for listening to me. How do you do this? Listen to people's pain all the time?"

Janes smiled. "It's my job. But I don't take it home with me. I try to allow that pain and suffering to pass through me. Most of what people feel is grief. A loss of something. Talking about it helps them get to acceptance. Maybe not right away, but eventually. Then they can heal and go on with their lives."

"My late uncle used to talk about acceptance. He would say that 'accep tance is the answer to all my problems today.'"

"A wise man," said Janes. "Anything else you want to talk about?"

"I think I'm good for now."

"Here's my card," said Janes. "If you ever want to talk again, give me a call."

"Thank you, so much." Windflower dried his eyes again, shook her hand and left. He didn't bother to talk to anybody, just walked out of the building and climbed into his car. He was glad he had done it, even happier that it was over, and feeling absolutely drained. He went back to work but sleep-walked through the rest of the day.

CHAPTER 50

After work he did everything he was supposed to do, helped Sheila get supper ready, got the kids organized to do their homework and then ready for bed. It was only when he was taking Lady for her final walk that he finally felt like himself again. He smiled at Sheila when he got back.

"Thank goodness you're coming out of that funk," she said. "I was worried about you."

"Just processing stuff," said Windflower. "I think I might need to talk to that counsellor again. Seems like a lot of things are churning around inside me. I can't even put my finger on it."

"That's a great idea," said Sheila. "We often hold things inside too much. Especially strong emotions like grief. I was a mess after my mother died. After about three months I finally went to see somebody."

"Did it work?"

"After about a year," she said with a laugh. "But it was worth it. I could accept it, the best I could anyway, and move on with the rest of my life."

"Interesting," said Windflower. "Anyway, I'm bushed. I think I have to go to bed."

He went upstairs and put on his pajamas. It seemed like seconds later that he was sound asleep. But that didn't last long. He woke in a dream.

This time he was in a familiar place, back in the bush near his home community in Pink Lake. It was summertime in Northern Alberta, and everything seemed alive. He could hear the insects buzzing and birds chirping. It was warm and hot and sticky, without a breeze. He saw a path in front of him and followed it until he came to a lake. There was a canoe on the shore near the water, and it seemed to be inviting him to get inside.

He pushed the canoe away from shore and jumped in. He paddled aimlessly for a little while and then saw a small island in the middle of the lake. He paddled towards it, beached the canoe on a sandy beach and walked onto the island. He didn't have to walk far before he saw a gathering around a fire. He walked over.

Sitting and standing around the fire were a number of

animals. There was a moose, a beaver, a rabbit and a large whitetailed deer. From above, an eagle fluttered and landed on a rock near the circle. Windflower felt pulled towards the fire and the circle of animals. He walked closer and the circle parted to let him come into the middle. None of the animals spoke, but Windflower could feel them messaging him somehow.

The message was that these were his allies in the spirit world. Their forms all represented aspects of himself. The beaver was perseverance and commitment. The rabbit was caution and carefulness. The moose was steadiness and security, and the deer was courage. The eagle was his extra vision, the ability to see beyond the ordinary and the wisdom to know when to step forward and when to hold back.

He felt all of them at once, their strength and support. Then another creature came into the circle. It was a boy, a young boy. The boy spoke. "I am young Winston," he said. "Some people call me your inner child. Your job is to protect me. Your allies do that for you when you're not around or not paying attention."

Windflower stood there, a little awestruck but taking it all in.

"Come with me," the boy said. He held out his hand, and Windflower took it. The boy led him through the woods until they came to a beautiful log cabin with a stream flowing past it on the back. But as Windflower got closer, he could see that the cabin was falling into disrepair. There were holes in the wood, and it looked like the roof was a little shaky. The boy led him inside. There was a fireplace, but it was cracked and crumbling, and his fears about the roof were confirmed. Mice scattered before him in what looked like the kitchen.

"This is your sacred place," said the boy. "It needs some work," said Windflower.

"That's what we've been trying to tell you," said the boy. "You need to pay more attention to what's going on inside of you."

With that, Windflower could feel himself being lifted up. He could see the boy standing outside the house and the animals in the circle around the fire. Then everything below him started to get smaller and smaller until he could only see darkness. He closed his eyes, and when he opened them again he was back in bed in his own house. Sheila was sleeping quietly next to him. That dream might have been a little strange, but the message was clear. He would phone Tanya Janes in the morning to set up an appointment. That decision seemed to free up something in him, and he was able to easily fall asleep again.

Tuesday morning was quiet when he woke, so he went downstairs and put the coffee on. He let Lady out in back and sat in the darkness for a few minutes, waiting for daybreak. By the time his coffee was ready, the sky had started to turn pink, and soon the whole of Grand Bank was bathed in a soft red glow. He picked up his phone, thinking he would check his mes sages. But instead he texted Tanya Janes and asked for an appointment.

That made him smile, like he'd accomplished something already today.

He was still smiling when Sheila came down a few minutes later.

"You look pleased with yourself," she said. "What have you been up to down here?"

"I have coffee. Which is enough to make me happy in itself. And I sent a message to my counsellor to request an appointment."

"I agree with the coffee part," said Sheila. "I'm proud of you for doing this. It will help all of us."

"How about if I help you by making some eggs?"

"Even better," said Sheila. "I'll go rouse the girls."

The rest of the early morning was peaceful and uneventful as he made breakfast and helped organize the girls and get them ready for school. He was about to go to the office when his cell phone rang. It was Quigley.

"We've got some great info out of Long Harbour," said Quigley. "At first, the two warehouse guys at the mine said they hadn't seen or heard anything. But our guys asked to see the surveillance tapes. That's when it all came out. Our three amigos were there. Meier, Gibbons, and Osmond in the car. Plus another guy who was driving a truck that pulled up to the door. Osmond set the whole thing up. One of the guys at the mine knew him from a stint in Millhaven.

Osmond paid them five hundred each to set up the machinery and leave."

"So, you think they melted all those gold bars there in Long Harbour?"

"That's a strong possibility," said Quigley. "Forensics is on the way over there to take a look around. They also said they saw them unload a number of large fish crates, the ones they use at the fish plants. They didn't see much more, but we got the license plate of a white truck with Nova Scotia plates. We have it in the system but suspect it's long gone."

"But what about what we found at the house in Grand Bank, or at least the traces of what might have been there?"

"Maybe someone decided to take a little sample for themselves," said Quigley. "That might have set up a dispute with the others. In any case, we've passed all this along to the higherups. It confirms what we've been hearing. They'll try to track down the truck and shipment in Nova Scotia and then on the other end in Europe."

"It sounds like there's not much more to do on our end," said Windflower.

"Except for finding Todd Osmond," said Quigley. "Not only will it solve some of our problems, but he likely knows how and where the shipment is being sent to Europe. Lots of people will want to talk to him."

"Got it," said Windflower. "Listen, is that trip to Halifax still a possibility? Once we get everything straightened out here, I'd like to take a break. And Sheila wants to go, too."

"Next week," said Quigley. "Barring any catastrophe. Just finalizing the agenda."

"Excellent, let me know."

"And remember dear friend, 'to thine ownself be true,'" said Quigley.

"'There's nothing either good or bad but thinking makes it so,'" replied Windflower.

CHAPTER 51

Quigley hung up. Windflower said goodbye to Sheila and drove to the office. He had barely gotten in the door when Betsy ran to greet him.

"There's been a shooting," she said. "Who? Where?"

"In Marystown, but I don't know who. Constable Gupta called and left a message, but it got cut off."

"I'm going to Marystown," said Windflower. "Call me if you hear any thing else."

He ran to the back, grabbed his vest and shield and rifle, and threw them in his trunk. He jumped in his car, turned on his lights and siren and raced out of town. He was on the highway when his cell phone rang. He answered it and put it on speaker. It was Gupta.

"What's going on?" he asked.

"It's Todd Osmond," said Gupta. "We had him cornered

at a house on Water Street, down by the Narrows. We had a full team but weren't fully loaded up. Tizzard had Avery set up as a sniper to give us cover, but Osmond must have spotted him. He had a longrange rifle. He shot Avery, and he managed to grab Tizzard. Right now, he's holding Tizzard inside."

"How is Avery?"

"I don't know," said Gupta. "He's gone to the hospital in Burin."

"Has Osmond said anything?"

"Nothing."

"Okay, stay there and don't do anything," said Windflower. "I'm on my way. Twenty minutes. Let's keep this line open. I want to know if Osmond says or does anything. And get Williams or someone else to get full gear for everybody. Take no chances."

"Okay," said Gupta.

The next twenty minutes were some of the worst in his life. The lon gest, too. But he made it to Marystown and took the road down towards Water Street. It was easy to spot the house where Osmond was holed up. There was a crowd of people behind a wooden barrier, and it looked like every police car in the Marystown area was somewhere in the perimeter. He noticed a media truck as well. It wouldn't be long before more of them showed up, too.

"I'm here," said Windflower.

"We're at the music store," said Gupta. "That's where we've set up our command centre."

Windflower drove to the store and got his vest and shield and rifle out of the trunk. He put his gear on and walked into the store. Gupta was there, along with Williams, who was in charge, and he spoke first.

"We've got the perimeter secure, and all exits are blocked. There's only two ways in and out, and we've got both routes secure as well. We've been going door to door and have everyone in the nearby houses out of the area."

"Thank you, Sergeant," said Windflower. "I'll take over from here. Has Superintendent Quigley been informed?"

"Yes, sir," said Williams. "We've also asked both Swift Current and Whitbourne to be in position on the highway."

"Avery?" asked Windflower.

"Shot in the upper body, sir," said Williams. "That's all we know so far. He was bleeding pretty badly. But no update from the hospital yet. And the media are calling, sir."

"Okay," said Windflower. "Can you arrange for a short media release? Simply say that there is a police operation in this area. The public is ad vised to avoid the area. The media can wait for anything else."

"Should we tell them that an officer has been shot?" asked Williams. "Not until we know his condition," said Windflower. "Is there someone over there?"

"Corporal Davies, sir," said Williams.

"Get him on the phone," said Windflower. Williams made the call and handed the phone to Windflower.

"Davies, what's going on with Avery?" asked Windflower.

"Hard to tell yet. He's still in emergency. He's lost a lot of blood. The doctors are with him now."

"Was he conscious when he came over?" asked Windflower.

"I wasn't in the ambulance, but he was fading in and out before that," said Davies.

"Okay, call me as soon as you hear anything, okay?"

"Okay," said Davies.

"Gupta, get me the megaphone out of my trunk. Here's the keys," said Windflower as he tossed them to Gupta.

"Maybe there's a phone in the house," said Williams.

"Good point," said Windflower. "Call the phone company and get the number, if they have one."

Gupta came back with the megaphone.

"Thanks," said Windflower. "I'll try this while we're waiting to see if there's a phone inside."

Windflower walked towards the house, careful to stay out of the line of sight of Osmond or anybody else in the house. He turned back and found Gupta.

"Is there anybody else in the house?"

"I don't know," said Gupta. "I didn't see anybody. Let me check on the radio." She made her call to the team on the radio channel.

"Somebody thinks they saw a woman inside," she said.

"The girlfriend? Or exgirlfriend," Windflower wondered out loud. "Check and see if anybody knows her name."

Gupta asked but shook her head at the replies.

"Tizzard said they had a tip. I think it was Bernard Thibault," said Windflower. "Take my phone. His number is in the contacts. See if you can get her name and names of her friends, anybody who might have her cell number."

Gupta made that call, and Windflower went back to moving towards the house. While they were waiting for more information, he might as well try to make contact.

He got as close as he dared and then turned on the microphone.

"Todd, Todd Osmond," he said through the megaphone. "It's Winston Windflower, RCMP. We should talk." He repeated the message three times. No response from inside the house.

He walked back to the command centre. Williams had good news. So did Gupta.

"We have a phone number for the house," said Williams as he handed Windflower a piece of paper. "The people living there are away."

"One of the neighbours said they might be in Florida," said Gupta. "Re tired. I guess they go down there most of the year. I have information on the girlfriend."

"Go ahead," said Windflower.

"According to Bernard Thibault, she's Marilyn Hodder," said Gupta. "I probed a little, and she used to be his girl."

"Whose? Thibault?" asked Windflower.

"A few years back," said Gupta. "He also said that she used to house sit for a place down on Water Street. He gave me the names of a couple of girls she hangs around with. I have one number."

"Interesting," said Windflower. "Call her and ask her for Hodder's num ber. Bring her over if you can find her."

Gupta went off on her task.

"Let's try the number. Williams," said Windflower. "Make the call."

Williams dialled the number using the portable phone they'd brought with them. "It mimics a land line," he said.

Everyone listened as the phone rang. Once. Twice. Three times. Ten times. No answer. The good news was it didn't go to voice mail. Either the occupants didn't have that service, or they turned it off when they were away.

"Try it again," said Windflower. "Every ten minutes or so. I'm going to call Superintendent Quigley."

CHAPTER 52

Windflower took his phone and went out to his car to call Quigley. He wanted that conversation to be as private as possible.

"Winston, what's going on? How is the officer who was shot?" asked Quigley when Windflower got him on the line.

"No news yet on Avery. We've got somebody at the hospital. He's still in emergency. Osmond is holding Tizzard. We think there's a girl in the house as well."

"Have you talked to Osmond yet?" asked Quigley.

"We've been trying," said Windflower. "We found the number for the landline in the house, but no answer so far. We've got a lead on a friend of the girl and are trying to reach her."

"That might be a way in," said Quigley.

Gupta came and knocked on the window of his car.

"One second," Windflower said to Quigley. He rolled the window down. "I've got a number for Marilyn Hodder," said Gupta. "But her friend is in St. John's. Do you want me to call Hodder?"

"Wait for a minute," said Windflower as he went back to Quigley. "I gotta go," he said. "We've got a number for the girl in the house."

"Okay, keep me in the loop," said Quigley. "You need anything?"

"Not right now," said Windflower. He hung up and followed Gupta

back into the command centre. "Let's text her," said Windflower.

Williams interrupted him. "The radio station is reporting that we are engaged in a stakeout," he said. "They are reporting that someone has been shot and an ambulance was seen leaving the scene."

"That's not good," said Windflower. "We'll have to put out a statement.

Can you get me Terri Pilgrim on the phone?"

While Williams went to find Pilgrim, Windflower noticed Gupta texting. "Have you made contact?"

Gupta passed him the phone and showed him the texts:
Hi, are you okay? (Gupta)
Who is this? (Hodder)
A friend. Is everybody safe in there? (Gupta)
Right now they are. Who is this? Are you police? (Hodder)

"That's the last message," said Gupta. "What should I say?"

"Tell her yes and give her your name," said Windflower. "Tell her you want to get her out safely."

Gupta sent the text.

Williams was back with Terri Pilgrim on the phone.

"Hi, Terri," said Windflower. "We need a media statement. RCMP in Marystown confirm that an RCMP officer has been shot. He is in emergency and receiving treatment. No further information is available at this time. The public is again advised to stay away from the Water Street area as a police operation is underway. The RCMP will also be closing access to and from the highway leading in and out of Marystown until this operation is complete."

"Got it," said Pilgrim. "I'll draft it up and text it back to Sergeant Williams."

"Thanks, Terri," said Windflower. "And can you dig up Avery's family information? He's not married, right?'

"No, sir," said Pilgrim. "I'm just pulling up his file. Next of kin is his mother, Linda Avery. I have her contact information. Do you want it?"

"Not yet," said Windflower. "Let's wait until we have more information."

He handed the phone back to Williams. "I'll look at the text from Pilgrim when it comes in."

Gupta was busy texting. He went to check that out.

"She's scared," said Gupta. "Said Osmond is unpredictable. She doesn't want to be there but is afraid to make a run for it."

"What kind of weapons does he have?"

Gupta texted again. A few seconds later she got a reply.

"He has a rifle with a scope," she read. "And he says he has explosives. He got them from a mine. Threatens to blow the whole place up if anybody tries to get in."

Windflower shook his head. That was not good at all. It might mean that Osmond could boobytrap the house and prevent them from entering. That wasn't their best option anyway. Their best option was to get some kind of deal with Osmond. But first, they had to find a way to talk to him.

"Text her that your boss is trying to talk to Osmond. Tell her we want to make a deal. Give up Tizzard, let her go, and we'll let him go."

"I'm not sure you can do all that," said Gupta. "With respect, sir."

"You're probably right," said Windflower. "Text her that we will call in ten minutes. See if she can get Osmond to answer the phone.

Gupta nodded and texted the woman inside the house.

Williams read the text statement to Windflower. "Good," he said. "Let it go. Can you get me Davies again?" When she did, he asked, "Any up date?"

"No, sir," said Davies. "The doctors are still in there. No one has come out yet. There are reporters outside here now.

We can keep them out of Emergency, but they are waiting for some kind of news or statement."

"A statement is coming, and I will get Williams to send it to you. Read it to whoever is there and tell them you are not authorized to speak any further. No questions. The statement will be on the wire, too, soon. And call me as soon as you hear anything."

"She said she will try," said Gupta. "Okay," said Windflower. "Now we wait."

Finally, the ten minutes had passed, and Williams called the number for the phone inside the house. It rang, and they waited. After about five rings, there was an answer.

"It's Osmond," said the voice on the other end.

"Todd, it's Windflower," replied Windflower. "Do you need anything? Food? Water?" He hoped to soften him up a little before getting to the real discussions.

"We don't have time for that," said Osmond. "If you want to see your friend again in one piece, I suggest you listen real close. And don't try to come in. I have enough stuff to blow this whole place skyhigh."

"I'm listening," said Windflower. "Is Tizzard okay? Let me talk with him."

"Easy, cowboy," said Osmond. "I do the asking, and you do the listening. I want a boat. Big enough for open water. Pulled right up to the shore as close as you can get to this house. In the boat, I want food and water. Enough for a week. You have four hours to make this happen."

"That's going to take some time," said Windflower. "We need you to release Tizzard and anybody else you have in the house."

"Don't worry about nobody else," said Osmond. "Your friend gets released when I'm safely in open water."

"Okay," said Windflower. "Let me see what I can do. But I need to know that Tizzard is okay. No deal otherwise. Let me talk to him."

"Here," said Osmond.

"Eddie, are you okay?" asked Windflower.

"I'm okay," came a faint response from Tizzard. "Hurt him and any deal's off," said Windflower.

"Four hours and the clock is ticking," said Osmond. "And you know what? Send me a large pizza and some Diet Cokes as a sign of good faith."

The phone line went dead.

CHAPTER 53

"**N**ow what?" asked Williams.

"I guess we order a pizza and try to find a boat," said Windflower. "Gupta, you can look after the pizza. I'll talk to Quigley about the boat."

"We're not giving him a boat, are we?" asked Williams.

"I don't know," said Windflower. "But even if we're not, we have to look like we are. At least to Osmond. We keep moving forward until we have a better plan."

He called Ron Quigley and gave him a quick update about Osmond's demands.

"There's a marina there in Marystown," said Quigley. "See if you can lease or rent a boat that would suit the purpose."

"Okay, we'll do that," said Windflower. "Coast guard?"

"I'll look after that from this end," said Quigley. "The

Constabulary in St. John's used to have a marine unit. Can you check with them and see if they can help?"

"Okay," said Windflower. "He also says he has explosives, likely got them from that mine in Long Harbour. Not really sure how to deal with that aspect."

"I guess the only good news on that front is that the explosives they use now are much more stable. Ammonium nitrate and fuel mixture. But still packing quite a punch. Too bad we don't have a bomb body suit here in Atlantic. But you know what, I'll get one shipped down from HQ. Might get there in four or five hours by chopper."

"Too late. He only gave us four hours," said Windflower. "But we can probably stall until it gets dark. He may not want to go out on the ocean in the dark."

"Good point," said Quigley. "I'm guessing nothing on Avery, or you would have said."

"Nothing yet. I don't know if that's good news or bad. But I have con tact info for his mother. I guess I have to call her now."

"Agreed," said Quigley. "It's not in our hands, and they have a right to know."

Windflower hung up. He got Gupta to check with the hospital and Wil liams to talk to the marina. He would phone St. John's himself.

Gupta came back first. "Nothing."

He phoned the number Pilgrim had given him. After a few rings, a woman answered.

"Is this Mrs. Avery?"

"Yes, this is Linda Avery. Who is calling, please?"

"It's Winston Windflower, ma'am," he said. "I'm calling from the RCMP in Marystown."

"Has something happened to Marcus?"

This was the hard part, thought Windflower. He took a deep breath. "I'm afraid he's been shot in the line of duty, ma'am," he said. "He's in emergency right now. I'm sorry I don't have any more details at this time."

"Oh my God," said the woman. "Is he going to die?"

"We don't know his condition yet, ma'am," said Windflower. "I will call you as soon as I have any news?"

"Oh my God."

"Do you have someone who can be with you?" he asked. "Someone you can call."

"Yes, yes I can call Moreen, his sister. She lives nearby. Is Marcus in the hospital in Marystown? Can I talk to anybody there?"

"He's in good hands at the hospital in Burin," said Windflower. "That's close by. The doctors are still with him. I can ask one of them to call you when they come out."

"Yes, please."

"Do you have any more questions?" He hoped she wouldn't.

"No, I don't think so. Can you give me your number? It's Wildflower, is it?"

"Windflower, ma'am," he said. "Here is my number." He

waited until she wrote it down and repeated it back to him. "Okay, ma'am, I will call you again very soon."

He sat there, stunned, after the call. "I never know how to end those calls," he said out loud to no one in particular.

"I thought you were great," said Gupta.

Williams came back with information from the marina. "They have a variety of vessels available. The guy was trying to sell me one. Then, when I told him who I was and what I wanted, he ran and got his boss. They don't want to get involved was the last word from him."

"Call Superintendent Quigley and give him the boss's number," said Windflower. "They'll sort it out on their end. I've got to call St. John's."

He searched his phone for the name he was looking for. Detective In spector Carl Langmead was an old contact. He'd worked with him on a few cases before. He hoped he'd be around today. He was in luck.

"Winston, nice to hear from you," he said. "I heard about the shooting on the news. Is your guy going to be okay?"

"Touch and go at this point," said Windflower. "We need your help."

"Whatever you need."

"Thanks, Carl," said Windflower. "Do you guys still have the marine unit?"

"Yeah, still going strong," said Langmead. "Mostly working with the coast guard to rescue tourists who wander off the beaten path."

"Can you see if they can be assigned to us?" said Windflower. "We'll need them in Marystown as soon as possible. I can ask my super to phone your chief if need be."

"Let me get back to you," said Langmead. "They should be fully operational. Still tourism season in St. John's. I suspect it'll take them at least four or five hours to get there, though."

"We're operating on a tight schedule, but send them anyway," said Windflower. "You should know, but not for public consumption, that we've got a hostage situation as well. They've got Tizzard."

"Oh my goodness, they got Eddie," said Langmead. "How is he?"

"So far, so good, but the situation is volatile," said Windflower. "We're hoping to buy some time, but if your crew can get here as soon as possible..."

"Understood," said Langmead. "Give me a few minutes and I'll get back to you."

Windflower hung up, and his phone buzzed. It was from Sheila. He read the text:

Are you okay? Call when you can. I love you, Sheila.

He walked outside and away from the building to call her. "I heard the news on the radio. Are you okay?" she asked.

"I'm okay," said Windflower.

"I heard an officer got shot."

"A young constable," said Windflower. "Avery. I don't think you've met him. He's new."

"Is he badly injured?"

"We don't know yet," said Windflower. "Listen, I can't really talk. But can you do me a couple of favours? Eddie Tizzard is in a bit of trouble. I can't really say more right now. He's okay, but...I'm going to call Carrie. Can you check in with her a little later?"

"Sure," said Sheila. "Eddie—"

Windflower interrupted her. "Can you also go over to Richard Tizzard's house and ask him to call me?"

"I will," said Sheila. "Winston, please be careful."

"I love you," said Windflower as he hung up. Time to make the next dreaded call. He called Carrie.

"What's going on over there?" she asked. "They said someone's been shot. Oh God, it's not Eddie, is it?"

"No, it's not Eddie," said Windflower. "But he's in a bit of a bind. He's being held hostage by Todd Osmond."

"Oh, no," said Carrie. "That's the guy Eddie was talking about. He said he's already killed at least one guy. Can I come over there?"

Windflower thought about it for a second. "Do you think that's a good idea?"

"I won't get in the way, but I can't just sit here, knowing what you just told me," said Carrie.

"You can come, but not in the command centre. I'll find another location for you over here."

"Okay," she said. "Thanks. I'll get a sitter and come over as soon as I can."

CHAPTER 54

Windflower hung up, wondering if he'd made the right decision. But it was done now. Hard to say no to Carrie. He went back and found Williams. "We'll need another location over here. Carrie Evanchuk is coming, and Tizzard's dad might come as well."

"Where do you want them?" asked Williams.

"Anywhere but here," said Windflower. "We have all these empty houses. Pick one."

"Pizza is here," said Gupta, coming back in with a pizza box and a bag that Windflower assumed had the soft drinks. "How are we going to han dle this?"

"I'll call him," said Windflower. He picked up the phone and called into the house.

"You got my boat already?" asked Osmond.

"No, that's going to take some time," said Windflower. "But I do have your pizza."

"Good, bring it to the door."

"No chance," said Windflower. "Send Tizzard out so that we know he's okay. We'll bring the pizza halfway. He can bring it in to you."

"No way," said Osmond. "How stupid do you think I am? I'll send somebody out, but it won't be Tizzard. Send the pizza."

Osmond hung up.

"What do we do?" asked Gupta.

"Let's wait for a few minutes and then send him his pizza," said Windflower. "Williams, have we got our snipers in position?"

"Yes, sir," said Williams. "One on each side of the house."

"Tell everyone that I'm going to walk halfway up the driveway and then walk back down. Everyone on alert. Any sign of movement from Osmond, we take him out, okay?" said Windflower.

"Got it," said Williams.

Windflower could hear Williams barking out orders as he put on his protective vest and got his shield ready.

"Everybody is set," said Williams.

"Let's call Osmond again before I go," said Windflower. Williams called and put it on speaker. "I'm bringing your pizza. Don't make any sudden movements, and don't send anybody out until I get back down the driveway. Understood?"

"Yeah," said Osmond and hung up. "Let's go," said Windflower.

He put his cell phone in his pocket and left it open so that he could talk to Williams if he needed to. He walked outside with his shield in front of him. He had removed his sidearm before leaving. If anything happened, he didn't want Osmond to get any more weaponry. He walked to the house and very slowly walked up the driveway. He thought he saw a curtain move but ignored it.

He deliberately walked step by step until he reached what he thought was halfway. He laid the pizza and the paper bag on the ground and then backed up slowly. As slow as he could keep himself, he walked backwards until the house was out of his vision. "Clear," he said, loud enough for Williams to hear. "Roger that," came the reply.

Windflower laid his shield down and crept to the side, where he could peek at the driveway. He saw the door open. It was the woman. He yelled into the phone. "Hold your fire. Hold your fire," he screamed. The snipers must have heard him because the woman ran down the driveway, picked up the pizza and paper bag and then turned and ran back into the house.

"All clear," said Windflower. He breathed a sigh of relief and walked back to the command centre. He didn't realize it at the time, but now he could feel that the tshirt underneath his uniform was soaking wet.

"Good job," said Williams.

Windflower nodded and sat down in a chair. He felt relieved that was over. But this situation was a long way from being resolved. His cell phone rang. He thought it might be Richard Tizzard. But it was Bernard Thibault. "I think I might be able to help," said Thibault.

"I don't think so, Bernard," said Windflower, then he thought about it a little more. "How?"

"I don't know for sure, but I know Marilyn Hodder. And I know Todd Osmond," said Thibault.

"Okay, come over and tell them to call me when you get to the road block."

His phone rang again. This time it was Richard. "Winston, what's going on?"

"Eddie's in a bit of trouble, but he's okay right now," said Windflower. "Thank goodness for that," said Richard. "He wasn't the one that was shot, was he?"

"No, that was a young constable, Marcus Avery," said Windflower. "He's in the hospital right now."

"Well, I hope he's okay," said Richard. "Tell me about Eddie."

"He's being held by a bad man," said Windflower, trying not to use the word "hostage."

"He was grabbed at the same time that Avery got shot. We're negotiating his release now."

"It sounds pretty tense," said Richard. "Does Carrie know?"

"Yes," said Windflower. "She's on her way over to the scene."

"Would you mind if I came over to be with her?" asked Richard. "I can get Brenda to drive me over."

"Sure, that would be fine," said Windflower.

CHAPTER 55

He hung up and paused for a moment. He didn't really want all the extra people around, but family had a right to know what was going on. And Richard could support Carrie if something happened. He stopped himself. He couldn't go there.

The next hour passed quickly and rather uneventfully. Quigley man aged to convince the marina owner to lease or lend them a thirtyfoot cabin cruiser. They were inspecting it now and then would load it with fuel and supplies before getting the word to bring it over to the scene. At Windflower's request, they were also outfitting it with a number of GPS devices. It could be followed on radar, but this would allow them to track the boat by satellite as well.

Quigley also reported that the coast guard had a patrol boat stationed around Trepassey that would be close by

Marystown in the next couple of hours. Carl Langmead had called from St. John's to let him know that the RNC marine unit was coming, but maybe not until late tonight.

Carrie was over at the second house, and Windflower took a moment to go see her. He didn't have a lot of words or much to tell her, but he did give her a big hug. She held on to him for a long time. He brought one of the other constables, Crocker, with him, assigned to look after the family members and be the conduit for any information.

"Right now, we're just waiting," said Windflower. "We're hoping he won't push us to go tonight. It's a bit dangerous to be out in the open water without really knowing what you're doing. Crocker will keep you up to date." He hugged Carrie one more time and then went back to the command centre.

A welcome sight at the command centre was a portable carafe of coffee and a box of donuts. "Courtesy of our local Tim Hortons," said Williams. Windflower poured a cup of coffee and was about to grab a Boston Cream donut when the main phone rang. Everyone jumped. Windflower picked it up.

"Halfway to deadline," said Osmond. "I'm here for my progress report.

Where's my boat?"

"It's not easy to get a boat like the one you're looking for," said Windflower. "We're working on it."

"Well, I have another request," said Osmond. "I'm going to need a pilot."

"That might be harder to do," said Windflower. "We can't put another person in danger. Besides, I don't know where to find one."

"I'm sure you'll figure out a way," said Osmond.

"That's not good," said Williams after Osmond had hung up.

"No, on a couple of fronts," said Windflower. "It means he's planning on leaving tonight. We have the coast guard that can track him and inter cept if necessary. But I was really hoping to have the Constabulary boat. We can be on that one ourselves."

He was pondering that when another call came in, this time on his cell phone. It was Davies from the hospital.

"What's going on?" asked Windflower.

"Doctors just came out," said Davies. "He was shot twice, once in the shoulder and one in his chest. Looks like it just missed his heart. But he has a punctured lung and has lost a lot of blood. One piece of good news is that the bullets missed his spine. That gives him a better chance of overall recovery. They are moving him to the ICU. They describe his condition as critical. They will monitor overnight and will know more in the morning."

"Okay," said Windflower. "Could you ask one of the doctors to phone his mother? Here's the number."

"The media knows that Avery is out of surgery," said Davies.

"Got it," said Windflower. "Tell them we will be doing something over here."

He called Quigley when he got off the phone with Davies.

"Avery is in ICU," said Windflower. "Two shots. One to the shoulder and one punctured his lung. He's in critical condition, and we'll know more in the morning."

"Probably as good as we could expect," said Quigley. "Next of kin?"

"I talked to his mother and asked the hospital to call her with an update," said Windflower. "Anything else?"

"Osmond wants a pilot now," said Windflower.

"Figured out he won't be able to find his way in the dark," said Quigley. "Yeah, kind of screws us up in a number of ways," said Windflower. "Langmead says the marine unit from St. John's won't be here until late tonight. And I don't like the idea of giving him another hostage."

"What happens if we tell him no?" asked Quigley.

"I'm afraid of what his response might be."

"It's a tough one," said Quigley. "Who are you thinking about for a pilot? Got any ideas?"

"I guess we start looking for a local fisherman or somebody who knows the waters," said Windflower. "Maybe look for a volunteer?"

"Might as well try."

"I have to say something to the media anyway," said Windflower. "They're camped out over at the hospital and know Avery is out of surgery."

"Okay, good luck," said Quigley.

That I am certainly going to need, thought Windflower as he pondered what he might say to the media. "Gupta, can you call Terri Pilgrim and tell her that I will speak to the media? Out at the roadblock in twenty minutes. And if we have a picture of Avery, put that on the wire as well."

That bought him a few more moments to think about what he was going to say. He walked outside and noticed that the sun was beginning to go down. The sky was red, even redder than it had been this morning. He hoped it would bring delight. He couldn't handle any more warnings.

Gupta came out to tell him that Richard Tizzard and Bernard Thibault were both at the family house. "I'm going to say hello," said Windflower. "Can you come with me to see the media? Introduce me and tell them I have a short statement and no questions."

Gupta nodded.

Thibault was pacing outside the house and ran to Windflower when he saw him approach. "How is Marilyn? Is she okay?"

"She seems fine right now," said Windflower. "Why don't you text her?

Do you have her number?"

That seemed to satisfy Thibault, and Windflower went inside where Carrie and Richard Tizzard were sitting in the living room. Crocker was standing in the hallway. The TV was on, but they weren't paying attention to anything.

Richard was holding Carrie's hand in an attempt to try to comfort her. Both of them rose to greet Windflower, and he embraced each of them in turn.

"Any news?" asked Carrie.

"Not much," said Windflower. "Young Avery is out of surgery but not out of the woods by any means. We've got support coming, but now Os mond wants a pilot to help him get out of here tonight. Are you okay over here?"

"We're fine," said Richard.

"Crocker, can you make a pot of tea?" asked Windflower. "Do you want any food?"

Both Carrie and Richard shook their heads.

"We're going to do everything we can to get Eddie back safe," he said. "We know," said Carrie. "It's just so hard." She started to cry, and Richard put his arms around her.

"I'll be back soon," said Windflower.

CHAPTER 56

Gupta was waiting for him outside, and together they walked towards the roadblock. The officers on duty pushed the barricades aside, and they passed through and stood with their backs to the roadblock. There were lights and cameras everywhere, and the crowd behind the media pushed closer for a better look.

"I'm Constable Samira Gupta. Acting Inspector Winston Windflower will be providing an update on the current situation. We will not be responding to any questions at this time and will provide additional information as it becomes available."

Windflower moved to the front, and it seemed like a dozen microphones and recorders were pushed towards him. He blinked in the lights and started to speak. "This is a very difficult moment for all of us, and we want to thank the community for your support during this period. The RCMP was attempting to arrest a suspect in a murder investigation when someone in the location shot an RCMP officer. Marcus Avery, twentythree, is in crit ical condition at the Burin Hospital."

He paused to compose himself. "His family appreciates your concern but requests that his and their privacy be respected while he is undergoing treatment. We are hopeful for a full recovery."

That was as much for the media as the general public. He continued. "We have the location where the suspect is located secure. We are now in discussions with the suspect to resolve the situation. We have two requests of the public. Please stay away from this area so as not to impede the oper-ation. Secondly, we require the services of a marine pilot or someone who can navigate a thirtyfoot cabin cruiser through the waters in this area. Please contact Constable Gupta at the number, which she will provide. Thank you all for coming today. We will provide another update when we have more information to share."

Windflower turned around and started walking back to the command centre. Gupta provided the media with the phone number and then caught up to him.

"Let's hope we get somebody," she said.

"All we can do is ask, and I'm sure that Osmond has the TV or radio on, so he knows we are looking," said Windflower.

When they got back to the command centre, there were calls waiting for Windflower to return. One was from Thibault. Windflower called him first.

"What's up?"

"They heard you on the radio," said Thibault. "He thinks you're stalling. He's not happy."

"You talked to Hodder?"

"Texted," said Thibault. "She thinks she might be able to get out. He's not really paying attention to her. She can get out the back if we can help her."

"What about Tizzard?"

"He's tied up in a chair, right by the front door," said Tizzard. "Osmond always has an eye on him. What should I tell Marilyn?"

"Tell her to hang on for now," said Windflower. "We can't risk getting too close. There might be an opportunity a little later on."

He hung up. His next call was to Crocker at the family house. "Richard Tizzard says he can drive the boat," said Crocker. "What do you mean?" asked Windflower.

"He says that he's worked in these waters before and wants to volunteer."

"Let me talk to him."

Richard came on the phone. "I saw you on the TV. When I first came over to Grand Bank from Ramea, I worked with a crew around here. I can do it, b'y. I wants to do it."

"Thank you very much, Richard, but I don't think I can let you do it."

"Why not?" asked Richard. "Listen, I know it might be dangerous, but it will be dangerous for anybody. I knows how to do it, and maybe I can help you and Eddie."

"I don't know," said Windflower. "But I will think about it, okay?"

"Okay, b'y."

That was something he hadn't expected. He honestly didn't know how to deal with it. The next call he got was totally expected. It was Osmond. "Time to stop screwing around. I saw that pitiful act on TV. Begging for a pilot. Pathetic. I want to see the boat now. Bring it right into the Narrows so I can see it from my window. And don't tell me you don't have it."

"We're getting it loaded up," said Windflower. "Fuel and supplies like you asked for."

"Bring it over. I want to see it," said Osmond. "Or else." The phone line went dead.

"What's the status on the boat?" he asked Williams, who was coming in with a large box of sandwiches.

"From your friendly local sandwich shop," he said, pointing to the box. "I think it's ready to go."

"Can you ask the marina to bring it over?" asked Windflower. "Right away."

"On it," said Williams, grabbing a sandwich from the box.

"Take these over to the family house," said Windflower to Gupta. "Then pass the rest around."

CHAPTER 57

Windflower took advantage of the brief calm in the command centre to call Ron Quigley.

"Any luck on the pilot?" asked Quigley.

"I have a possibility," said Windflower. "Richard Tizzard has volunteered."

"Eddie's father?"

"Yeah," said Windflower. "He's got the experience and the expertise. We may find someone else, but it will take time. I'm not sure I can let Richard do it, though."

"Tough call," said Quigley. "What's Osmond like?"

"He sounds a bit more frantic. Wants to see the boat. I'm not sure we'll be able to slow him down."

"You may not have any other choice," said Quigley. "Is Richard Tizzard calm enough to do this?"

"He's pretty solid. I just hope Eddie doesn't freak out when he sees him."

"Can you get a signal or a message to him somehow?" asked Quigley. "To Eddie, that is."

"Maybe," said Windflower. "Bernard Thibault can text the girl who's inside with Osmond. Give him a headsup. That only leaves my biggest fear, that we're sending in another hostage for Osmond."

"Not sure you have a whole lot of choice," said Quigley. "Any chance of going in?"

"I don't think so," said Windflower. "The intel we have is that Osmond has Tizzard tied up and doesn't take his eyes off him. And we can't risk getting close enough for a shot."

"I support you, no matter what your decision is."

"Thank you, Ron," said Windflower, and he laid the receiver down. He called Crocker. "Can you bring Bernard Thibault and Richard Tizzard over to me at the command centre?"

A few minutes later, Crocker led Thibault and Richard into the command centre.

"Bernard, I need you to get a message to Hodder. Tell her that we have a pilot and that it's Richard Tizzard, Eddie's father. See if she can get that message to Tizzard. Okay?"

"Okay," said Thibault. "I'll see what she says." He went to a corner of the room to do his texting.

"So, you're taking me up on my offer," said Richard. "Good. I'm the right man for the job."

"I appreciate you doing this," said Windflower, "but you have to prom ise me not to take any unnecessary chances. Let the process unfold. We will be tracking the boat, both physically and electronically. Osmond is dangerous and volatile. Just drive the boat as if you aren't connected in any other way. Can you do that?"

"Yes, b'y, I can do that," said the elder Tizzard. "You're not afraid?"

"At my age there's little to be afraid of," said Richard. "'Death is not extinguishing the light; it is only putting out the lamp because the dawn has come.'"

Windflower smiled despite the desperate situation they found them selves in. He went to the older man and gave him another hug.

"Please take him back to the other house," he said to Crocker. "We'll call you when we're close to being ready," he said to Richard.

Thibault came over to talk with Windflower. "Marilyn is going to try to get the message to Tizzard," he said. "She also says that she thinks she might know where Osmond is going."

"Where?"

"She won't tell me unless you help get her out," said Thibault. "She's afraid to go with Osmond."

"You've got to be kidding me," said Windflower. "In the midst of all this?"

"I tried to talk her out of it, but she says no go unless you agree to help her get out."

Windflower thought for a minute. "Okay, tell her that we'll help her. Just before it's time to go. But don't make any moves before that. You'll text her when it's time."

Bernard sent the text while Windflower waited.

"She thinks he's going to Chapel's Cove," said Thibault. "He's got a cab in there that he talked about a few days ago. Said it was a great place if he wanted to lay low for a while."

Windflower looked up Chapel's Cove on the map. According to Goo gle, it was now part of a bigger community called Harbour Main–Chapel's Cove–Lakeview. But there were a number of cabins and houses for sale. It looked very quaint and picturesque. But Windflower wasn't looking for the views. It was located off the TransCanada Highway between Whit bourne and Holyrood.

Williams came in as he was putting down his phone. "Boat's ready, sir.

The marina is sending it over. Should be here in fifteen minutes."

"Great," said Windflower. "We've got a possible first desti-nation. Apparently, Osmond has access to a place in Chapel's Cove."

"That's a beautiful spot," said Williams. "The comedian, Rick Mercer, has a house out there."

"How do you know that?"

"It's in his book," said Williams. "About fortyfive minutes from St. John's."

"Let's contact both Whitbourne and Holyrood detachments, since we don't know who has jurisdiction, and we'll want each of them involved," said Windflower. "You do that. See if they know anybody from there who can help us track down which house or cabin Osmond is connected to. Put them both on alert that he might be heading their way by boat. I'll call Quigley again."

Once he got Quigley on the line, he said, "We think we know where Osmond might be going." He told Quigley about Chapel's Cove and that they were contacting the other RCMP detachments.

"One step at a time," cautioned Quigley. "We don't know for sure that's where he's going."

"Absolutely," said Windflower. "But he will be leaving here within an hour or so, by the looks of it. We have things locked down over here, so we have to think about next steps as well."

"Good. I'll call St. John's and have their unit head directly for Chapel's Cove. They could be there before him, by the sounds of it. I'm going to leave the coast guard where they are to monitor where he goes. And I've got the RCMP chopper on its way to St. John's. They should be there soon if we need them."

"Okay," said Windflower. "You probably won't hear from me again until something moves."

"Good luck, Winston. Be safe."

"The boat is coming," said Williams.

CHAPTER 58

Windflower and Williams went outside. "Do you have the radio connection?" asked Windflower.

"I do," said Williams. He opened his phone and punched in some num bers. He handed the phone over to Windflower.

"Hello," said a voice from the boat.

"It's Windflower. Can you run the boat up and down through this area a couple of times and then dock it a little farther up?"

"No problem," was the reply.

He and Williams watched as the cabin cruiser floated up long the shore line and then turned around and came back down, once and then again.

Windflower went back inside. The phone was ringing,

and he picked it up. "Good. You got the boat," said Osmond. "Now, I'm ready to go."

"We're still waiting for the pilot to arrive," said Windflower. "And we've got time..."

"Time's up," said Osmond.

"Listen," said Windflower. "We've met all of your deadlines, and we'll meet this one. So far, you've done nothing for us."

"Not my problem," said Osmond.

"How about a sign of good faith?" said Windflower. "Let the woman go before you leave."

"She wants to stay with me," said Osmond. "I'm her sugar daddy."

"What about if she wants to leave?"

"Pull the boat up to the shore directly across from this house. Have the pilot wave to me when he's ready. And there better not be anybody else on board. Tizzard goes first if there is," said Osmond.

Windflower stayed silent. He didn't bother going back on Marilyn Hodder. No point in riling Osmond up any more or getting him suspicious.

"And I want a police van driven right to the front door of the house," continued Osmond. "A driver and nobody else. They will take me and my party to the boat. Got it?"

"Got it," said Windflower. Now, they had about twenty minutes to get everything together. He sat with Williams and Gupta to plot it out.

"Gupta, I want you to drive the van," said Windflower. "Don't say a word and don't get out of the van for any reason. You are simply the trans port. Okay?"

"Yes, sir," said Gupta.

"It's going to be tricky because whether we want it or not Marilyn Hodder will likely try to get out the back as soon as you show up. Williams, I want the snipers in place, and if Osmond turns towards Hodder, and they can get a clear shot, take it," said Windflower. "But you'll have to be in direct contact with them and give the order."

"Got it, sir," said Williams. "As soon as we're done, I'll talk to them."

"Okay," said Windflower. "When we're set, I'm going to take Richard Tizzard down to the boat. I will monitor the house from the sidelines. Let me have a radio with the control channel. I will coordinate. Go and set everything up. I will broadcast in five minutes."

Windflower called the person on the boat. "Bring it back up this way," he said. "I'll tell you when to stop." He watched until the boat came closer, and when it was almost directly across from where Osmond was, he called out. "Stop. Bring it right up to the shoreline and park it. Then get out of there." The boat stopped near the shore, and a man got out. He ran as fast as he could back the way he came. Windflower went down to the family house.

He pulled Thibault outside. "We don't want her to do this," he said.

"I think she's made up her mind," said Thibault. "She's stubborn and will make a break for it whatever you do."

"That's what I thought," said Windflower. "Text her and tell her to wait until the last moment before making her move. We'll have people lined up then. But once she starts, she can't stop. Or even look back. Just run until she's out of view from the house."

"Okay, I'll tell her," said Thibault.

Windflower went back inside and went to Richard. "You sure you want to do this?"

Richard didn't answer him at first. He went to Carrie, and they hugged tightly. "It'll be okay."

Carrie didn't pretend she wasn't upset. Tears were running down her face. Windflower hugged her too.

"Let's go," said Richard.

They walked back to the command centre.

"We're going to the boat now," Windflower said into the radio. "This will be the channel for updates moving forward. Gupta, do you have the van? Over."

"Roger that," she said over the radio. "Williams, is everybody in place? Over."

"Roger that," said Williams.

"I'm going to call Osmond and tell him we are going to the boat and that the van is coming to pick him up. Over and out."

"Are we ready yet?" asked Osmond when he answered Windflower's call.

"I'm escorting your pilot to the boat," said Windflower. "And the van will be at the house very soon."

"Let's go," said Osmond.

Windflower took his portable radio with him as he walked Richard down to the boat. Richard went on board and started the motor while Windflower stood by.

"Boat is in position. Gupta, move out, over."

"Roger that," said Gupta.

When he saw the van move towards Osmond, he waved at Richard and started walking back towards the command centre. He stopped halfway between the two houses and watched as the van came close to Osmond's house. The front door opened, and Osmond pushed Eddie, with his arms tied behind him, out in front of him.

"Hold fire, hold fire. Over," shouted Windflower into the radio. Osmond emerged seconds later with a bag over his shoulder, pushed

Eddie into the van and jumped in beside him. He held the door open for a few seconds as if he was waiting for someone and then slammed it shut.

The van sped down the driveway. Windflower could spot a figure running from the back of the house.

"It's the woman, don't shoot. Over," he shouted again.

He could see Williams running towards the woman and pulling her off to the side.

"Hodder is secure. Over," said Williams.

Windflower had turned his attention back to the van,

which was now at the side of the boat. Using Eddie as a shield, Osmond carefully got out of the van and ran onto the boat. He and Eddie disappeared, and shortly afterwards the boat started moving back out into the Narrows and then out for open water.

"Osmond and Tizzard are gone. Williams, please advise coast guard to begin monitoring. Over," said Windflower.

He watched as the boat with his best friend and Eddie's father motored away until only a glimpse of them remained. He walked back to the com mand centre, where Williams was trying to calm down a very agitated Marilyn Hodder.

"Marilyn, I'm Windflower. Where do you think he's going?"

Hodder, who was shaking and shivering, did not respond. She was clearly in shock.

Gupta came in as he was sitting down with Hodder. "Can you get her a blanket from the bedroom? And some tea," asked Windflower.

Gupta came back with a blanket that she wrapped around the woman. "Marilyn, we need to know where he's going," said Windflower.

"I–I think he's going to Chapel's Cove," stammered Hodder. "He's got a cabin out there."

"Have you ever been there?" asked Windflower. Hodder nodded.

"I want you to go with Constable Gupta," said Windflower. "She's going to get you a cup of tea and ask you some more questions." He pulled Gupta aside and whispered in her ear. "See if she can tell us where the cabin is in Chapel's Cove. And what else she can tell us about Osmond and his plans." Gupta nodded and took the woman into the kitchen.

CHAPTER 59

Windflower called Quigley.

"He's gone. With both Eddie and Richard Tizzard," said Windflower. "We've alerted the coast guard. The Hodder woman escaped. We're interviewing her now."

"Good," said Quigley. "I'll let the RNC marine unit know. They were heading towards Chapel's Cove."

Gupta came in as he was talking to Quigley. "Just a sec," said Windflower.

"I've got a location and maybe some more intel on where Osmond is ultimately heading," said Gupta.

"Let me put you on speaker," said Windflower. "It's Gupta," he said to Quigley, indicating that she should go ahead.

"Hodder says the cabin is actually a blue house that is just off the main road, overlooking the water," said Gupta.

"Okay, we'll relay that to Whitbourne and Holyrood," said Windflower. "Call them when we're done."

"She also thinks that he's heading for the Cayman Islands," said Gupta. "Overnighting in Chapel's Cove and then heading out in the morning as soon as it's light. Hodder says that he has something he plans to sell down there. She hasn't seen it, but it's in a bag that he carries with him wherever he goes. She says it looks heavy."

"Might be gold," said Quigley.

"Might be," said Windflower. "But I'm more worried about Eddie and Richard. We can't let Osmond take them down there with him."

"Agreed," said Quigley. "If he's going to Chapel's Cove, we have to get him before he leaves."

"Let's work on that," said Windflower. "We've just got to clean up around here, and we can help."

"There's not much you can do from that end," said Quigley. "I'll take over from here. Easier for me to coordinate with the other detachments."

This was a hard pill for Windflower to swallow. His people were on the line. But he knew Quigley was right. And Quigley was his boss.

"You have to keep me in the loop," said Windflower. "I will," said Quigley. "Every step of the way."

That didn't make Windflower feel any better, but there

was little else he could do, he thought as he hung up with Quigley.

"Okay, I guess that's it for us here," said Windflower. "You look after Hodder. We'll get Bernard Thibault over to help you with that. Get them to stay around town once you've finished your interview in case we need her for anything else."

Gupta went back to the kitchen as Windflower opened the radio channel.

"Stand down. Stand down," he said. "Suspect has left. We need to in spect the house and then move to mopping up the scene. Over."

As he walked over to the family house, he could see RCMP officers moving from every direction towards the roadblock. He saw Williams there and knew he could count on him to start winding things down and doing the search of the house where Osmond had been holed up.

Carrie stood up and ran to him as he entered the house. He hugged her again. "Go over to the command centre," he said to Thibault. "You can leave, too," he said to Crocker.

"Where is he taking them?" asked Carrie.

"We think it's Chapel's Cove," said Windflower. "Osmond's got a place there. But we also have some info that says he's headed down south as soon as he can."

"Mexico?" asked Carrie.

"Cayman Islands," said Windflower. "But we're working to make sure that doesn't happen. Quigley is on it now, and we've got the coast guard and the Constabulary and both Whitbourne and Holyrood engaged."

"But they still have to get Eddie out," said Carrie. "And now Richard too."

She left out the word "alive," thought Windflower. "True," he said. "But we think we know where he's going in Chapel's Cove. They'll be set up and ready for him."

"So, now we wait," said Carrie.

"Yes," said Windflower. "Do you want me to stay with you? Someone to come home with you?"

"No, I'll be fine at home. I mean, I won't be fine, but the kids will keep me busy."

"Okay," said Windflower, coming closer for one more hug. "You have my number. Call me any time. I will call you if I hear anything."

Carrie shivered a little and then let him go. He walked out of the house and went to look for Williams. He found him at the house that Osmond had just left.

"Anything?" he asked.

"Not much," said Williams. "I think we should get forensics to take a look, just in case."

"Agreed," said Windflower. "Call them and set that up. I also think we can reduce the perimeter to just this area."

"Okay," said Williams. "That means we can let everybody but one person go. What will we say to the media?"

"Good question, I don't want to talk to them, but I'll get Terri Pilgrim to put out something to say the area is safe again. If you're okay here, I'm going over to Burin to check in on Davies."

"I think we're good," said Williams.

Windflower walked back across the roadblock area, where the barri cades were already being taken down. Some of the media who were still hanging around yelled questions at him, but he kept walking to his car. He called Terri first.

"Terri, can you put out a media notice?" he said. "Say that the police operation has been concluded and that there is no longer any danger to the public. We will provide further information as it becomes available."

"Is everybody okay?"

"Right now, everybody but Avery is okay," he answered. "Although Tizzard is still with Todd Osmond. We're hoping to catch up with him very soon."

"Do you want to see a draft of the statement before I send it?"

"No, just send it out when you're ready," said Windflower. "You can tell anybody who asks that we will not be responding to any questions at this time."

CHAPTER 60

His next call was to Sheila. "Winston, how are you?"

"I'm fine. Eddie is still in trouble, and so is Richard."

"Richard?" said Sheila. "How is Richard involved?"

"I'll tell you when I get home. Right now, I'm going to the hospital to see Avery. I'll be home afterward."

"Okay, I love you," said Sheila.

"I love you, too."

He drove in the dark to the Burin hospital, saying a quiet prayer for Marcus Avery along the way. He parked in the emergency area next to a cruiser that he assumed belong to Davies. That was confirmed when he saw him in the waiting room.

"Any update?" Windflower asked.

Davies shook his head. "Not since I talked to you. I hear he still has Tizzard."

"Yeah," said Windflower. "Nothing on that either. Are any of the doctors still around?"

"Doctor Fogwell was here a few minutes ago. He may be in the doctor's lounge."

Windflower got directions to the doctor's lounge, walked down the hall and knocked on the door.

"Sergeant Windflower," said Doctor Les Fogwell. "Although I guess it's inspector now, isn't it?"

"Acting inspector," said Windflower. "Nice to see you again."

"Always bad circumstances when we see each other, though," said the doctor. "We really should do something about that. I'm guessing you're here about Marcus Avery. Do you want to go see him?"

"That would be good, thanks."

Doctor Fogwell led him through the swinging doors in Emergency to the small ICU unit at the back.

Windflower was always surprised by how bright the ICU was. That made the operation of the many pieces of equipment and rapid movement of medical staff easier, but it felt uncomfortable for anybody who wasn't a patient. They, of course, were usually so sedated that they didn't care. Avery looked like he fell into that category, if he even knew where he was. He was hooked up to two machines and had three tubes protruding from his body. To Windflower, he looked pale and barely breathing.

"He's lucky, if one can call this condition lucky," said Fogwell. "The surgeon said that one inch either way and his spine and spleen and more would have been damaged. As it stands, his lung got nicked and collapsed, but he still has a chance."

"How would you rate his chances?"

"I would say forty percent," said the doctor. "But I'm not a surgeon, and I'll be the first to admit that I don't know much about recovering from being shot. We don't get much of that thing around here. Nor in Elliot Lake, where I interned."

"So, we wait?"

"And pray, if you're so inclined," said Fogwell. "We'll know more in the morning. I'm going off soon, but I can call you when I come back in."

"That would be great, thank you, Doctor," said Windflower.

He left and went to talk with Davies, who was now drifting off in his chair.

"You should go home," said Windflower. "I'll call Williams to get someone to relieve you." He reached for his cell phone.

"If it's all the same to you, I'd like to stay," said Davies. "I can snooze here if I need, and the nurses keep bringing me coffee. I feel helpless to do anything, but maybe I can be of some service."

"Okay," said Windflower. "You have my number. Call me if anything happens."

Helpless, he thought as he walked out of the emergency area and to his car. He hated the helplessness of this whole situation. There was nothing he could do to help Avery or the Tizzards. He could pray, and he would do that on the way home. But before he did that, there was one thing he could do.

He called Gupta. "Are you still at the scene? I need the phone number for Avery's mother."

"Give me a sec," said Gupta. "Here it is."

Windflower called the number.

"Hello," said a voice at the other end of the line.

"This is Acting Inspector Windflower calling from Marystown. Is Mrs. Avery there?"

"Inspector, this is Moreen, Marcus's sister," said the woman who answered. "Is there any news on Marcus?"

"Not very much," said Windflower. "But I just visited him and thought I'd call your mother."

"One moment, I'll get her."

"Yes?" said Linda Avery.

"Mrs. Avery, it's Windflower from Marystown again."

"How is Marcus?"

"He's still about the same," said Windflower. "I just went to visit him and talked to the doctor there. They think they'll know more in the morning. But I wanted to tell you that he was sleeping peacefully when I was in to see him. I thought you'd like to know that."

"Thank you for telling me that," said Avery's mother. "We've been worried sick about him. Now that I know he's resting, maybe we can get some rest, too."

"Okay," said Windflower. "We have a man on the scene at the hospital.

If I hear anything I will let you know right away."

"Thank you so much, Wildflower. Goodnight."

"Goodnight, Mrs. Avery."

Maybe he wasn't helpless after all, thought Windflower as he started his car and drove back to Grand Bank.

He had no idea what time it was when he got home. Sheila was waiting up for him. She didn't say a word, just held him. Finally, he let go and started crying. He didn't stop until Sheila told him his bath was ready. He went upstairs and sank himself in the hot water. He refused all offers of food and drink and after ten minutes in the bath put on his pajamas and went into bed. Sheila held him again until he fell asleep.

CHAPTER 61

His phone woke him in the morning. He glanced at the time: 6:35. "Windflower," he said.

"It's Davies, sir. Avery is moving a little, but still out of it. The doctors said that's a good sign."

"That is good news," said Windflower as Sheila stirred behind him. "Is Doctor Fogwell in yet?"

"Yes, I just saw him," said Davies. "Hang on, I'll see if I can find him."

"Good morning, Inspector," said Doctor Fogwell. "I was about to call you, but your man beat me to it. Avery is better this morning. He's still heavily medicated but starting to move. Some of it is muscular reaction, but an improvement."

"So, his odds are increasing?"

"We have to wait for the surgeon to take a look, but I'd say sixty percent at this point," said the doctor.

"Can you do me one more favour?" asked Windflower. "Can you call his mother? Davies has the number."

"I have it too," said Fogwell. "I will certainly do that."

"Thank you, Doctor," said Windflower. "Can you pass me back to Davies?"

"Yes, sir?" asked Davies.

"Go home, Constable," said Windflower. "That's an order. Call over and get someone to relieve you."

"Yes, sir. Thank you, sir," said Davies. "Is there any word on Corporal Tizzard?"

"I'm going to call Superintendent Quigley right now," said Windflower.

"I will send a report in and make sure it gets circulated. Now go home."

"Some good news?" asked Sheila.

"Young Avery looks like he's going to make it," said Windflower.

"That is great news," said Sheila. "I'll make some coffee, if you need to make calls."

"That would be great." Windflower sat up in bed and called Quigley. It went to voice mail. He padded into the bathroom and ran a hot shower. When he came out there was still no reply, so he went downstairs to see Sheila. She handed him a cup of coffee.

"Thank you," he said.

"No news?"

"Not yet," said Windflower.

"Breakfast?"

"I am famished," said Windflower. "I don't even remember when or what I last ate. It's all a bit of a blur."

"I'll make some eggs," said Sheila. "You relax for a few minutes. Once the girls get up there won't be time for that."

"I think I'll go outside." With Lady at his heels, Windflower got his jacket and smudging kit and went out on the deck.

He lit his mixture and let the smoke encircle him for as long as he could. Then he started to pray. He realized once he began that while he had a lot of people to pray for this morning, he also had a lot to be grateful for. It looked like Avery would be okay, and that was a great blessing to all of them. No one else had gotten hurt in a very dangerous situation, and every one on his team performed their duties with calm and confidence. He also knew that no matter what happened at work, when he came home, he had a beautiful wife and two adorable daughters who loved him completely.

His final set of prayers was for the Tizzards, Eddie, Richard and Carrie too. He didn't yet know what would happen, but that wasn't up to him. He would be kind and supportive and do anything for that family, part of his family too, he also realized. He prayed that they be given the help of the universe and all their allies to go through this storm and hopefully come out safely at the end. He finished his prayers and called Lady to come back inside.

The smell of bacon and eggs and toast made his mouth

water, and at Sheila's request he went to rouse the girls. They were happy to see him and wondered where he had been all last evening.

"I was just working," he said. "In Marystown."

"Okay," said Amelia Louise.

"We're glad you're home," said Stella.

"Me, too," said Windflower. "Get dressed. Breakfast is ready."

Windflower and Sheila had a few moments to enjoy their breakfast by themselves before the tornado of the two girls came downstairs. Windflower got them their breakfast and was starting to clean up when his cell phone rang. It was Quigley. He went into the living room to take the call.

"Ron, what's going on?"

"They're both safe. We got them both."

"What happened?"

"We tried to set it up last night in Chapel's Cove, but somehow Osmond sussed it out," said Quigley. "Or maybe it was his plan all along. He got Richard to moor the boat in the middle of the harbour and turned off all the lights. We couldn't take a chance on getting near it because we had no way of knowing what was going on the boat. We had to wait until it got light."

"They're both okay, right, Eddie and Richard?"

"A little worse for the wear, but fine as I understand it. Richard insisted on taking him and Eddie back on the boat together," said Quigley.

"What about Osmond?"

"He's in custody," said Quigley. "Being transferred into St. John's."

"How did it all go down?"

"Well, I got it third-hand, but I understand that in the morning Richard went on deck first to get the motor going," said Quigley. "Then Osmond came up. The people who were watching said that it looked like there was a bit of a struggle, and Richard knocked Osmond into the water. Once that happened, he lost his weapon and turns out he can't swim either. We had a dingy from the RNC marine unit, and they fished him out."

"That's amazing," said Windflower. "Richard Tizzard is amazing."

"What's going with Avery?"

"I saw him last night, and he was in a lot of trouble but fighting back," said Windflower. "This morning he's a bit better. The docs give him a sixty percent chance of a full recovery."

"Good news all around," said Quigley. "You should do some media today. Got some good stuff to share."

"Why don't you come down and share the spotlight?"

"Nah, you got this," said Quigley. "You and your team did an excellent job."

"Thanks, Ron."

"You deserve it," said Quigley. "You rose to the occasion.

Like I told you before. 'Some are born great, some achieve greatness, and some have greatness thrust upon them.'"

"I think that's a compliment," said Windflower. "'A fool thinks himself to be wise, but a wise man knows himself to be a fool.'"

Quigley laughed. "Enjoy your day. Unless you have other plans." Windflower laughed too and closed his cell phone.

CHAPTER 62

"Good news," he announced. "The best news. Both Eddie and Richard are fine. And I guess Richard is a bit of a hero."

"Yay," said Sheila.

And the girls yelled "yay" too.

"What's your day like today?" he asked.

"I've got a couple of calls to make, but not too bad, why?"

"Why don't you take the day off and we'll all go to Marystown," said Windflower. "I've got to do some media, but that'll only take an hour. What do you think?"

"Yay," said Amelia Louise.

"Yay," said Stella.

"I guess the yays have it," said Sheila. "I'll make my calls now if you finish cleaning up."

"I will, but I have one more call to make," said

Windflower. He went back into the living room and called Carrie.

She had already gotten a call from Eddie, so she basically knew what had happened but was still grateful for Windflower's call.

"We're coming over today, the whole carload of us," he said. "Maybe we could drop by for a visit if that's not too much for you?"

"That would be very nice," she said. "We should be home. We don't get out much."

Windflower told Sheila about the possibility of visiting Carrie.

"That would be great," said Sheila. "We'll get to see the baby, too."

While the girls and Sheila were getting ready, he called over to Marystown and got Terri Pilgrim to get started on a media release. "Let's do it for eleven-thirty if we can. And can you see if Corporal Tizzard is up to attending, along with his father, Richard, if he's still around, too."

"I'll check with Corporal Tizzard and see what's possible," said Pilgrim. "In any case, I'll see you later this morning."

He had one more call to make, to the RCMP office in Grand Bank. "Isn't it grand news?" said Betsy when she answered the phone. Windflower wasn't surprised that she'd heard the news already. She had her own connections. "And that young constable is coming along, too."

"Yes, it appears that everything is getting back to normal," said Windflower. "I'm going over to Marystown to do some media, if anybody is looking for me. See you tomorrow, Betsy."

The drive to Marystown was short and pleasant. Everybody was in a good mood. Why not? They all had the day off, thought Windflower. Well, he would too once he did his media work. He dropped Sheila and the girls off at the mall and drove to the RCMP office. Everyone there seemed to be in a good mood as well, with lots of smiles and cheery good mornings. He went to see Terri Pilgrim and found both Eddie and Richard Tizzard waiting for him in his office. Terri showed him the media release, which he scanned and approved. "Let me know when everyone is ready for us," he said as he walked into his office. "Oh, Terri, can you get me a quick update on Constable Avery? Talk to Doctor Les Fogwell if you can. Thanks." Eddie looked tired and a little strained from his adventure, while Richard was his usual animated self. "Good morning to the conquering heroes," said Windflower.

"Not me," said Eddie. "I was like a tied-up dummy most of the time. Dad is the hero."

"So, tell me the story," said Windflower. "How did you manage to over power Todd Osmond and make your escape?"

"I didn't do much at all," said Richard. "He told me to go up on deck and get everything ready to go, so I did. When he came up, he was a bit shaky and started to stumble a little. I just gave him a hand to fall over. Just a little push, and there he went, ass over kittle."

Both Windflower and Eddie laughed at the simplicity with which Rich ard told this story. There was obviously much more to it than what he described. But that was his style, always humble, thought Windflower.

"Well, to all of us you are a hero," said Windflower. "How are you feeling, Eddie?"

"What's that saying, Dad?" asked Eddie. "Ridden hard and put away wet? But I'll be okay with a couple of days' rest. I hear you're coming for a visit afterward."

"The whole gang is here," said Windflower. "They all want to see the baby. Me, too."

"That'll be nice," said Richard. "Maybe I can hang around and get a ride back with you."

"Absolutely," said Windflower. "Weren't you scared when all of this was going on?"

"No, b'y," he said. "Like I told you before, I know I'm in the last years. I also had faith in you and the other RCMP officers to figure this out. I've learned that 'faith is the bird that feels the light when the dawn is still dark.'"

"I forgot to ask about this before," said Windflower. "Did Osmond have a bag with him? What happened to that?"

"Into the water with him," said Richard.

"They had divers on the way when we left," said Eddie. "Ron Quigley seemed very keen on recovering that bag."

The three men made some small talk until Terri came in. "Constable Avery is continuing to improve," she said. "They have moved his condition to serious from critical and are reducing his sedation levels. Those are all promising signs, according to Doctor Fogwell."

"Thank you, Terri. Is the media ready?" asked Windflower.

"In the main boardroom," she said.

Windflower and the father and son walked down the hallway to the boardroom. Richard tried to move to the back, but Windflower gently nudged him to come along with him to the front. Eddie and Richard stood just behind him.

He gave the prepared statement about the situation being resolved and that Todd Osmond was in custody awaiting a number of charges including attempted murder and forcible confinement. The statement ended by thanking the community and the media for their support.

"I also want to give you an update on the constable that was wounded during this situation," he added. "Constable Marcus Avery is making progress in his recovery. His condition has been moved from critical to serious. He is not out of the woods yet, but he is receiving excellent medical care at the Burin Hospital. We want to thank the staff there for everything they have done and are doing for Constable Avery."

Windflower paused and looked behind him. He motioned for Eddie and Richard to come stand behind him.

"We also want to acknowledge two individuals who played a critical role in resolving this situation. First of all, Corporal Eddie Tizzard, who showed great courage and bravery under very trying circumstances. Thank you, Corporal," he said.

"And the real hero today is Richard Tizzard, yes that is Corporal Tizzard's father, who not only volunteered to assist the RCMP but is also directly responsible for the apprehension of an armed and dangerous criminal at very grave risk to his own safety. Thank you, Richard."

Both Eddie and Richard beamed at these last comments and then stepped back while Windflower took questions from the assembled media for the next few minutes. At the end, they all wanted pictures of the three of them, which Windflower and the Tizzards happily agreed to.

Back in his office, Windflower called Sheila. They were done at the mall and starving, according to the girls. "I'll see you later," he said to Eddie and Richard as he drove back to meet them.

The girls were arguing quite strongly for McDonald's, but Sheila was having none of that. After much discussion, they reached a consensus on Chinese food. The local restaurant had a lunch buffet, and that meant everyone could have what they wanted.

Windflower ate far too much, especially the chicken balls in that deadly red sauce. But it was so good that he couldn't resist just a couple more. After lunch, they drove to Eddie and Carrie's place.

The time with the Tizzards was a bit wild and wonderful. The girls fawned over the new baby, and little Hughie got himself into everything. Carrie had made a chocolate pudding dish with whipped cream that he managed to spread on just about every surface in the house.

The drive home was a much more subdued affair, probably because of the pudding, thought Windflower. He was happy for a few moments of peace and quiet as they traveled along the highway and right up to Richard Tizzard's front door. Sheila and Windflower got out to give him a hug.

Back at home, the girls occupied themselves with a puzzle they'd been working on while Sheila returned some phone calls. Windflower was actually dozing off a little on the couch when his cell phone rang.

"Good coverage of the media event today," said Quigley. "It's every where. Nice touch to acknowledge Richard Tizzard."

"He deserves it," said Windflower. "Did you find Todd Osmond's bag?"

"That's one of the things I was calling about," said Quigley. "The divers recovered his weapon and the bag. There were six gold bars inside. We're getting them traced but are pretty sure they're from the Toronto heist."

"Wow, how much are they worth?"

"Each one is worth about $65,000," said Quigley. "A nice

little haul. We're likely sending him to HQ very soon. Lots of people want to talk to him about the rest."

"Still not worth it," said Windflower. "'All that glitters is not gold.'"

"True," said Quigley. "'But many a man his life has sold.' Anyway, enough about Osmond and gold. Don't you want to hear what else I wanted to tell you?"

"Sure," said Windflower.

"I've got you booked to speak on Tuesday at ten o'clock. Can you be in Halifax?"

"I'll be there," said Windflower. "I gotta go tell Sheila and the girls." He hung up. "Hey, everybody, who wants to go on a trip?"

ABOUT THE AUTHOR

Mike Martin was born in St. John's, NL on the east coast of Canada and now lives and works in Ottawa, Ontario. He is a longtime freelance writer and his articles and essays have appeared in newspapers, magazines and online across Canada as well as in the United States and New Zealand.

He is the awardwinning author of the bestselling Sgt. Windflower Mystery series, set in beautiful Grand Bank. There are now 15 books in this light mystery series with the publication of *Too Close for Comfort*.

A Tangled Web was shortlisted in 2017 for the best light mystery of the year, and *Darkest Before the Dawn* won the 2019

Bony Blithe Light Mystery Award. *All That Glitters* was short-listed for the LOLA 2024 Must Read Book of the year award.

Some Sgt. Windflower Mysteries are now available as audiobooks and the latest, *Darkest Before the Dawn,* was released as an audiobook in 2024. All audiobooks are available from Audible in Canada and around the world.

Mike is Past Chair of the Board of Crime Writers of Canada, a national organization promoting Canadian crime and mystery writers, and a member of the Newfoundland Writers' Guild and Capital Crime Writers.

Mike loves to hear from readers. You can contact him at sgtwindflowermysteries.com. You can follow the Sgt. Windflower Mysteries on Facebook.

ALSO BY MIKE MARTIN

THE SGT. WINDFLOWER MYSTERY SERIES

THE WALKER ON THE CAPE

THE BODY ON THE T

BENEATH THE SURFACE

A TWIST OF FORTUNE

A LONG WAYS FROM HOME

A TANGELED WEB

DARKEST BEFORE THE DAWN

FIRE, FOG AND WATER

A PERFECT STORM

SAFE HARBOUR

BURIED SECRETS

DANGEROUS WATERS

ALL THAT GLITTERS

BETTER SAFE THAN SORRY

TOO CLOSE FOR COMFORT

CHRISTMAS IN NEWFOUNDLAND: MEMORIES AND MYSTERIES
BOOK 1

CHRISTMAS IN NEWFOUNDLAND: MEMORIES AND MYSTERIES
BOOK 2

A FRIEND FOR CHRISTMAS

THE CHRISTMAS BEAVER